HorrorQuake

HorrorQuake

EDWARD NEWTON

A
GRINNING SKULL PRESS
Publication

PO Box 67, Bridgewater, MA 02324

DEDICATION

For Treina, Kobe, Gage, Oliver, and Bennett

ACKNOWLEDGMENTS

Thank you to California, for being a quake away
from monsters running amok.

def. earthquake
earth·quake
ˈərth-ˌkwāk
noun
1: a shaking or trembling of the earth that is volcanic or tectonic in
origin
2: upheaval

4.0 Richter

[The Garcias]

Upheaval.

That's what Rosie had called it when Hector announced a road trip for a December vacation instead of their usual holiday routine. The idea of leaving home for three weeks left his teenage daughter apoplectic. The deviation from pattern rocked her entire life to its core. Yet Hector pressed forth with his plan, and now they're on the road, burning up miles.

The RV handles like a dream. An RV is like putting wheels on a luxury home and setting sail on fair winds. Hector imagines the vehicle as a modern-day pirate ship traveling across the seas of desert dunes in the Mojave, luxury accommodations becoming of only the bravest and most successful roguish scalawags! The idea to pull the kids out of school for an extended holiday vacation and hit the open road is Hector's best idea in years.

The 35' long beauty has a pop-out living space, state-of-the-art entertainment system, electric fireplace, high-tech dinette, lumbar seating, panoramic kitchen window, power skylight, solar panels, in-motion satellite, and two 15,000 BTU ACs. The vehicle is the result of someone taking a dream and slapping four 22.5" wheels with aluminum rims on the son of a bitch. It's only missing a Jolly Roger flag flying from the antenna.

They'd left yesterday and stayed in a Walmart parking lot in California City the previous night. The route east includes some scenic byways, such as this one through Death Valley along California Highway 190. The real adventure is along these less-traveled roads through the unpopulated stretches of America.

"Remember when we saw *Deliverance*?" Linda asks as they drive deeper into the remote California desert. "This is like *Deliverance* in the desert. A scary, sandy sequel."

"We're not in a sequel, Linda," Hector says. "No one's plucking a banjo on their front porch."

Hector had worked on arranging the itinerary over the last few weeks. He's absolutely anal about plans and schedules. A decade of coordinating deliveries across America had kept him on a tight schedule. But what does the sign say as they pass, while Rosario asks him another crazy question about how long they will be gone? He missed the details, but his eyes had picked out a very intriguing phrase.

Ghost town.

Hector had passed dozens of such attractions over the countless miles of road he'd driven in his lifetime, but he'd always seemed to have been on a timeline to get from point A to point B. He's still on a schedule, but it's of his own making. And he who makes can *un*make. The same rule could apply to his son when the little brat gets on Hector's last nerve.

Hector watches the roadside signs as they continue along the highway. Most billboards showcase the endless sex and gambling offered in Vegas. McDonald's signs, one after another. More evidence the world is going to hell faster than his *abuela's* Friday night fajitas went through his digestive system.

Linda goes back to check on the kids. Hector grins at the road, the asphalt humming along in that sweet harmony under his tires. The only interruption is the faint sound of a song through the radio speakers and one low rumble beneath the bass of banal pop tunes. Thunder?

Hector gazes at the blue sky. Not a cloud in sight. Sonic boom? He doesn't spy a plane.

Linda returns, plops into the passenger seat, and speaks to Hector in a conspiratorial tone. "Rosie has to use the bathroom."

"Well, she's fifteen. I don't think she needs permission."

"She wants to stop at a rest area or a gas station."

"We filled up only an hour ago," Hector says. "We're driving around in a mobile hotel room. There's a bathroom right in here."

Linda leans forward so the radar ears of their son, Chuy, can't pick up the adults' conversation. "She has to go number two." Hector shoots his wife a glare. "She won't go in the R.V." Hector moves his eyes from road to wife to road to wife. Linda shrugs. "What? She might make an embarrassing noise or make a… You know…" Linda mouths the word *stink*.

Before Hector utters a four-letter word that would get him into more shit than Rosario is dealing with, he sees another billboard that doesn't advertise casinos, brothels, or other places of sin. The billboard scene features a western town from the time of the gold rush, an old-fashioned setting like the spaghetti westerns he used to watch with Papa. Below the image reads the tag line—"Come visit a real GHOST TOWN. Skidoo, CA. Next right."

"We're going to take a detour," Hector decides. He has never deviated from the plan before. The idea makes him feel both exhilarated and anxious. "Can she hold it for a bit?"

Linda disappears into the rear to check on Rosario's excremental emergency. Chuy plops into the passenger's side seat as soon as his mom's ass is out of the saddle. His son is only eight but already has enough attitude for two teenagers. In the six years since Chuy learned to talk, Hector has lost almost all his hair. The kid is an endless font of irritation.

"I don't know about this plan, Pop."

Hector hates it when the kid calls him "Pop." He's not a fucking soda. But Chuy knows he hates it, and if Hector admonishes him, the kid only calls him it more. Hector bites his lip before he issues a rejoinder and stares straight ahead, waiting for the exit. His temper used to blow at the slightest provocation, but his explosions have only ever exacerbated Chuy's responses. So Hector stews in silence.

"You didn't allow for any surprises," Chuy eventually continues as Hector resists provocation. "What if they're hosting a Pokémon convention in Nevada? What if we find out The Rock is signing autographs in Vegas? What if we need to check out the world's best juicy lucy from my *Freddie the Foodie* blog?"

Hector wonders what the hell a juicy lucy is, but he doesn't take the bait. Instead, Hector manages to hold his tongue long enough to arrive at the exit for Skidoo. Chuy shoots him a surprised glance as Hector steers the big RV onto the narrow off-ramp. Hector comes to a complete stop at the sign even though it doesn't look like anyone has come this way in a very long time.

"What're you doing?" Chuy barks. "This isn't on the agenda."

"Sometimes you have to take the road less traveled, son," Hector says—the first time he's ever given such advice to his thunderstruck offspring.

Chuy sits silently, watching as they unexpectedly detour into the wilds of the desert. The quiet from the passenger seat is pure bliss—Hector would take a thousand wrong turns if it meant making Chuy's neverending vomit of sound suspend its steady gush, even for a few minutes. Hector hums a Christmas song as he leaves the well-traveled road in the dust.

"*Daaaaaaaaaa-aaaaaad,*" Rosario calls from the back.

The call of nature is more like the caterwaul of a dying banshee. Fortunately for Hector's ears, the sanity of all passengers, and probably the survival of one pair of underwear, a gas station appears in the distance, a generic sign sticking up into the crystal-clear sky that simply reads "GAS."

"Coming right up," Hector calls back.

He smiles to himself. The unplanned diversion isn't a move Hector usually makes, but he's eager to experience a real ghost town. The call of the past has always fascinated him, and an entire settlement frozen in yesterday enthralls him more than any other destination on the official itinerary. This detour is a temporary diversion worth deviating from the plan.

4.1 Richter

[Carl]

Nothing much surprises Carl Kennedy after 70 years. He has seen the capability for terrifying evil and unexpected charity in humanity—frequently in the same person. Good and bad are grammar-school words for little kids who aren't old enough to wear big-boy pants. Anyone with some dirt behind their ears knows a person can't explain the world in three or four letters. The intellectual assholes who think they're wallowing in more profound thoughts than the next group of fools like to say the world isn't black or white but painted in shades of gray. Gray's just another fucking four-letter word.

Who cares about the color of things? The world isn't about color, no matter what the goddamn media wants you to believe. It's about fearing the indefinite, and everything comes down to being unknown. Humans are powerless in the face of a dreadful fate. Death gets everyone in the end. So best not to dwell on what comes tomorrow or worry about today because those moments are only closer to the finish line.

Carl likes to think of yesterday. He could *understand* the past, at least his part in it. He could handle his memories of the war and the things he'd done to survive. Carl's wife had been a loyal woman who'd lived a life that ended too soon and with more pain than she deserved.

He'd buried her out back in a plot marked with a humble stone. While he misses her still, it's all behind him.

No kids. He'd be chained to his children's futures all his days. Carl could never handle all that unknown. Mary had desperately wanted children, but he'd resisted long enough that disease had finally tabled further debate. There are enough damn Kennedys out there to carry on the family name without Carl contributing to the clan.

He doesn't know what day it is. It could be a Monday, and it might be a Friday. He hasn't glanced at a calendar in years. He knows the seasons by the weather changing, and sometimes a customer clues him into a holiday with a "Merry Christmas" or "Happy Easter." Otherwise, he prefers being free from marking the passing days. He can't check off the moments he has left if he doesn't measure the turning weeks.

Carl's station simply says "GAS" on the sign. No need for a proper name. He only sees a handful of people regularly, and they'd all given up making small talk with Carl Kennedy a long time ago. Tom brings him supplies—Carl eats from canned food he adds to his orders and expired items off his shelves. He only takes cash inside the store, and the pumps have a credit card reader—if that doesn't work, there's a number on the pump for travelers to call. Carl doesn't give a shit if they get gas or not. Billy Hammel comes by occasionally to make change. Chuck delivers fuel when he needs it. Mostly, that's it. Other than the occasional stranger passing along a route almost as empty as the ghost town down the road.

Carl sits on the front porch of the small station. He stares at the quiet stretch of road in each direction off the approach. A hawk cries as it flies overhead. The wind whispers as if it has a secret it doesn't want to share. Carl loves the quiet and the stillness. Minutes stretch into hours out here and hours into days. The world moves too fast everywhere else. Here, things go at a pace to accommodate the elongation of a solitary existence.

The day has involved more activity than Carl usually likes in a day. Billy Hammel delivered fuel earlier. Tom wasn't on the route today— some stranger in his place—and Carl told him he'd wait for supplies until Tom returned. The substitute Tom went on toward Skidoo, deeper into the desert. Someone in a little blue fucking electric car stopped, tried to buy a soda, and expressed utter confusion when Carl told her he only accepted cash. She was too young to understand a world without credit cards. He didn't have a receptacle for her battery-powered embarrassment, either. She left empty-handed.

Now, an RV comes trundling down the road. Carl hopes the thing keeps going, but, of course, it starts signaling a half mile up the way like anyone else needs to know about the left turn. The dad gets out of the driver's seat, and Carl thanks God Almighty that the fella isn't some emasculated bitch who lets his woman drive the massive machine down the road while he plays Pac-Man or whatever grown men are swiping on their phones for hours on end nowadays.

The mother and a daughter burst out the back door and make an erratic run toward Carl. He is familiar with the Gotta-Shit Shuffle. The girl has to go. They will present the legendary ever-lovin' request to use Carl's facilities.

"Bathroom?" the mother asks. The girl's so close to messing herself that she can't speak.

"Restroom's closed," Carl grumbles as he watches the dad pump gas.

"She can't hold it any longer, sir. Please."

The girl begs the old man with her eyes to put her out of her misery, maybe by changing his answer or using the large ceramic coffee mug in his right hand to knock her unconscious.

"Her abilities don't affect the facilities."

The mom peeks through the screen door and examines his shop. She gauges the shape of the building and the use of the place. She can tell he lives here. And he doesn't live here without a working restroom.

"You have a bathroom in there, sir," the mom accuses.

"You have a bathroom in there, ma'am," he counters, pointing a crooked finger at the RV.

The mom gives him a glare, indicating the evil potential in all living creatures. Carl is legitimately surprised by her fierceness. The woman leans closer and looks Carl right in the eyes. He isn't easy to stare down, but she does it.

"You let us use the bathroom, old man, or she's gonna take a shit right here on your porch, and I'm going to turn around and leave it for you to clean up."

"Maaaaaaaawwwwwm," the girl cries, her face turning scarlet red.

But Carl is a little impressed. Irritated, but impressed.

"Through the screen door, behind the counter, second door on the right," Carl says.

The girl waddles through the door like a stuffed turkey. The mother follows her inside. Carl sighs as if he's been significantly put out by their interrupting his nothingness. He gets up and goes in. The mother browses in the shop as she awkwardly waits for the teenage girl to finish shitting in Carl's private bathroom. Carl only has snacks with fat, sugar, and calories, designed to slowly plump you up before the holiday slaughter. The mom spins a metal rack holding postcards 'round and 'round. She holds up a cardstock photo of Skidoo circa the 19th century and raises an eyebrow in the universal expression of "How much?"

"Quarter," Carl grumbles. The cheapest goddamn thing in the whole shop. "We only take cash."

The woman digs inside a pocketbook attached to the back of her phone. She withdraws one quarter and hands it over.

"Plus tax."

The woman glares, digs back into her pocketbook, and finally extracts a dime. "Keep the change."

The girl emerges from the back with an interesting expression of gratitude and embarrassment. "Thank you, sir." Her tone of voice suggests he'd saved her life or something. Carl nods. Acknowledgment and dismissal. The women depart. The RV, reloaded and refueled, drives off.

They head in the direction of the ghost town.

Carl stands up, intending to check his bathroom for befoulment, when his legs turn momentarily to spaghetti. He leans on the countertop containing his cash register, the postcard rack, and nothing else. Carl is 70 and hasn't been to a doctor in 40 years, but he's always felt fit as a flea. Now, his legs threaten to betray him. He doesn't feel dizzy or weak. Then what was that? Stroke? Aneurism? The onset of diabetes?

It felt like the whole world had turned to jello momentarily, giving a subtle jiggle.

Earthquake.

4.2 Richter
[Pi]

Pi suffers Josh Henry's company because she has no other way to get home for the holidays. Her parents wouldn't buy her a plane ticket, and she barely has enough money to buy food. She's a poor college girl who uses public transportation when she needs to get anywhere. But Josh was leaving before her semester ended, so she tested out of her classes and joined him on the thousand-mile road trip across the southwest. She hadn't ticked off even one mile before she'd started to imagine ways of disposing of Josh's corpse and driving the rest of the way to Cali alone.

What does her sister see in this douchebag?

Day 2 and Josh had to take this detour to some godforsaken ghost town in the middle of nowhere. Pi doesn't believe in spirits. She doesn't believe in anything that wouldn't add up. Ghosts aren't quantitative. No measure of mass or photographic evidence of existence. More fairy tales. Made-up diversions that belong on the fiction shelf along with the inherent goodness of humanity and the achievement of racial equality and Jesus Christ himself.

"Can't we avoid getting sidetracked by tall tales?" Pi complains as they turn off the main route.

"C'mon, Pee," Josh taunts. "Where's your sense of adventure?"

He calls her "Pee" instead of "Pie," and Pi can't tell if he's mispronouncing her name, making fun of it, shortening it from one syllable to one goddamn *letter*, or if he's merely that stupid. His intelligence is quantitative. Barely.

"My kind of adventure is proving the veracity of data, not taking wild excursions to entertain the impossible."

"It's an old town," Josh says. "I thought you liked old shit."

She's studying to be an archaeologist, not a historian. This idiot doesn't know the difference. Pi isn't interested in facts and figures but rather in the old truths buried and waiting for someone to discover them. A tourist attraction isn't going to reveal anything unique about the evolution of man. As evidenced by Josh, the progression of the development of *homo sapiens* may be going backward.

"The original settlement of Skidoo fell into the desert long ago," Pi says. "The ghost town on the site of the old boomtown is as fake as my sister's hair color."

Josh frowns. "She's not a natural blonde?"

"We're Asian, Josh." Pi glares at Josh as he seems astonished by the follicle revelation. "She's not well-endowed by merely natural means, either."

Josh blinks dumbly as he drives forth. His face is handsome, she supposes, if one likes the simplicity of a square jaw and a smooth complexion. His nose is perfectly proportioned and as straight as his sexual preferences. The guy's too vanilla to have ever encountered androgyny or polyamory. He probably couldn't even pronounce those words.

Pi wants this road trip to be over. As much as she can't handle her own family sometimes, she could accommodate Josh Henry even less. Her patience for stupidity is legendarily thin, and this excursion to a ghost town in the middle of the Mojave is about to send her over the edge.

Josh parks the Toyota RAV4 in a small lot south of town. Only three other vehicles occupy the two dozen spaces. The morning is nearly over, and Josh thinks he might see an old-time shoot-out at noon. Pi doesn't have the energy to explain this is a mining village, not an Old

West outlaw town. He eagerly hops out while Pi remains in the SUV.

"You go on," she says. "I'm going to catch up on some school-work."

Mid-nineteenth century isn't her field of study—Pi prefers things further dead and long gone. Indiana Jones didn't pan for gold. He raided temples and uncovered ancient artifacts. Dr. Piccadilly Lee—good thing Josh doesn't know Pi's full name if he thinks "Pee" is amusing—wants to be the next adventuring archeologist. But *Finders of the Fake Ghost Town* isn't exactly the title of a rip-roaring adventure serial.

Pi flips open her laptop. There's no cell service out here in the middle of nowhere, but she picks up a Wi-Fi signal free for customers. It's labeled "Ghost Productions, LLC" because they have even incorporated the supernatural in the 21st century. Pi sighs. If she could write her papers longhand and turn in a bound copy, she'd have placed her last assignment in Professor Landon's inbox before she'd left. Instead, she's sitting in the desert plucking out the conclusion so she can email the project before the end of the week.

The Toyota suddenly jostles like someone gave the vehicle a shove. Or a strong gust of wind made the machine shudder. Pi looks out of the windshield, but the world is as still as a statue. Nothing moves outside the SUV. Even the American flag hanging off a pole at the edge of the parking lot doesn't stir one bit.

"Didja feel that?"

Josh is standing outside Pi's open passenger side window, and he scares the ever-loving shit out of her. She almost bashes him in his pretty face with her laptop.

"Were you bouncing the back of the fucking S.U.V.?" Pi accuses.

"I didn't bounce anything," Josh huffs. "I was coming back to get you. The old-timey saloon is a hoot."

"I'm not looking for a hoot, Josh. I want a ride home, and you've taken me on this goddamn detour. Now the whole world shifted under my ass. Was that an earthquake?"

"I'm from Colorado. What do I know about earthquakes? Let me ask someone from California. I think my girlfriend is from there. If only her sister were here."

"Funny, asshole. I know how an earthquake feels. I wasn't expecting one in the middle of the desert."

"I don't sit around waiting for a blizzard in Colorado, but you can tell a storm's brewing when the wind blows."

"You can blow me, dickhead," Pi mumbles under her breath.

Josh had already stepped away and walked to the driver's side, unable to hear her through the windshield. She is ready to get the rest of the way home. Too many more hours on the road with Josh and she might murder this asshole.

"I'm not sticking around the Mojave if they're going to have earthquakes."

"Driving toward the San Andreas fault will make you feel better?" Pi asks.

Josh starts the engine. He cranks the bass, making the whole vehicle throb like a persistent headache. She can't hear the following words from his face over the obnoxious volume, but she reads his lips: "Can't worry about it if I can't feel it."

Pi turns away so he can't read her lips right back and says, "Probably what my sister says about your performance in bed."

They put the ghost town in the rearview mirror. Pi can't say she's sorry to cut the detour short. She didn't want to come out here anyway. She's felt a hundred tremors worse than the one that shook them up. Pi isn't going to be spooked by a tiny little rumble.

She is grateful the shake scared Josh silly, though—anything to end this exhausting escapade with the idiot sooner than later. Pi doesn't like considering the future, as strange events always make her nervous and anxious. But tomorrow can't be any worse than today.

She must convince her sister to make Josh Henry another ex, crossed off the list of possible additions to the Lee family tree. Pi couldn't have any intellectually deficient nieces and nephews wandering around with Josh's supremely irritating expression of confusion on their faces. Maybe that's why she enjoys the company of relics more than friends—the ancient remains don't have faces.

4.3 Richter

[Brock]

Brock Hayes drives the speed limit precisely. The Inyo County Police Department pays him to uphold the law, and he can't defend it if he thinks he's above it. That's what his dad always said, and Brock, Sr., had been the best damn cop in all of Southern California. The man had followed every rule to the absolute T.

Brock isn't going to eek one extra mile an hour over the speed limit, either. The driver riding his ass seems to think putting the diesel engine of the prisoner transport bus in the patrol car's trunk would get Officer Hayes to drive faster. However, the federal penitentiary employee who wants to get to the destination a few minutes early is sorely mistaken in his ability to intimidate Brock Hayes.

"Jesus Christ, brah, my grandma has a heavier foot than you, and she's been dead ten years," Deputy Donnie Davis declares derogatorily from the passenger seat. "You should've let me drive."

Brock hates it when Donnie calls him "brah."

"The speed limit is fifty-five," Brock says. "The needle's right between the fives, Davis."

"Ri-i-i-ight."

The transport bus they're escorting across the Mojave flashes headlights and starts to fall behind. Officer Hayes eases off the gas and slows. The bus pulls alongside the road in a spot designated by a sign for scenic pictures. The sand has been hard-packed to support vehicles, but it's barely big enough for both the bus and the patrol car.

The driver leans out the window and hollers at Brock as the police officers step out of their patrol car. "One of the passengers has to go," the burly driver calls out. "The guards need one of you to escort."

The two officers exchange glances, and Brock exhales. "Hey, I've had to suffer your slow-ass driving for two hours. You draw the short straw automatically, brah."

Brock heads over to the bus's door. It opens with a pneumatic hiss. A scowling woman in bright orange coveralls wears a puckered expression, either indicating the precipice of peeing or the perpetual petulance of the incarcerated. Her flat breast features a number and the last name—"Smith." Brown hair, brown eyes, brown skin. The side of her face features a spiderweb tattoo. Brock wonders how many times she has regretted that choice over the years.

"C'mon," Brock commands. "Must be a pretty big emergency to make them pull aside."

"I warned them of the mess they be cleanin' if they didn't let me take a piss."

"Great," Brock mumbles. "This way."

"Ain't a woman supposed to do this part?"

"Precious few females in my precinct. You got me," Brock says unenthusiastically. "We can stand here while you wet yourself, or you can accept the circumstances."

"Let's move it before I don't have a choice anymore."

"Don't worry, I'm not going to sneak a peek," Brock promises.

"I don't care if you watch the whole thing, you kinky bastard."

Brock escorts the handcuffed woman off the road a short distance. The desert has certain creatures that could bite someone in the ass, so he rounds the nearest clump of cacti and stops. "This is far enough. I'll give you some priva—"

Inmate Smith doesn't require privacy. She drops trou before

Brock can spin on his heel, squatting in the sand right before him. "I shower with twenty other women twice a week. My ass gets more views than your social media. Don't give a fuck if you stare all goddamn day, mister."

Brock turns his back too late, witnessing the woman beginning to urinate like a wild animal right there in the sand. Brock stares into the desert scene, scant creosote bushes and stubby cacti on otherwise barren dunes rolling into the distance. The image is deceiving—the endless desert recalls deadly heat, but the landscape is now comfortable in the dry December season.

There isn't even a breeze. The air is so calm. Brock can hear the rumble and wheeze of the bus on the other side of the dune's slope and the bramble of bushes. Otherwise, there's only silence. Thin cirrus clouds are ghostly fingers reaching across the crisp blue sky. The sun is big and heavy as it travels down toward the west. A single lonely bird circles overhead, too far to see its species. It reminds Brock of a vulture intuiting an impending buffet of death.

The world before him reveals no hint of modernity. Brock could be staring at the world as it existed a million years ago. The rolling dunes feature timeless sands, ageless vegetation, and bright skies without a powerline or airplane contrail visible as far as he can see. The desert is a world unaffected by progress and untouched by corruption.

Brock finds the peacefulness out here alluring. The simplicity of form. Life must be hearty and ruthless to survive in this environment. Only the nastiest buggers thrive. Primitive rules. The kind Brock can understand. Not the complicated conditions of modern civilization, where someone like Jessie Hindman can break his heart. Brock longs for the black-and-white rules of desert survival instead of the tangled web of civilized life.

"It's nice out here," the prisoner says behind him. The faint sound of spattering liquid accompanies her raspy voice. The bathroom sound effects reveal she isn't done and hasn't run. Escape would result in death—there's no water for a hundred miles. "No walls. No locks. No fences."

"Things are waiting to kill you if you step near their territory," Brock warns. "And you'll die of dehydration if exposed to the elements for too long. It feels cool enough, but the desert air wicks the water out of your flesh."

"I ain't running, if that's what you're thinking," Smith assures. "I'm squatting."

"We don't have to talk."

"I don't get to talk much," she sighs, her exhale becoming a rumble of flatulence. "Conversation is too civilized, and I'm a caged anim— Holy shit!"

Officer Hayes stumbles forward. The whole world gave him a jolt. Like the sand beneath him had shifted. *Earthquake.* He's felt quakes before. A 4.8 had hit not too many years ago, shaking him while having coffee at Jessie Hindman's. This one wasn't as strong as that, and even then, he'd only spilled a little coffee on the kitchen floor.

"Almost stepped in my own puddle," Smith says behind him. "Fuck was that?"

"An earthquake," Officer Hayes replies. He peeks over his shoulder. Smith is standing up. Done. Her pants are back up. She's discreet to a certain point. Not just a wild animal.

"One thing I always depended on when the world turned upside down was that the ground at least hadn't fallen out from under my feet. Now…"

"The valley follows a fault line," Brock explains. "It's what created the whole area in the first place. Little quakes like that happen now and again."

"Little?" Smith quips. "I'd have pissed my pants if I hadn't emptied already."

"We need to enjoy the silence," Officer Hayes advises as he escorts her around the dune they'd used to give her privacy from Deputy Davis and the bus driver. *Silence…* Brock realizes he hasn't noticed the rumble of the bus since the tremor. He can't hear the huffing of the big diesel engine.

They round the dune, and the bus is missing. Deputy Davis and the Inyo County police cruiser are gone, too. Brock stops short, and Smith stands beside him, jangling her handcuffs. They both stare as if Copperfield himself has performed a personal disappearing trick roadside in the Mojave. The two are standing along the highway alone, not another soul in sight.

The only thing to indicate they aren't a million miles from civilization is a billboard a hundred yards down the road advertising Skidoo. Just Officer Hayes, Smith, and a ghost town.

4.4 Richter

[Landry]

Landry Honanie works at the Skidoo gift shop. The ghost town runs with only two employees most days. One lucky person sits and guards the cheap China imports against foolish shoplifters who would risk incarceration for a fifty-cent plastic cactus. The other patrols the attraction to make sure no stupid tourists are trying to graffiti the one-room schoolhouse, swipe the props from the saloon, or use one of the rooms in the bordello for public intercourse. The patrol isn't much more entertaining than guarding this shit on the shelves, but occasionally it was fun to chase some horny Utah brats out of the whorehouse with their pants around their ankles.

The clock moves in slow motion. Finally, the minute hand reaches the four. Closing time. Landry locks the front door. After a quick sweep and a fast countdown of the till—only the two kids from the RV bought anything today, and they used their parents' credit card—Landry shuts off the lights and leaves through the back. The ghost town is an *actual* ghost town.

Landry comes around the front. The main street—the only road—is empty. The RV family left a few minutes ago. The asshole who had arrived a while ago with a girl Landry's age—she hadn't even left the vehicle—boogied out as soon as the first tremor hit. No one else had visited Skidoo all damn day.

Bucky will need help locking the buildings up and down the deserted street along Skidoo. Bucky is old as hell. Charity Pellman swears he's one of the founders of Skidoo. Landry isn't sure if she's joking or doesn't realize the town had initially operated a century and a half ago. Maybe she's being funny, although Charity isn't known for being a joker. Bucky isn't 150, but he might be closer to that than he is to zero.

Bucky probably hasn't even finished locking up the jail. Or maybe he's fallen asleep on one of the bordello beds again.

Landry starts in the one-room school. The RV family left their names on the blackboard. Rosario. Linda. Chuy. Hector. Sometimes, Landry thought of the names tourists left behind as epitaphs. How many had died right after leaving Skidoo, so the last thing they'd ever printed on this Earth was the message on this old blackboard? Landry traces the heart the girl named Rosario used to dot her "i." Then Landry erases the rest of the white chalk to make a blank slate again tomorrow. New names, new faces, same old shit. Every day.

Next, the jail. No Bucky. The asshole with the nice car had left a business card between the bars of the single jail cell. A picture of the photogenic bastard highlighted his fake tan and a fabulous head of blond hair. "Josh Henry, paralegal. Dyson, Dytel, and Dickson." Landry is sure the card would say "Dyson, Dytel, Dickson, and Douchebag" someday. When Landry's dad rebuilt Skidoo and made the town a tourist attraction, folks still appreciated the past and honored what had come before. Now, the public rewards vain motherfuckers like Josh Henry for an attractive appearance and a fake smile. Welcome to the face of the future.

Landry crumples up the business card and tosses it in the otherwise empty trash.

After a few more buildings, the saloon is the only structure remaining. If Bucky is sleeping while Landry locks up the whole town, the old man will get seriously bawled out. Bucky better be down and out from a severe heart attack if he's not on his feet with a broom in his goddamn hands.

The main interior of the saloon features a bar top along the back with antique liquor bottles filled with colored water. Tables around the place feature cards preserved under the lacquer—poker games frozen mid-play. A piano along the wall plays automatically. Landry flips the switch, and silence blankets the building. No sound from Bucky at all. The old bastard must be asleep in a bed upstairs.

Landry ascends the stairs. The grand stairway owes less to Douglas Honanie's attention to historical accuracy and more designed according to something Landry's dad had seen on an episode of *Gunsmoke* the month of its origination. Handsome detailing by Douglas Honanie's hand turned the wood in a gentle curve up to the second floor. Bucky liked to doze off in the bordello for an hour or two in the afternoon when it was slow. Today was slow, but Bucky is usually responsible enough to be awake again to close on schedule.

The rooms upstairs are empty, including the public restrooms. Bucky isn't in any of the bedrooms or bathrooms. One of the beds exhibits signs of use. Landry recalls a line from an old nighttime story—*Who's been sleeping in my bed?* If Bucky had been here, he's gone now. Landry frowns. This is the last building on the list. Every building is locked up. Still no Bucky. Had the old fart gone back and reopened one of the locked-up buildings? Does Landry have to retrace his steps through every one of the doors along Main Street Skidoo?

The second story of the saloon offers unparalleled views of the ghost town. Employees park in reserved spots out back of the mercantile. Landry spots the dirty white Nissan that has been in the Honanie family for years. Dad handed it down to Landry last year. The car remains right where it's supposed to be. Beside the Nissan is a blue Chevy pickup as old as Landry. Bucky's truck. So, he didn't take off without telling Landry.

Then where the hell is he?

"I swear to God, if the old bastard lost his marbles and wandered off into the desert, I'm gonna leave his ass out there."

Landry walks down the second-story hallway and looks out the window opposite the one overlooking the employee parking lot. The desert stretches into endless miles in that direction. At the edge of the landscaped part of Skidoo sits a facade of a mining entrance with a cutout in the center mimicking an entry to the shaft. A replica mining car features in the cutaway. The face is painted plywood, weathered and worn. Dad always worried a strong breeze would someday blow it over. Landry believes it'd be a mercy. They ought to allow the faded set piece to expire.

As Landry sweeps both eyes across the landscape, the whole saloon gives a sudden lurch, making the lonely Skidoo employee stumble backward before tumbling forward. At 22, Landry has experienced enough tremors to know an earthquake when one rumbled through. Staring out the second-story window, the flimsy plywood facade of the mine entrance flopped back and forth a couple of times before succumbing to gravity. The scenery the size of a building facade topples forward to land on its face.

It was an aftershock. Landry had felt the first slight tremor a while ago. Enough to send the supremely douchy Josh Henry skedaddling out of Skidoo. Nothing of concern to anyone who's experienced dozens of such rumbles. But this one had been enough to topple the fake mine shaft front that had stood for decades. Maybe not a minor reverberation after all.

Landry needs to find Bucky. Maybe the unsteady old duffer toppled over during the last quake and hit his head. Perhaps he'd been out back of one of the buildings when he suffered a fall. Landry didn't think anything dangerous about the former tremor, but being 22 isn't the same as being 80. Bucky could be in trouble…

Landry exits the saloon and stops short on the front boardwalk running down Main's dusty avenue. How many times has Landry stared at this exact panorama? A thousand times since he was a baby? But something is different. Something amiss. Landry has seen the scene almost daily for a lifetime, yet the exact difference from before avoided an easy answer. Then the missing thing jumps out at Landry like a phantom manifesting in the ghost town. A change as plain as the wine-swollen nose on Bucky's wrinkled face—the one-room schoolhouse is *gone*.

That building had not been merely a facade like the mine entrance. Landry had been standing right inside the classroom only a few minutes before. As quickly as Landry erased the names of the RV family from the blackboard, so too had the entire school been erased from the line of buildings down Main Street. Gone. A whole building *disappeared*— just a space of empty sand between the jail and the mercantile.

It is gone without a trace.

4.5 Richter
[Pastor Montgomery]

Pastor Montgomery Childes is on his way back from a convention in California. The Lutheran parish members of the St. Joseph Church will appreciate the insights he gathered from the West Coast retreat. The president of the ELCA herself had spoken at the conference in Glendale, California. Inspirational and educational, Monty feels he's learned a lot of new things to share with his congregation.

These conferences were never the extravagant affairs of the Catholic callings. Father Mike at Mary Mother of the Lord Cathedral in downtown St. Joseph, Missouri, often brags about being flown to Vatican City every so often for a lavish retreat. Pastor Montgomery's Lutheran followers had pooled enough to pay for gas and a stay at the Red Roof Inn in Glendale. Now he is returning to Missouri, a road trip across half of America.

He's eager to get home. He hasn't seen his wife, Daphne, in a week. His dogs are surely missing him. His daughters no longer live near Missouri—Cheri is an RN in Chicago, and Ashley is in Miami for school. They'll all be together for Christmas. Soon enough. But Monty can wait patiently…he's never been in a rush to move forward. He likes to think of Cheri and Ashley as little girls, always in awe of their daddy, needing him to serve as their anchor and keep them steady. But nowadays, he's lucky if they text him once a week.

As much as he looked forward to returning to his bed, Monty had decided on a detour on his way home. Pastor Pauline from down in Oklahoma had told Monty about the last time she'd had to drive that route (she was flying this year—a wealthy congregant had died and left a chunk of money to the church. Sciatica was the devil on her back this year, and she refused to drive all those hours.). A few years back, Pastor Pauline stopped in the Mojave desert, and she said she felt like Jesus in the desert.

"I parked my car by the side of the road and walked out across the burning sands. I've never felt such heat, such thirst. The sand and sun had me all turned around. Two hours in the heat, and I felt like Satan was coming for me," she'd said. "It was a religious encounter, Montgomery. I felt like I was living the Lord's experience. Straight out of Matthew, chapter four."

The conference that year had been in July, and the desert heat would have been unfathomable. Pastor Pauline is lucky she hadn't died of heat stroke. Monty firmly believes in miracles but subscribes to the idea that God helps those who help themselves. Wandering around in 120-degree heat is a great way to prove natural selection rather than divine intervention.

It isn't July, but December. Monty isn't going to fry like an egg on a skillet. The temperatures are very comfortable, especially for a guy used to the bluster of a Missouri December. Pastor Pauline's story about the desert piqued Monty's interest, so he detours to travel deeper into the desert rather than the straight route along I-15 to Vegas would've taken him. Monty wants to get a feel for the Jesus experience without the heatstroke.

He pulls over a couple of miles past where Panamint Valley Road turns into Highway 190 and goes through the middle of Death Valley. This area is as desert as it gets. Monty gets out of the car and marvels at the endless amounts of sand. He thinks about Pastor Pauline getting lost out here in the wavering heat, and maybe it *is* a miracle she hadn't died. Everything looks the same for miles in every direction.

Monty imagines Jesus wandering around the wilderness for 40 days and 40 nights. Monty kicks off his shoes and steps into the sand. Maybe the Lord had sandals, maybe not. He walks a little off the road until sand and cacti surround him. There is no sign of a road or power line or modern convenience. His stomach tightens as he considers Pastor Pauline's tale again—what if he gets turned around and lost for 40 days? What does Montgomery Childes know about survival in a rugged environment?

Nothing.

He turns, prepared to head back, and pauses. The ground moves under his feet. "Holy..." he mutters as he dances with the desert underfoot. The earthquake was a tiny tremor but alarming for a guy from Missouri. Monty plants his feet apart in a stance, waiting for an aftershock. How long between quakes? He isn't any more expert on seismic events than desert survival skills.

Monty marches the ten yards back over the roadside dune to his car. Or at least where he'd left his car five minutes before.

Monty stands dumbfounded, wondering if he's gotten lost, as Pastor Pauline had one July years back. He can't be hallucinating because of heatstroke because it isn't hot. He couldn't have taken a wrong turn—he'd only journeyed a few feet off the road. But his car is *gone*. He'd pulled it to the side of the road in a flat spot on the sandy shoulder. Now, there is nothing.

His car is missing, but the highway remains. This must be the spot, isn't it? The dizzying effect of the incomprehensible makes his mind swim. Logic fails. Monty looks back. Were two roads running parallel, and had he gotten turned around by the tremor? He shakes his head. Surely, there can't be another highway so near in the middle of nowhere.

Someone must have *stolen* his car!

He'd left the keys in the ignition and the door unlocked. He hadn't passed more than one or two vehicles in the last hour, so he hadn't expected highway robbers out here along this remote expanse of desert road. Yet the car has disappeared. Either this is the oddest and greatest practical joke ever pulled, or someone carjacked him.

His shoes… Even his shoes are gone. He'd left them by the car, and they'd also disappeared. What sort of thief engaged in grand larceny would take the time also to commit a footwear felony? The idea boggles Monty's mind.

Then he hears it.

All Creatures of Our God and King.

Monty's daughter, Ashley, loves animals. Growing up, she would go gonzo over every critter and wayward pet. There was always some living thing in a box or a tote in the parsonage. The hymn "All Creatures of Our God and King" was her favorite when she was little. She'd sing it loudest of the congregation. Monty loved hearing her voice. Now that she is grown up and studying marine biology in Miami, he'd made the hymn her ringtone.

He hears it now, faintly, like it was coming from some distance. He'd left his phone on the passenger seat of the missing car. Monty pauses and holds his breath, trying to silence the thudding of his panicked blood rushing in his ears. Is it his imagination? No. He can hear it over the utter stillness of existence, a sound from another world. Maybe he is trapped in a nightmare and can listen to what's happening outside the dream. But Monty can't wake up. He's sure he's not dreaming.

Is he hallucinating in the desert? Is this a religious experience like Pastor Pauline had experienced? He's only been out of his car for a few minutes. Right? Or had he tripped and fallen during the earthquake and knocked his head? Maybe it has been longer than a few minutes. The day looks the same, but maybe it's the *next* day? He checks his head for bumps or cuts—all fine.

Then the hymn stops. A quietness settles over Monty's place in the world. This is true silence. He is sure he hadn't imagined the ringtone. Maybe his phone was tossed out the window when the thief had taken his car. He searches his surroundings and finds nothing. He waits for the ringtone to come again. Silence.

Pastor Montgomery Childes stands barefoot by the side of the road in the desert. No one and nothing in either direction for many miles.

His car has mysteriously vanished. No plan. No way to contact anyone. Except…

Monty closes his eyes and starts to pray.

4.6 Richter

[The Garcias]

Linda Garcia hadn't been eager to spend the holiday vacation packed into an RV with her husband and kids. She'd wanted to spend Christmas at home in the traditional way—make a big dinner, decorate the tree, and watch the Charlie Brown special for the umpteenth time. The Church of the Everlasting Light featured a live nativity scene on the Saturday night before Christmas, and it was her favorite thing. Chuy could've been singing in his school's holiday program with a bunch of other off-key eight-year-olds—instead, they sail the concrete byways of southeastern California. The world looks more like the Sahara than a winter wonderland.

Yet the adventure has turned out to be pleasant enough. Exciting even. Hector had boldly turned off his planned route. When was the last time he'd been spontaneous? Probably the night Rosario had been conceived. They had even scheduled Chuy's impregnation with the clinical help for insemination—and hadn't she wondered what Hector had thought of his best-laid plans on the frequent occasions Chuy tried to drive his father mad? Hector hadn't scheduled a detour to a ghost town, but he had taken the turn.

A ghost town. Not on Linda's bucket list of destinations to visit before she died. That list is long, but Hector always promised to tick every last place off the list. They had postponed many endeavors since she first waved a positive pregnancy test in front of Hector's face. But this year, she is checking one spot off her menu. They are heading for the Rockies for a white Christmas.

Surprisingly, she could mark off one recent addition to the list already—Skidoo, California, had been the place she'd never known she'd wanted to go. But hadn't it ended up being a place of fresh surprise? The old-fashioned town harkened back to how things used to be—things like the romance in Linda and Hector's marriage.

The kids had asked to get snacks at the gift shop while Linda and Hector entered the saloon. Hector gave the kids his credit card. Linda gazed at the bottles of fake booze and wished they contained something more potent. But while the colored liquid in the props was impotent, Hector Garcia certainly wasn't.

"Upstairs is the bordello," he said in his sexy voice—at least, he *thought* it was his sexy voice. Hector waggled his eyebrows as he used to when...

"What are you suggesting, Mister Garcia?"

"Have you ever made love in an old west whorehouse?" Hector teased.

She has now. They'd had a quickie on one of the beds while the kids shopped for cheap imported souvenirs. Linda hadn't been satisfied sexually in so many years she didn't want to think about it, but she had had to stifle her cries so she didn't alert the whole damn place she was enjoying this fake-ass ghost town a LOT more than she'd ever expected to.

Hector is *full* of surprises today.

Now, she sits in the passenger seat as he whistles happily to himself. She smiles coyly, and he gives her a wink. This trip feels like their honeymoon to Vegas all those years ago, where they'd had such a great time. Then Chuy plops down on her knee and starts complaining about his sister, and the whole illusion comes crashing down.

"She's giggling over some message from Chaz *again*."

"Never mind your sister," Linda scolds. "Enjoy the scenery. Check out all this natural splendor."

"A whole lot of nothing," Chuy grumbles. "Except those two idiots."

Hector stops the RV at the intersection that will return them to the highway after their extracurricular activity in Skidoo. Along the main road, two figures are walking toward them like images of something that doesn't belong in this scene. In the summer, two hitchhikers would die in minutes in this desert environment. In the winter, it only seems eerie.

"What are they doing out here walking?" Hector asks.

"I think one of them is a cop," Chuy says.

"Maybe they need a ride," Linda says.

"At the rate they're moving, it's going to be nighttime before they get here," Chuy whines. "Let's go. I'm borrrrrrred."

"Well, they're in the opposite direction we need to go, and I can't turn this R.V. around on this narrow highway," Hector says. "What if they need help?"

"We aren't going to sit and wait for them forever, are we?" Chuy complains.

"I'll check it out," Linda says. She is still buzzing with energy from Hector's unexpected performance at the bordello, and she needs the excuse to stretch her legs for a minute.

"I'm coming with you," Chuy says.

"Wait here," Linda tells her son. "I'll be right back."

Chuy crosses his arms and plops into the passenger seat—his classic windup to an epic pouting session. No one is better than Chuy at spreading his misery to others. He's like the grand champion of feeling sorry for himself. Linda smiles to herself as she leaves the mess for Hector to deal with.

The world is quiet. Their neighborhood in LA bustles with activity all the time. They live near the freeway, cars zooming along at all hours of the day. The airport is near enough for a jet to drown out all conversation once or twice every hour. Their apartment is in a building with a hundred others, sounds emanating across the cubicles in a constant backdrop of noise. Sirens, televisions, music, shouting, gunshots, beeps and blasts, and bass and banging. All the time.

Here, the silence is almost disturbing. The lack of sound makes Linda wonder if the world beyond this barren landscape has ceased to exist. They could be the last survivors of some cataclysmic Armageddon and they wouldn't even know it. She checks her phone; there are no bars. No service. They are at the end of the world.

The two figures walking toward the RV along the highway act as further evidence of Armageddon. The scene reminds Linda of a hundred post-apocalyptic movies where a few survivors live to make a new life in a barren wasteland. Maybe these pedestrians are zombies from a terrible horror movie or mutated monsters from some sci-fi schlock. But Linda doesn't believe she's in some hack's idea of a horror movie, so she starts walking toward them.

Linda feels more alive than she has since she was a newlywed. She and Hector had a whirlwind romance—they'd met, fallen in love, and married within months. She remembers the swoon she'd felt during their first year together. The feeling was wonderful and lasted for a while. Then Rosario had come along. A baby zapped her libido. When Rosie was old enough for Linda to feel ready to rekindle some romance, it was time for another pregnancy. Baby number two was twice as debilitating.

But now, she skips for a few steps as she moves along the roadway. She glances back. Sure as hell, Hector Gonzales is checking out her ass! She puts a little more sway in the hips as she continues. If Hector wants a show, she'll give him something he can enjoy.

Linda pauses halfway between the RV and the two people walking toward her. Something is off about the two figures approaching. One is a black man in a police uniform, and the other is a brown woman in an orange jumpsuit. Guard and prisoner? An unfortunate choice of cosplay? Is the desert air playing tricks on her eyes?

She cups her hands and uses her loudest "mom voice": "Do you need help?"

The woman in the orange jumpsuit flips her off, but the cop waves his hand high over his head. Is that a yes? The cop hollers back, but it arrives in a whisper. Rat-a-tat-tat? Riddle me backpack? Riverbank clap-trap?

Nothing she imagines makes sense. She cups her hands to shout back another question, and the earth shakes beneath her feet.

There had been a tremor back at the ghost town. Linda had seen some white boy turn tail and run like he didn't trust the quake not to shake his bowels loose. A little rock 'n' roll like that in LA was just another Tuesday. Linda hadn't panicked. They'd finished their tour of Ski-doo and skedaddled—after a session of getting diddled. Now, a tiny aftershock rumbled through.

Nothing major.

Indeed, nothing to make her turn around and run back to the RV.

But the pair of strangers walking toward her? They give her the creeps.

She waits for them rather than making a further approach. Why had she come out here anyway? Why hadn't she stayed at the RV and waited for them to arrive? She suddenly felt silly standing out here all alone. The whole stroll was entirely pointless. She is so full of energy she wants to burn up a little by walking in the fresh air. And letting Hector have an eyeful of second helpings.

She feels like that young woman all over again.

The whole future is looking bright.

Then the ground opens beneath Linda and swallows her whole.

4.7 Richter
[Bulldog]

Suraya Ahmadi sits high in the big rig, heading down the highway at full speed. She takes the back way to SoCal through the Mojave in the winter because the roads are deserted and the temps moderate. Suraya feels like she owns the road as she roars over the sands, a lonely voyager on a sea of rolling dunes. In her life, she has rarely felt in control of her destiny. Now, she's the master of the roadway.

The other truckers think she looks more like a "sir" than a Suraya. Her mother still worries over her being on the road in an eighteen-wheeler—"Sur, the men. They take what they want." It sounded as bad in Pashto as it did in English. The men didn't take anything from Suraya. Most of them think *she* is a man.

Squat, wide, frumpy, she had earned a nickname long ago when she started rolling over the miles of highway. The truckers in her circle call her Bulldog. Maybe they didn't mean it as cruel, but it feels like it. Instead of being stuck with it, she embraces it. Her bark and her bite are ferocious. Bulldog is fifty going on not-giving-a-fuck. Too damn old to give a shit about what a bunch of assholes call her.

Bruno Mars comes on the radio, and she starts singing a terrible duet of his newest song. Suraya doesn't know if it is about having sex, being sexy, or wanting sex, but Bruno could sing about whatever he wants. She wouldn't slow down if the president were thumbing a ride along the stretch of lonely desert highway, but she'd give Mr. Mars a lift anywhere he wanted. Bulldog likes chocolate, and Mars is her favorite treat.

Suraya suddenly craves candy and decides to stop at the next gas station for snacks. Chocolate melty snacks.

A voice crackles on the CB as another trucker reports on road conditions. "The way's out east of where one-ninety intersects Panamint Valley Road."

Suraya just passed Stovepipe Wells heading west. She's traveling right in that direction. She grabs the handset. "Fuck you say," Suraya grumbles, trying to tamp down her Pashto accent as much as possible. "Headin' right in that direction."

"That you, Bulldog?" The voice belongs to Dex Geist, who goes by "Jesus Geist" or "Holyman." "You best head back, sweetheart." Suraya was no sweetheart. "If you can manage to turn that big ass around."

He meant her rig, but he also referred to her actual backside. Holyman forgot Bulldog could have some bite. She would take a chunk out of him the next time their rigs met. Suraya could make a grown man cry.

"Could you see what's the holdup?" Suraya asks.

"I saw the 'Road Closed' sign and took the detour. End of story. You want a closer look, then keep comin' over on one-ninety, Bulldog."

Holyman signs off. He couldn't care less if Suraya turned around or barreled through the roadblock. She would lose at least two hours if she went back. And she couldn't turn around right here anyway. She needed a place wide enough to make a U-turn. An intersection. The closest location would be the turn-off to the ghost town she always saw the signs for along this route. Skippy? Skidmarks? *Skidoo.*

The intersection is another mile up the road.

Suraya comes up on a spot along the highway where she can pull aside, but it isn't big enough to turn around without jackknifing the big rig. Parked alongside the road, she pulls out her cell phone to call the local authorities and ask them if she can circumnavigate the roadblock. No signal. She curses and climbs out of her cab. Holding her phone over her head, she walks in a circle, trying to get a bar. Nothing.

She hates technology. Everyone depends on wires, lights, and enchanted airwaves transmitting all sorts of hoodoo. Suraya hates being dependent on these goddamn machines all the time. The old Pony Express had the right idea—man and animal and the elements. The only machine they had to worry about was one made of flesh and bone. Now, everything is made of magic and mayhem.

Suraya pauses. She examines the sandy sidebar along the road. Barely long enough for her sixteen-wheeler to fit. No other tire tracks in the dirty sand. But two sets of footprints come from the desert alongside the road. Then they track off along the shoulder toward the west. Suraya gazes into the wilds and wonders where the two pedestrians had come from and where they are going. Another time of year, they wouldn't have gotten a half-mile before they dropped dead of heat exhaustion.

Suraya exhales. She climbs back up into the truck's cab and returns to the road. She ramps the rig up to full speed. The intersection is coming up, and she plans on turning back. She spies an RV in the distance, the only vehicle in sight along the highway in either direction along the juncture. It better get out of her way. Pissed off and counting off the hours she would be losing, she barrels toward the Skidoo intersection to turn around and make the voyage back. *All* the way back.

Suraya sees two figures alongside the road, surely the pedestrians who made the footprints along the shoulder. One wears a bright orange jumpsuit. At first glance, Suraya registers the color as a construction sign, but it's a woman who looks like someone from a prison television show. The other is a cop, the bland, dark blue uniform blending into the shimmering asphalt of the highway. As she closes in on them at high speed, the cop turns toward the sound of the approaching semi-truck. He shouts and points at the roadway. The prisoner waves her handcuffed arms over her head in warning. They hop and dance like they'd witnessed Jesus Christ making crocuses out of the cacti. No

Holyman here. Holyman had taken the detour.

Then Suraya sees what all the commotion is about. The sand swallows up the asphalt route another hundred yards down the road—a sinkhole. The road is out! Her trailer is empty, but the truck is still heavier than hell. She can't stop in time. Bulldog's only hope of saving her tail is to go around. How steep is the ditch? How much rock and bric-a-brac clog the roadside? Would she hit the sand like a mouse in a glue trap?

She doesn't have any other choice.

She pulls the wheel hard to the right. The wheels leave the pavement, but the condition of the road ahead has already promised that inevitability. Suraya sees thick cacti before the truck grille plows like a combine through harvest corn. Sand blasts upward like she is riding a whale that has breached and splashes back into the sea. She jerks hard against the seatbelt, cinched tight and holding the big ass Holyman had teased her about firmly against her seat.

Suraya slides through the sandy surface like so much snow, without traction on the soft surface. Then sand gives way to windswept rock, and the tires grab hold, giving her enough grip to turn in a wide arc leading her back toward the highway. Another lurch as the wheels plow more sand like she's breaking through a fresh snowbank. Past more soft terrain is finally the road, her wheels return to pavement.

She brakes until the rig comes to a complete stop on the highway.

Somehow, she'd made a wide arc around the missing section of roadway. A twenty-foot section of asphalt is gone, like the road crews had been working toward the middle from each end, and this is the last piece of highway to finish. A slight depression in the sand indicates a sinkhole had swallowed the roadway.

Suraya climbs out of the cab. The cop and the convict followed her wheel tracks around the missing section of the road and arrive huffing and puffing at her side. They point at the missing portion of Route 190, lips moving but neither making a sound. What had they seen? What had happened? Why are they pointing at the missing section of the road?

Then Suraya hears the wails of true misery. A haunting sound she's blessedly heard little of these last twenty-five years. But she'd listened to its ominous warble enough for the first half of her existence—the caterwaul of shock and grief. Two kids are sprinting away from the RV at the Skidoo exit toward the place where Suraya has come to a stop. Behind them, a man leans against the recreational vehicle in a visible state of shock. The young people scream the same word again and again and again.

The word chills Suraya to the bone.

"Mom! Mom! Mom! Mom!"

4.8 Richter
[Pi]

Pi can hardly stand another minute with this asshole. He about shit his shorts when the earthquake gave them a lurch in Skidoo, and they left in a hurry. They resumed their voyage west along the highway until they came to a roadblock. A concrete barrier stretched across the entire road. The genius had thought he could get around the barricade and only got them stuck in a pile of sand.

They wasted an hour trying to get the SUV unstuck. Josh scratched his head and hemmed and hawed. He waved his phone in the air, trying to get a signal to call for a tow truck, but services are nonexistent here, at the edge of obscurity. Josh had borrowed the vehicle from his sister in Omaha because he hadn't wanted to put so many miles on his new Mercedes.

"Maybe we ought to walk somewhere," Josh wonders aloud.

"Where to?" Pi asks. "We're in the middle of fucking nowhere!"

"Back to the ghost town," Josh suggests. That place is ten miles back and would take hours to arrive. Returning to an empty town in the dead of night doesn't seem like a good choice.

"That will take us way too long. The place will be closed."

"There was a gas station back there."

"It's already late afternoon," Pi notes. "It'll be dark soon."

"Then we keep going west. There must be something up ahead. We go past the roadblock and see what's on the other side. Maybe a road busy enough to catch a ride?"

"I'm not betting my whole night walking along a desert highway on a goddamn hunch, Josh. Let's try to get the car unstuck before we go hiking in the dark with the coyotes and vultures."

That seems to motivate Josh. Scared of earthquakes, he isn't any braver regarding nocturnal predators. He examines their sandy situation and considers ways of righting the ship rather than abandoning it.

Not conceding the role of rescuer to the so-called "man," Pi scrounges through the trunk for some sort of tool with which to dig. She feels like she's at some archeological site, rummaging through an area no one has explored in a long time. She finds an ancient packet of ramen noodles, a baby rattle chewed like a dog's toy, and an old flip phone. She uses the phone as a scoop and shovels sand from around the tires.

Josh uses his hands for something other than glad-handing potential clients and clears a path from the tires to the roadway. Between the two of them, they create a rut leading backward out of the sandbox. Pi gets behind the wheel as Josh leans against the front bumper and shoves with all his inconsiderable might, hoping that with enough force he could gain enough traction that would get them moving incrementally back to the road.

Eventually, they get the SUV back on the pavement. Pi hops into the passenger seat, and Josh climbs behind the wheel. He won't let her drive his sister's vehicle. Because he's the man. Supposedly.

Pi notes the billboard to Skidoo. They retrace the miles to the place where they'd already been. Then how many more miles of backtracking to get around the closed road? What a colossal waste of time. And even more hours she would have to spend with Josh until she can finally escape. Being stuck in her mother's house with the douchebag would feel like freedom after being trapped together inside this car for so many hours.

"What the—"

The road ends unexpectedly. There is no roadblock this time. Josh slams the brakes, but he isn't going to swerve left or right and hit the sand again. He keeps going straight, even though the pavement simply disappears.

Those two words are all Josh manages before they topple off the edge of the world.

The RAV4 pitches off the end of the road and falls nose-first down a sinkhole ten feet deep.

The airbag hits them like a professional boxer with a massive glove. Pi feels twin rivulets of blood leaking down her face, and she sees stars. Not the night-sky kind, but the punch-drunk type. She hasn't felt like this since her sister socked her in the nose when Pi had called her ugly back when they were tweens.

"What the hell," Josh slurs.

Pi pushes the deflating bag out of her face and wipes away the blood leaking from her nostrils with the back of her long sleeve. She checks Josh. He's half-stunned, his nose broken and crooked, and his eyes streaming tears. She turns the other way, and all she sees out the passenger side window is sand. Earth also blocks the windshield. Her chest strains against the seatbelt, cinched tight on impact, holding her against her seat. Otherwise, she'd be smashed against the dashboard as the Toyota currently is oriented at 90 degrees off normal. The nose of the vehicle points straight down.

"Earthquake opened a sinkhole. Probably along a fault line," Pi observes. "We gotta get outta here."

"Gotta get outta," Josh repeats in a mumble. He's half-stunned and in shock.

Pi adjusts the rearview mirror and tilts it to see behind her. The back window stares up at the sky. The back hatch allows the only escape out of this. If the earth can open and swallow them without warning, it may close again as unexpectedly. Swallowed whole. Pi shudders. And she starts moving.

"Let's go," Pi says, releasing the seatbelt and falling forward, trying to brace herself against the windshield and dashboard but still banging her forehead on the visor.

"Fuck, I'm stuck," Josh panics, pulling on his seatbelt like a rip-cord.

Hell of a time to reveal poetic talents, Pi thinks.

Fuck, I'm stuck repeats in her brain over and over, like a song that replays in perpetuity.

"Settle down," she says, finding the button for his buckle and pressing it. He's still cinched. She pushes again, harder. Still belted. She yanks and pulls while pressing the button. Locked tight. *Fuck, he is stuck.*

The RAV4 shifts, tilts, and then drops farther down. Down the gullet. Pi pictures them swallowed. Jonah-and-the-whale shit. But it's a sinkhole. How deep do they go? Is there any getting out of such a trap? Or is it game over? The Toyota could be her coffin.

FuckI'mstuckFuckI'mstuckFuckI'mstuck.

"Knife?" Pi asks. She knows the answer. They already searched the car for anything to help dig them out. She has cataloged the entire inventory of the SUV. Josh's eyes are wide, dark sinkholes into his head. He shakes his head. No knife.

"You need to wiggle out," Pi says, pulling the belt back.

Flung forward, all his weight strains on the straps. Maybe if he could ease up on the belts… He braces his hands against the steering wheel and pushes himself back into the seat. Pi feels some slack and grabs for the button again just as the SUV falls another couple of feet, slamming Josh against the belt once more and smashing Pi against the windshield. Her foot strikes the side window, and a crack appears across the pane.

Pi envisions sand pouring in like she's stuck at the bottom of an hourglass and this is some kind of *Batman* villain trap. She gazes over Josh's shoulder through the rear window and can barely see anything. The SUV is deep enough that sand has started to cascade over the back hatch. If they fall any deeper, the collapsing sand will make the rear door too heavy to open.

"Josh, I gotta go for help," Pi says, pushing off against the windshield and grabbing the passenger seat's headrest. "We're running out of time."

I'm *running out of time.*

"Nononononono," Josh cries. "Don't leave me. Please don't leave me. I'm gonna be buried alive. I don't want to be buried alive!"

"I can get help," Pi promises, pulling herself through the seats toward the back. "There won't be any help if we're both stuck."

Josh grabs her by the back pocket of her jeans. "Don't go."

Pi has her left foot wedged against the center console, and Josh's hand on her ass pulls her back, making her knee bend painfully. He's going to get them both killed. She isn't going to die down here with Josh Henry. But he's anchoring her to the front of the vehicle, ensuring a double death in this sandy pit. *Fuck, I'm stuck,* she thinks.

She isn't going to die down here.

Pi brings her right leg up into Josh's face. She has no plan, but survival instincts have taken over her reactions. She isn't going to give up. Either one person is going to have a chance, or neither. She hears the crunch of a knee against an already ruined nose, and Josh screams like a banshee. His hand loosens enough so that she gets some traction on her left knee while gaining a foothold with her right shoe. Her back pocket rips free. Then she's moving forward, upward, toward the sky.

Pi ascends through the back seat and into the trunk area. This piece-of-shit SUV might be old, but it still has an automatic back hatch, and Pi has the spare keys in her front pocket. She presses the fob, and the rear door starts to open. She shoulders the door when the latch releases and forces it fully open.

Josh is still screaming as Pi claws up the side of the sandy hole. Standing on the back bumper, she can just reach the edge of the sinkhole. She climbs up and out as Josh continues his caterwauling behind her. She's never heard someone make such noise. Those awful screams will echo in her nightmares for the rest of her life.

At least she has the rest of her life.

Pi scrambles away from the sinkhole like a crab crawling across a beach. She stops at the edge of the asphalt, where the highway continues opposite where they'd fallen into the hole. Pi stops and stares up at the sky. She can still hear Josh screaming, although the sound grows increasingly muffled. After a few minutes, she knows the sound has stopped. The window couldn't have lasted much longer, or sand pouring in the open back hatch would've buried him shortly after her escape.

But she can still hear him in her head.

Screaming.

4.9 Richter

[Carl]

Carl flips the sign on the front window promptly at five. The gas pumps are completely autonomous and will still work with a credit card. If anyone needs full service or necessary sundries, they either keep driving or wait until morning. Carl never comes out of his quarters to help a customer after hours. *Never.*

The back of the gas station features a small apartment tucked away as such that most people wouldn't guess living quarters even existed on the premises. Carl doesn't own a vehicle, so there's no telltale sign of occupancy once the lights are out. He never goes anywhere after work except front to back—a routine unvaried since Mary died. A monotonous repetition meant to stretch his experiences out exponentially.

In the mornings, he gets up well before sunrise to take a long walk along the trail through the valley behind the station. He uses a walking stick to ward against pesky varmints who might want a bite. Nature abhors invaders to this inhospitable domain. The temperature is deadly in the summertime, and darkness affords only a brief window to experience the outdoors. Now December, Carl usually wears a light jacket for his morning endeavors.

After work, he follows a strict regimen. After locking up, he always makes a small supper featuring items from cans—boiled potatoes, a portion of beef, and a helping of vegetables rotated between corn, peas, and carrots. A glass of black tea over ice cubes serves as his beverage of choice. On Saturdays, he enjoys one bottle of beer after his meal. On Sundays, he allows himself a dessert in the form of a prepackaged confection from the convenience store—cookie or cupcake.

He doesn't possess a television or fancy phone. The last electronic convenience he'd owned was a can opener that died not long after Mary, and he'd tossed it in the trash in favor of a hand-held one. Electricity ran only necessities like lights and A/C. Refrigerator. His ancient shortwave radio. Nothing else had a cord. His stove and hot water ran off the propane tank out back.

The world had already gone dark, the sun setting before he even closed up shop at this time of year. Darkness in the valley falls completely, scant artificial light disturbing the landscape. The signs all turn off automatically at five, so the front of the station features only the faint digital glow from the electronic screens and credit card readers on the pumps. Overhead lights, which might aid late-night travelers in re-fueling, remain dark. Carl refuses to sacrifice the ambient darkness for convenience's sake.

Out back, only the stars light the world. Carl keeps a weathered old rocking chair on a cracked concrete pad beside a small table flecked with peeling green paint that provides a perch for his tea. A tattered awning offers some shade during the summer. He settles in and stares up, lost in the stars.

Out here, tiny twinkling points pepper the sky, so many it reveals the night sky isn't black at all but a kind of gray. The myriad stars off-set the vast emptiness between. The view is a tapestry of the past, a pic-ture of things long ago. The light from the stars is all ancient history. The illumination arriving now started countless years ago on the long journey to Earth. Everything above is the past. The white pinpoints are holes too small to breathe through, the night a heavy blanket slowly suffocating the world.

Carl sighs.

The world rumbles, as if reminding him of the insignificance of a tiny flesh-and-bone mote upon the cosmic stage. He's been feeling tremors all day. There's a strange regularity to the quakes, a rhythm uncommon to the random rumblings of Earth. Carl hasn't ever been concerned about earthquakes—not much around here to shake. The gas tanks have emergency precautions against rupture or leaks. If something shook the world hard enough to cause Carl a problem, it would likely be big enough to drop Los Angeles into the Pacific.

These quakes aren't severe enough to shake up much. They might scare a tourist or two if someone like the girl who used his bathroom earlier is still close enough for the shake and shimmy. Not her mother, though. That lady was tough as tanned leather. The girl was the first person to invade Carl's personal space since Mary died, but she left no trace after she relieved herself. Only a few squares were missing from his roll and the faint scent of a pretty perfume she must've sprayed self-consciously after evacuation.

Carl's first company in how many years?

He sighs and takes a sip of tea. The quiet out here is nearly absolute. Nocturnal animals remain silent in the twilight. There's no wind tonight, abject stillness a blanket over the world. The shake-shake of the quake was the only disturbance Carl experienced as he finished his tea.

The shortwave radio squawks as he swallows the last drops from his glass.

He hardly uses the radio. It's more for emergencies in case he gets bitten by a rattler or suffers a spell like Mary had started to experience once her sickness seriously took hold. Occasionally, he reaches out to fellow folks out there in the world, as social as he ever gets nowadays.

Carl grabs his empty glass and makes his way inside. The shortwave radio sits against one wall. The place is small—a living room with a kitchenette along the east wall, a bedroom off to the right, and the bathroom on the left. That's it. He eats on a folding tray he tucks behind the easy chair when he's not using it. Simple furnishings for a simple life. The only decorations are a framed picture of Carl and Mary's wedding and a painting of Jesus on the cross that Mary had picked up at a flea market decades ago.

Carl places his glass in the sink as the radio squawks again. "—nybody out there?"

Carl recognizes the voice. Sandy Tompkins. Carl has participated in a few conversations between three or four old bastards like himself over the years—vets who talked about the war. Well, the other guys talked about the war. Carl mostly listened. He's not much of a talker. Sandy's a talker. He was usually the one jabbering when Carl finally turned off his radio and went to bed. 7:00 p.m. sharp.

"I'm here," Carl says into the transmitter.

"That you, Carl? Say, you getting any military activity down there in the desert?"

Sandy hails from the mountains of Montana. Altitude gave him a great range of transmission. Usually, Sandy's voice was clear as a bell, but today, the message comes across as scratchy and faint.

"Quiet as a mouse," Carl says. "Nothing different."

"Nothing?"

There were the slight tremors coming through every little while. That's unusual. But not anything to wonder about with someone from Montana. Sandy doesn't know an earthquake from a tsunami.

"Nothing."

"Helluva snowstorm up here. I mean, it's December, so you gotta figu—" Sandy cuts out for a few seconds, then he comes back. "—lling up the National Guard to a local ski resort. Reports of blackouts caused by someth—"

Sandy cuts out again. Carl starts to figure he's lost him for the night. It's almost seven, and Carl needs to get to bed. He reaches for the shortwave to turn it off when the speaker blasts piercing feedback. Carl flinches. His fingers pause at the power switch as Sandy manages four more syllables—"...breach..."

"...frost..."

"...monster..."

And Carl, never prone to being spooked, shivers.

5.0 Richter

[Shiv]

Shiv had seen some shit in her day. She'd *done* some shit in her day. Ain't never seen the earth swallow someone whole. The ground had opened and gulped that woman like a grape.

Then it closed back up as quickly as a mouth shuttered after uttering something you can't take back. Because the past could seal it up in a steel box and preserve it forever. Some things, once said or done, can't ever be undone. Didn't Shiv know a thing or two about that?

Night has fallen on this scene of misery. Shiv remains handcuffed, and the dumbstruck cop shows no sign of coming up with a plan for fixing the situation. He doesn't have the key—it's as gone as the transport bus that was hauling her ass from one prison to another. This fine piece of badge was the unlucky bastard who escorted Shiv on a bathroom break because she'd drunk too much OJ for breakfast. Her overfull bladder saved their asses while the rest of the convoy disappeared.

Shiv stares at the place on the highway where the desert ate a lady. Now she understands where the transport bus and the escort police cruiser had gone. When they'd returned from her pissing in the sandbox like some mangy alley cat, the cop looked like someone had smacked him in the face with a dick—unable to understand the circumstances that led to the unfathomable event. How did a bus full of prisoners and his goddamn partner leave them stranded in the desert?

They hadn't left. Shiv and the cop were the ones who walked away. The bus and the cruiser were back where they left them under a few tons of sand.

What the fuck is happening?

None of her fellow travelers are focused much on the mystery of what or why but on the immediate emergency of saving a mother suddenly swallowed by the sand.

A man frantically digs at where the woman went under, bent over and paddling through sand like a dog desperate for a bone. He calls her name over and over for longer than anyone would've been able to hold her breath—"Linda! Linda! Linda!" He's gone mad and appears intent on driving the rest of them there with his delirious mantra.

A kid sobs uncontrollably beside where the highway's pavement crumbled and comes to an end for a swath of ten yards. Every few minutes, he runs to his father's side and shovels furiously with his hands until grief overtakes his ability to dig again. A teenage girl wanders near the RV where Shiv stops to park her handcuffed ass—the girl holds up a cell phone as high as she can, walking around in a circle like she could get a signal out here in the middle of nowhere. Shiv might be as hard and cold as any bitch in America, but she doesn't tell this grieving daughter that it's too goddamn late for Mommy.

The big rig driver parked the truck at the intersection where the RV idles. The truck's headlights point to where the woman disappeared, illuminating the dig site. The driver has been trying to hail anyone on the CB radio, but there's still no response after exhaustive attempts. Shiv initially thought the trucker was a burly male, but she revises her initial judgment after the driver finally gives up and climbs out of the cab. The trucker trudges toward the rescue team with more bad news.

The cop diligently helps the father dig. The effort is pointless yet poignant. There will come a time for them to give up, but the time isn't now. This family can't handle quitting on their lost member. Not yet.

An earthquake caused the sinkhole. A couple of aftershocks followed, and Shiv worries another sinkhole might open in the earth directly below her. She remains near the two large vehicles parked along the intersection, ready to grab onto either one like a massive life preserver in case she starts sinking. Would that even help? She considers the missing prisoner transport bus and longs for terrain less sandy.

How did her life lead to this point? Tasha Smith was a dull girl from a traditional Indian family living in Chicago. But she fell in with the wrong crowd in high school. Maybe because she didn't get enough attention from Daddy. Maybe because Mom was a self-righteous bitch. Her prison-issued mental health provider wanted to blame everyone except the one who'd stabbed an old man.

Shiv made the worst possible mistake by following her group of anarchists to a red state. Or maybe killing a harmless old man was her Number One wrong decision. But he'd been ancient and almost expired anyway. Tasha Smith tossed away the next sixty years of her life while the victim only lost maybe five or ten of his. Hardly fair. Fucking red states.

The riots seemed like a great idea. Tasha's group referred to the planned public events as "The Takedown." They meant to force change. America's black and brown people deserved reparations for the atrocities of America's past. Civil protests had gone unanswered as the general public ignored the marches. The right had demonized public demonstrations utilizing kneeling at public venues. Every passive initiative attempted to prompt action had been neutered and vilified. So, Tasha became involved in The Takedown. They staged riots to punish those who sought to squash atonement for this country's shameful history.

Tasha traveled around the states. Some faceless philanthropist funded their efforts. Influential people in America sought to support their efforts—evidence they were doing the right thing. She'd demonstrated in Chicago, Detroit, Seattle, Portland, and San Francisco. Then she made the mistake of participating in a riot in Jackson, Mississippi. She was throwing bricks through a storefront window when the elderly owner of the establishment confronted her. Tasha doesn't even remember what went through her head as she wrestled with the frail man. A short stub of sharp metal was among the pile of bricks along the sidewalk. As the old man pulled her hair and kicked at her shin, Tasha grabbed the shiv and stabbed the feisty geezer in the chest.

She left him dead in the street.

One dead white man didn't make up for all the past sins, but at least *someone* paid. Nevertheless, she didn't feel any better after dealing out a small dose of retribution.

She wasn't a killer then. The jury sent Tasha to prison for a murder that was more of an accident. She hadn't *wanted* to kill anyone. That hadn't been her plan. It kind of just happened. But five years behind bars *made* her a killer. Her nickname might've originated with the death of one old man, but it had been sharpened and honed by three more bodies since. None of those three had been remotely accidental.

Shiv could make a weapon out of anything she could fashion into a pointy end. Three bitches in five years thought they could take her out. Shiv realized behind bars that inmates don't worry about historical reparations. They are more interested in carnal needs and exerting power. Making victims of perpetrators. Not this woman. Those predators had ended up dead without Shiv ever considering the color of their skin. White, black, or brown, they all died screaming and leaking red.

Did the mother who'd been swallowed up by the earth even get a chance to scream?

The truck driver doesn't ask about Shiv's orange jumpsuit or the handcuffs. Her attire isn't the weirdest damn thing around here. The trucker puts one boot up on the front wheel of her rig, engine still idling in a rumble in the night, headlights shining on the desperate men and their fruitless efforts.

"We need to get moving," Shiv says. "There might be another quake. More sinkholes."

"Maybe," the driver concedes. "The road's out right there. And the road's out the other direction. I was about to turn around, but now there's no going back. I won't get lucky enough to get around that patch again."

Shiv nods at the intersection. "Sign says there's a gas station going the other way. And a tourist attraction. Think there's a way out?"

"A ghost town," the driver says, as if that is the pinnacle of dead ends.

"Better than sitting ducks along the road, waiting for another sink-hole to swallow our asses."

The driver nods. She gazes at the father, digging desperately for his wife, calling her name repeatedly. "Soon. Give them another minute."

Shiv nods. She isn't in charge and doesn't have a choice. She only hopes they have another minute…

5.1 Richter

[Pastor Montgomery]

Monty sees a figure in the distance moving away from him. After nightfall, the stars in the clear sky illuminate the world with an eerie silver light. He can see the highway clearly, the yellow line looking golden in the starlight. The cacti, dunes, and tumbleweeds along the route make for shadows and strange shapes looming on either side of the road. The individual at the edge of the darkness might be something other than human. Or it's nothing living at all—only a trick of the night.

Monty wonders if it's a mirage. Any story of getting lost in the desert involves a mirage. Monty remembers his daughter, Cheri, questioning once—when she was just a teenager—about the story of the devil tempting Jesus after wandering forty days in the desert. "Maybe he was hallucinating from dehydration," she had suggested. "Or was it a mirage from the heat?" Monty and Daphne should've named her Thomas since she was always doubting.

Monty isn't a skeptic. He decides the figure in the distance isn't of questionable existence but rather an answer to his prayer. He'd stood roadside where his car disappeared for a few minutes, praying for help. Maybe God would send a motorist who would stop for a barefoot hitchhiker. Or would divine intervention make his phone ring again so Monty could find it and call for help? Perhaps He could arrange a miraculous return of Monty's inexplicably missing car. Monty would even accept waking up in his bed to find this had all been a nightmare. When none of the above presented after a few minutes, he remembered his reaction to Pastor Pauline's desert tale—the Lord helps those who help themselves.

Monty started walking.

He might have gone a mile or two. The sand on the side of the road is soft, but it's murder on his arches. He wishes he had never taken his shoes off. His soles ache terribly. The bottoms of his feet are raw, like exfoliation taken a step too far. Quite a few steps too far. Monty tries to remember how far his GPS mapped to the next gas station, but he can't recall.

He might be stuck out here for the next forty days and forty nights. He doesn't know the first thing about surviving off cacti and roasted lizards. His other daughter, Ashley, was into saving creatures, not cooking them on a spit.

He decides the figure in the distance isn't his imagination. Monty starts moving faster, ignoring the aches in his arches and the rawness underfoot. Another aftershock makes him stumble, and Monty pauses, hands out to his side like Jesus on the cross, as if the world is a tightrope and he fears falling off the side. The tremors subside again, and he starts forward in a jog.

"Hey!" he calls out. "Hey, you!"

The figure doesn't slow down. Maybe the stranger is too far away to hear. The silence of the desert seems absolute, as if sound could carry for miles and miles, but the desert plays tricks on the ears. He thinks of the hymnal ringtone assigned to Ashley and wonders. Had that been real? Is this true now? Maybe the desert is playing tricks on his eyes. Perhaps the devil is testing Montgomery Childes.

"Hup!" He resorted to his grandmother's cry when she'd wanted to wrangle the cousins in from the neighborhood ballgame or a gathering of youngsters in the old, abandoned lot next to her apartment complex. Twenty different families had their kids mixed together, so a generic

"Kids!" or "Hey!" didn't get anyone's attention. Or it got everyone's. She'd holler "Hup!" to get her grandkids' notice.

Monty cups his hands and hollers at the top of his lungs. "Hup! Wait up!" He's sprinting like a marathon runner catching up to the lead contestant. He hasn't moved any faster than a brisk walk in a decade, not since Cheri "Race me, Daddy, race me!" Childes would run for the fences in their backyard. "Hup! Wait up!"

The figure becomes more definite. Someone of smaller stature. Short hair. A child? The person stops and turns. She waits for Monty to catch up. As Monty gets closer, he sees she is a young woman. Asian. Maybe five feet tall, but she's no child. She observes Monty's approach with her head tilted to the side, as if she's studying a curious natural phenomenon.

Monty stumbles up to her. His feet feel as if he's run over hot coals, and raw blisters cover his soles. He's sucking wind like he's made it to the peak of Everest without an oxygen supply. Hadn't the devil taken the Lord to a mountaintop and tempted him with the whole world— "All this I will give you," the devil said, "if you will bow down and worship me." But Jesus replied to the devil, "Away from me, Satan! For it is written, 'Worship the Lord your God, and serve him only.'"

This young woman looks as far away from being a devil as Monty can imagine.

He noticed she had taken a step back when he stopped. Ten feet separate them. He realizes she's keeping her distance. He probably looks like a lunatic. Exhausted, he can't even form a word for a few seconds. She stares. She wears shoes, and Monty tamps down his envy. The young woman looks ready to sprint if she deems him dangerously deranged.

"I've been yelling after you for half a mile," Monty says between huffs and puffs.

"I thought I was hearing things," the young woman says. "What were you saying?"

"Wait up, I said. 'Hup, wait up.'"

"I thought I heard, 'Fuck, I'm stuck.'"

Monty winces at the curse. Not many folks have the guts to swear in his presence. But he realizes he doesn't look much like a pastor right now, drenched in sweat, barefoot, breathing heavily, probably with a glint of madness in his eye.

What a strange phrase. Why would the woman mistake his words for being stuck? Stuck where? There's nothing in any direction.

He wipes his sweat on a pant leg and holds out a hand. "Pastor Montgomery Childes."

The young woman stares at his hand but doesn't step close enough to shake it. "Pi Lee."

"Why are you out here walking in the middle of nowhere?"

Pi looks him over. Any young woman must be cautious around a male stranger alone, without anyone else in sight. It doesn't help he's sweaty, confused, barefoot...and black. There's always that extra glimmer of caution because he's black.

"You really a pastor?" Pi asks. "What church?"

He can maybe blame her for being a little prejudiced, but he can't blame any young woman for being cautious. He hopes Ashley or Cheri would show the same reservations.

"Saint Joe's. Missouri."

"What are you doing in the middle of the Mojave?"

"Matthew four, verses one through four. 'Then was Jesus led up of the Spirit into the wilderness to be tempted of the devil. And when he had fasted forty days and forty nights, he was afterward an hungred. And when the tempter came to him, he said, "If thou be the Son of God, command that these stones be made bread." But he answered and said, "It is written, Man shall not live by bread alone, but by every word that proceedeth out of the mouth of God."'"

"That's a mouthful," Pi says. "Only a church dude would know all that. But why are you barefoot and running down a fucking highway?"

"My car...," Monty starts and then clamps his mouth shut, stopping the words. If she thinks he might be crazed judging by his appearance, his recounting how his car disappeared along the roadside would confirm her fears. "It's, uh, broken down."

Pi narrows her eyes and glares. "You give me the truth, mister, or you can stay the hell right here. I've got a can of pepper spray, and I'm really eager to try it out."

"The truth is different for different people, Pi," Monty says. He doesn't want to tell her. If she thinks Monty is crazy, she'll leave him alone. And he doesn't want to be alone right now. The world is shaking, and he's worried it's falling apart.

"Isn't 'Thou Shalt Not Bullshit' a commandment?"

Getting pepper sprayed in the middle of the Mojave without water to flush out his eyes sounds like torture, only a little this side of Christ suffering on the cross. But this young woman seems to be some sort of a human lie detector. Of course, Monty is terrible at fibbing. She's right, after all—Thou Shalt Not Lie.

"My car…," he mumbles. Pauses. "It disappeared."

Pi nods curtly and turns back in the direction she was walking. "Right. Mine, too." She moves slow enough so Monty and his aching feet can keep up.

5.2 Richter
[Brock]

Officer Brock Hayes is exhausted.

Emotionally. Physically. Mentally.

They trained him for tragedy, but this isn't anything anyone ever mentioned in any crisis management class he ever attended. The world opened and swallowed Linda. Then the sandy mouth closed back up and sealed her inside the desert grave. He helped Linda's husband dig and dig as the man repeatedly cried out his wife's name. Their hands are raw from the abrasive texture of the sand and the desperate motion of their fingers, but the ground isn't going to give up its treasure tonight.

Finally, Brock grips the grieving widower's shoulder. "Sir. Enough. We can't do it ourselves. We need to get some heavy equipment out here."

"I need to get her out of there," Linda's husband cries.

"We'll get to that, but we need help," Brock says. He nods to the young boy and the teenage girl sobbing near the RV in the distance, illuminated by the semi's headlights. "And *they* need *you*."

The grief-stricken man stares into the distance toward his children. His eyes are the hollowed orbs of stark incomprehension, the gaze of someone loosed from the tethers of routine life—the mark of a man affected by great tragedy, unmoored from the comforts of predictability and sense. Occasionally, a man stares into the abyss of true existence, and the enormity of its complete nonsense gazes back.

Brock shakes his head. Those dark thoughts aren't what he needs right now. Whatever happened to this woman, Brock must keep his focus tight. He needs to make sure no one else suffers her fate. If the earthquakes caused the sinkhole, then there have been more tremors since. He was concerned the whole time they were digging in the sand that the ground would open again under them both.

Then the ground rumbles.

Brock and the grieving widower scramble backward from where Linda disappeared. The earth doesn't give way underneath them, but at the edge of the semi's powerful headlights, another section of roadway disappears, swallowed by the sand. A puff of grit expels in a terrestrial burp. If the highway exhibited any possibility of escape before the quake, now it is no longer an option.

"We need to get somewhere safer," Brock says. "You have to think about your kids, sir."

"My kids are safe," the man mumbles. "But my wife…"

"I don't know if any of us are safe," Brock says. "I don't understand what's going on, sir."

The distraught husband and father blinks, and Brock can see him struggle to turn his thoughts away from the tragedy, like a man trying to wake up from a nightmare. It's always a harrowing experience, watching someone suffer shock. Brock delivered plenty of bad news during his time on the force, and he never got used to it. Someday, he knew someone else would be the bearer of bad news, and he'd be the recipient. His parents are still alive. All four grandparents. Three brothers and two sisters. Six nieces and nephews. All alive and well.

He can't relate to what this man is experiencing.

He dreads the day that it will come.

"Right," the widower finally admits. He turns away from agony and despair and focuses on Brock. A lifeline to something that makes sense. "Promise me we'll come back for her."

"Let's get somewhere safe, and then we can do whatever you want, sir."

"Stop calling me 'sir,'" drones the haunting voice. "Hector Gonzales."

"Mister Gonzales. Sure. Come on, let's step away a bit."

If it were a flood, Brock would seek higher ground. If this were a snowstorm, he'd seek shelter. But the very earth doth quake, and the ground swallows people whole. The world expands in every direction for miles and miles with no end. Where could they run? They couldn't go back east, as a sinkhole had swallowed the road. The truck driver said they couldn't go west due to a blockade. Brock suggested someone should call for help when he started digging beside Mr. Gonzales, and no one could get a signal on any device. "Road's out both directions," the truck driver said. No going back, and no going forward.

Skidoo is the only option left. Brock patrols the county and responds to calls about the occasional tourist who causes trouble at the roadside attraction. Usually, the instigator is less than pleased when a big black cop shows up. He's endured many mumbled derogatory names as he stepped out of his cruiser.

His cruiser…

Had his car and his partner suffered the same fate as Linda Gonzales? An entire bus? Isn't that the only explanation for the disappearance? What else could've happened to them? They wouldn't have abandoned Brock and the convict in the middle of the Mojave. The desert must have swallowed them, also.

A sinkhole beneath the mother of these children and the prison transport and the county cruiser? Random natural occurrences claiming lives in two separate incidents? Coincidence?

A chill runs up Brock's spine.

Brock walks a little faster toward the big vehicles parked at the intersection.

Mr. Gonzales goes to his kids, and the remaining members of the Gonzales family huddle in a group and cry quietly in the night. Brock takes the driver of the big rig aside. The convict watches as Brock leans his head close to the trucker. Brock isn't going to include his prisoner in the decisions they must make. And Hector Gonzales isn't in any shape to help make choices. That leaves Brock and a very grumpy-looking woman to figure out this situat—

"Does anyone know what the hell is going on?"

The truck driver doesn't even flinch at the sound of a voice coming from the darkness. The woman's spine is solid stone. The headlights from the truck had blinded Brock, so he didn't even see the stranger as she approached from the west. A young woman emerges from darkness as if she personifies the night and is some terrible goddess who maybe wreaks her havoc on the mere mortals of the physical plane.

"Shit," Brock swears, his hand moving reflexively toward his holster. He pauses. The young woman is defenseless, slight, and looks a mess. Her ethnicity may be Asian, but she's as white as a ghost. Like a specter risen from the grave. For a moment, he wonders if Linda Gonzales had survived this after all. But this young woman isn't old enough to have birthed a teenager. She's barely older than the grieving girl huddled near the RV.

"Where did you come from?" the truck driver asks.

The girl thumbs a finger behind her. "From the west."

"You came in from the west?" Brock asks, hopeful reports that the roadblock had been a mistake. "Are the roads open?"

The girl shakes her head. "I had to turn around and come back. The road's out a few miles down. We walked all the way."

"Damn," Brock curses. "We?"

He looks around in the darkness, his eyes adjusting enough to see she's not alone.

A man staggers forward. He isn't wearing any shoes. Barefoot, he leaves a faint trail of bloody prints behind him.

"Jesus Christ," the trucker swears—although it sounded like she said, "Jesus Geist."

"Pastor Montgomery Childes," the barefoot man corrects. A preacher.

"You were out hitchhiking, pastor?" Brock asks.

"My car," he starts. Pauses. Brock knows what he will say and why he's hesitant to voice it. It's crazy. "A sinkhole swallowed it."

"Mine, too," the young woman adds solemnly. "It sucked up our whole S.U.V."

Our. These two weren't driving together. That means any fellow travelers didn't make it.

"Those aren't the only two incidents," the trucker says. She nods toward the devastated Gonzales family. "They lost their mom."

"Oh, holy shit. Really?"

Brock nods grimly. "Then it's happening all over. We need to get to someplace with solid ground."

"We're in the middle of a fucking desert," the trucker grumbles.

"The town. That ghost town," the young woman suggests.

"Yeah," Brock agrees. Plan made. "Skidoo."

5.3 Richter
[Landry]

Landry pulls into the gas station along the route, the only thing along this stretch of the highway except for some side roads to remote homesteads and the ghost town at the other end. After checking for a cell signal and getting nothing again, Landry sighs and tosses the phone on the passenger seat. Someone needs to know about the disappeared schoolhouse and the missing Bucky, but Landry can't get ahold of anyone. Communications have vanished along with buildings and coworkers.

Landry doesn't like the old man who runs the gas station. Not that the two have ever shared more than a few words. Usually, Landry uses the credit card reader at the pump to refuel and avoids interaction with the grumpy old fart. On the rare occasion that requires some sort of snack for the day, Landry limits interaction with Carl Kennedy to a brief exchange and makes a hasty exit. Carl keeps the conversation down to grunts and sighs and the total for the piled goods on the counter—not a thank you or a good day after the transaction. And cash. Only cash.

Who carries cash nowadays?

It's after-hours, and Landry knows Carl has closed the station for the night. The man works like someone set by an old-time clockmaker who uses gears and shit that winds up. He's never open past five o'clock. And it is way past five. Yet Landry pulls into the station because home is still an hour away, and someone needs to know about Bucky's disappearance sooner than later. Maybe not about how the schoolhouse disappeared. At least not over the phone.

Certainly, an ancient relic like Carl has an old-fashioned phone with a cord. Lines along poles stretch out from the station and feed the place power. They must have also brought communication to the remote area this way. Skidoo had landline phone service until a few years ago when the lines had fallen into such disrepair that the phone company refused to upgrade the service. Dad had given up and bought a cell phone dedicated to official business. The company cell isn't working. Neither is Landry's personal phone.

Landry has to report Bucky's disappearance pronto.

Landry had wandered around Skidoo, calling Bucky's name for longer than was prudent. The eerie otherworldliness of the situation hadn't quite settled in yet. The idea of the missing building was disturbing and maddening, but Landry disregarded it because it might be a sign of going crazy. Landry doesn't want to be crazy.

Mom had gone crazy. Landry *won't* end up like Mom.

Dad avoided the subject whenever it came up. Landry occasionally asked what had happened to Mom and how she'd deteriorated so quickly. Dad wouldn't give a good answer. Once, when Landry had incessantly pressed him for information, Dad had snapped that her condition was "hereditary." Landry has lived in constant fear of going crazy ever since.

Disappearing buildings is nuts. Missing coworkers is cuckoo.

Carl lives behind the gas station. The old bastard might not talk to anyone passing through, but the folks who live and work in the area gossip about one another. Landry is sure the local busybodies have much to say about the Honanie family—Dad's strange obsession with a ghost town, Mom's mental breakdown, and their peculiar offspring who defies labels. But the chatterboxes also talk about Carl Kennedy. The widower lives alone behind the station and never goes anywhere. *Ever.*

So, Carl *must* be home. Landry is only twenty-two years old and doesn't want to deal with adult problems alone. Pounding fists on the station's back door will get Carl's attention. It's after seven, but still early as hell. Is the old coot already in bed? Maybe he turns in impossibly early, the nocturnal habits of the elderly as mysterious to Landry Honanie as disappearing schoolhouses. The night has turned into a nightmare.

Finally, the door opens, and Landry steps back, unsure what to brace against. Is this the scene from one of those stories one sees on the news where an old man shoots a young intruder dead for trespassing on his land? Landry prepares to be staring down the barrel of a shotgun. Instead, Carl is empty-handed, armed only with a loaded glare.

"Why the hell are you pounding on my door in the middle of the night, asshole?"

Asshole? Middle of the—Landry sighs. What a colossal dickwad. "My name is Landry Honanie. I work over at the ghost town."

"I'm not standing at my door at this godawful hour to hear you jabber about your whole life story. Why are you bothering me?"

"There's an emergency," Landry says through teeth biting back a sharp retort. "I need to use your phone."

"Don't you young people have a phone attached to your ass nowadays?"

To my ass? Landry thinks. *What would be the use of a phone attached to my rear end?*

"Why would I subject myself to this experience unless I had to, sir? This conversation is about as pleasant as making small talk with a rattlesnake. I need to call the cops to Skidoo because Bucky Sakeva turned up missing today." *And I lost an entire building,* Landry thinks but doesn't say.

"Missing?" Carl accuses, like Landry lost the most valuable thing in the museum. "How can you lose someone in a small town like Skidoo? There are only so many places he could be."

"I know, sir," Landry replies with a clenched jaw. A frustrated Landry had already exhausted all personal resources to turn up the missing person. Maybe the best choice would've been to keep driving until *actual* civilization. Carl is about as much help as a tumbleweed blowing in the wind. "That's what I'm trying to tell you. He vanished into thin air!"

"People don't just disappear, kid."

"Don't you think I know that?" Landry snaps. Then sighs. "Bucky isn't the only thing that disappeared."

This is crazy, this is crazy, this is crazy—the words echo inside Landry's mind. But Bucky is missing, and the time to find an elderly man lost in the desert grows short. Carl might think this sounds nuts, but maybe it'll snap the old bastard out of asking pointless questions and take some damn action.

"A building went missing," Landry says.

"A… building?" The grumpy grampa didn't have a clever fucking quip for that. "What's that supposed to mean?"

"The schoolhouse. It was standing on Main Street, where it's been since before I was born. One minute it was there, and the next, it was gone. Without a trace. Like the world swallowed it up whole."

Carl stares at Landry as if trying to figure out truth from fiction. A lot of people wore a similar expression when examining Landry Honanie. What's real and what isn't? Boy or girl? Simpleminded or sagacious? Fashion fiend or total fiasco? Landry faced puzzlement every day. But Bucky's fate didn't usually rest on other people's shortsightedness.

The world gives a shake—a slight tremor. Desert people like Landry and Carl hardly register the little quakes. But haven't they been rumbling all day? One spooked off a midwestern tourist right quick. Wasn't there another right after Bucky went on his last patrol?

Did the quake have something to do with Bucky's disappearance?

What does Landry expect next? More ridicule? A rude retort and Carl sending the bothersome nuisance away? More pointless banter while Bucky might be in mortal danger? An escalation of confrontation until Carl retrieves the aforementioned loaded weapon and points it in Landry's face? A change of heart and a promise to find Bucky?

Or none of the above.

"Come on in." Carl opens the door wide and steps aside, allowing Landry entry into his home. "I've got a shortwave radio in the back.

Maybe we can raise someone on there who can put us in touch with the local authorities."

Landry steps inside, grateful for the lifeline. And wondering, *What the hell is a shortwave radio?*

5.4 Richter
[Bulldog]

Suraya climbs up into the cab. The convict sits in the passenger seat, hands folded on her lap with metal cuffs jangling. The cop and the new girl head toward the RV, followed by the shuffling, barefooted minister. No one in the Garcia family is fit to drive. Brock offered to lead the way since he knows the lay of the land, and Suraya said she'd follow. The woman in the orange jumpsuit has decided to play Chewie to Bulldog's Han Solo. The cop has more significant worries than whether he might lose a prisoner if she starts to run. Only a fool would take off and try to escape across the desert after what happened to the woman now buried under the highway.

The desert is hungry...

Suraya grips the steering wheel tightly.

"You gonna be trouble?" Suraya asks.

"I'm kinda known for trouble," the convict says, holding up her cuffs. "But only when I need to be."

Suraya couldn't worry about no criminal in handcuffs. Mostly, these assholes from prison have a bark much worse'n their bite. Bulldog knows about bite.

The danger she finds concerning is out there, not in here.

"What do they call you?" Suraya asks.

"Shiv."

"That ain't your name."

"Ain't the name my mama gave me, but I hadn't stabbed anybody back then."

"That's why I like babies."

"And what do they call you? Mack?"

"Bulldog," Suraya says. Also, not what her mother called her.

"Love it," Shiv compliments.

The RV heads south-southeast from the highway down a cracked and narrow two-lane road. The headlights pick up the barren landscape on either side—decrepit plants that look like tumbleweeds still rooted to the soil and the stony rise of the occasional slope. The sensation of dread and the desolate setting make Suraya feel like she's driving through the terrain of some post-apocalyptic sci-fi movie. She wouldn't be surprised if Mad Max came around the corner.

Along the way, Suraya tries to raise any other drivers on the CB. Interference seems to affect her reception, but she gets sound through the static at a high point along the narrow roadway. She picks up Holyman again.

"Jesus is coming back for us, Bulldog," he proselytizes. "I hope you made peace with the Lord."

Suraya shoots a glance at Shiv. The passenger doesn't look like anything in the world could frighten her. Suraya thinks of herself as having a tough spine, but this other woman is scary—precisely the person Suraya wants as a ride-or-die after the crazy shit she'd seen tonight.

"What did you see, Holyman?"

"The world cracked open and let out the monsters, Bulldog. Big fucking beasts heralding the end of days. Satan is coming, and these are the goddamn horsemen of the apocalypse. Abominable kaiju in the north, great Kraken in the Atlantic, monsters from under the earth, and flaming nightmares descending from above. These are terrible horrors sent to raze the earth to prepare for the advent of the devil."

The world cracked open. The desert swallowed a woman.

"What the hell did you *see*, Holyman?" Suraya repeats into the handset.

"I didn't see it," comes a staticky reply. Holyman is breaking up again. "Tooter up in Montana said he hit a godawful storm. Blizzard came up outta nowhere. Said some tourists at a ski resort reported giant creatures in the snow wreaking havoc in the Rockies. They described it like King Kong had fucked a yeti. Hundred-foot-tall monsters."

"Bullshit," Suraya interrupts.

"I heard Tooter die, Bulldog. He must've held the mike open the whole time. 'It's picking me up!' he hollered. Had to have been picking up his whole rig cuz he was still transmitting! His last words were, 'The sky. I can see the whole sky.' What does that mean? Really, what does that even *mean*?"

"Impossible," Suraya replies. But didn't a sinkhole open in the desert and swallow someone whole? Impossible is her entire day.

"Remember Hippychick? Total lunatic, sure. Believes in all kinds of beads and chakras and séance kinda bullshit. She's crazy, but she ain't certifiable, y'know. She ain't an imaginary-friend or a hiding-bodies-under-the-floorboards kinda nutjob. I talked to Hippychick an hour ago. She'd finished making a run to Miami. She was headed back up the Atlantic coast when a hurricane came out of nowhere. She said all the chatter on the radio station from one of the towns along the coast was about an impossible freak storm over the ocean—arcane weather that arrived without warning. People called the station, claiming to see spooky shit in the storm. There was something in the water. An honest-to-God sea monster. Tentacles reaching out from the ocean and stealing whatever they touched. You believe that B.S.?"

"I don't know," Suraya mutters. She doesn't want to believe it. "Hippychick was probably high."

"Then we're all high. Because this shit is real, Bulldog. Real as the devil himse—"

And the CB cuts out. White static. Blue noise. Dead air.

"Monsters?" Shiv asks.

"He's a fanatic. Holyman believes anything. Tooter's probably pulling a joke. Maybe Hippychick is in on it."

"Crazy jokes about sudden snowstorms and impossible hurricanes at the same time a crazy fucking sinkhole swallowed a woman up? And probably what happened to a whole prison bus and a patrol car? The preacher's car disappeared, too. And you heard what that kid said about her S.U.V. The desert almost ate her up."

Suraya doesn't answer. She strangles the steering wheel and stares forward. The taillights of the RV in front of her at least make sense. She's been chasing taillights for a long time. There's a specific order in that. Following a path. Everyone is in line—none of this unexpected bullshit.

The RV's brake lights come on.

"Damn."

Suraya pumps the brakes. The headlights pick up the silhouette of a ghostly station in the distance. The RV apparently has plans to detour into the lot. Suraya would rather keep going and get out of here instead of slowing down, but she also didn't want to be alone in a desert full of earthquakes and sinkholes and… And whatever Holyman was talking about. Suraya isn't sure she wants to get off the paved highway and stop in the empty parking lot. A sinkhole seems as apt to appear under the asphalt of the road as a concrete lot, but something about the highway makes her feel safer. Despite reservations, she follows the RV as it turns into the gas station's lot.

The world shakes—another tremor. The truck dances on the tires like a bouncing cab in the backlot where one of Suraya's trucker buddies had picked up a lot lizard and was banging her relentlessly in the bunk in the back. But no one is having any fun in this gas station parking lot.

Shiv still looks badass, but isn't there an undertone of fear to her stony expression?

Then a sinkhole opens right under the semi-truck.

"Hell!" Shiv hollers, grabbing the center console to steady herself.

The hole appears under the middle of the truck and trailer, so the space exists between the dual rear wheels to the back of her cab. The sound of crushing metal and breaking parts drowns out both women as they curse. The middle of the truck falls into the hole, folding the trailer and truck until it resembles the Titanic sinking, the Mack truck grille facing 45 degrees off regular and the rear lights shining up toward the night sky.

"Shitshitshit," Bulldog swears, flinging open the driver's side door, ready to jump. But there's a hole out her door and no ground below her. The floor of the crater is something other than earthen. Bulldog doesn't want to see what's out there, but she's already staring into the abyss.

And the abyss stares back.

The truck bridges the outside circumference of the hole, jack-knifed so the front and back point at upward angles. The view outside the windshield gradually shifts more and more skyward. Soon, this ship will break in two, and the truck will sink into the sand. This rig has 100% fewer lifeboats than the Titanic had. They must get out. And like Jack from the fucking movie, the door isn't the answer.

"You got something you can use as a hammer?" Shiv hisses like a cornered badger.

Suraya reaches back and fumbles in her lockbox behind her head until she grips a flare gun she has for emergencies if she finds herself stranded on a particularly lonely stretch of highway. It's heavy and metal, and Suraya could use the grip to pound against the glass.

Shiv lives up to her nickname. She pulls a tapered metal rod the size of a fat permanent marker from the folds of her orange jumpsuit. The tip is pointed and still rather blunt—a work in progress. But the end is narrow enough to serve its purpose. She holds it against the wind-shield as a chisel, and Suraya swings the handle of the flare gun and smacks the shiv. The whole windshield becomes malleable, with spider-webbed glass shards held together by the laminated layer. The women shove and shoulder the heavy laminated glass out of its housing. The flexible sheet falls to the side and into the darkness below.

The women crawl out onto the truck's hood to the front grille. Suraya uses her bulldog hood ornament as a foothold and jumps up and forward, rolling away from the sinkhole onto solid ground. The preacher runs to the edge of the sinkhole and helps Suraya to her feet.

The truck's hood sinks below the surface of the sand, and Suraya's truck is entirely inside the sinkhole.

Brock and the mourning widower squat next to the perimeter of the pit. Shiv is still down the hole. The men shout into the hole, telling her to jump. Then, like fishermen hauling in their catch, they reel her in, Shiv caught by the links of the handcuffs hooking her wrists together.

They drag her backward and collapse beside Suraya. The sinkhole groans and moans, the dirt closing on itself. With a great *ka-thump* of bass, the ground shuts tight.

The world swallowed Suraya's truck whole.

5.5 Richter

[The Garcias]

Chuy Garcia has a memory from when he was young. Maybe a baby.

The sun was bright and warm on his skin. His family was at a park, and Mom was holding his hand. He saw a happy puppy wagging its tail. A man had a cone, ice cream dripping on the sidewalk. Rosie was talking, her voice like a song. He was too young to understand words, so the language was all feelings. Tacit emotions. The world as translated in feels. If it were a text message, the whole thing would be written in emojis.

At Chuy's age, in his memory, his mother was all the emojis. She encompassed everything. In the universe before Chuy learned how to talk and understand and communicate and wonder, the only truth was that his mother was a god. Creator and protector. She answered every prayer. In the snippet of the past, she stood tall and beautiful and immortal. She could do anything, and she would go on doing everything forever. He had continued to think of her as interminable until...

The Earth swallowed her whole.

The world ate her up as quickly as Chuy smacked a mosquito flat and rubbed the bug into nothingness.

Now, he sits beside Rosie in the RV and watches as his father stands outside. Dad gets too close to where another sinkhole just closed. Chuy presses his face against the window as Dad and the cop remain too near the spot where the ground swallowed a whole semi-truck. Chuy stops breathing. What if the ground sucks in his dad next? What if the world eats *both* of his parents?

"What's he doing?" Chuy whines.

"He's fine," Rosie says. "Nothing's going to happen."

"Get back, Dad!" Chuy shouts inside the RV. Dad can't hear his voice through the thick glass.

"Shut up, Choo. He's fine."

"He's gonna get swallowed up!"

"He isn't going to die. We can't lose them both."

Chuy turns away from the scene outside and glares menacingly at his sister. "Mom isn't dead! We'll find her."

Rosie stares at her brother, blinking in the stupid way she does when he tries to explain the history of baseball or the biography of one of the great old-time players. Like she can comprehend individual words but has trouble when Chuy starts stringing them together in a sentence that's too long. There isn't anything too long about his latest senti-ment—"Mom's alive."

"Choo, she's buried in the ground."

Tears run down her face like streams running down the glass dur-ing a springtime rainstorm. Chuy used to be afraid of storms, so Mom would sit beside him at the window, and they'd watch the rain. "Nothing to be scared of," she promised. She was right about the storms. They ought to have feared the ground.

"There are natural caverns under the desert running in a complex cave system right under our feet. Mom's lost in an underground maze. We'll find her as soon as we get help. Emergency services will have sonar or radar or whatever it takes to find her. Easy, peasy, your face makes me queasy."

"Choo, I'm sorry. That's not right. There aren't caves under the sand. She's not—"

Chuy holds up his index finger and almost jabs it up her nose. "You shut the fuck up, Rosie, or I'll punch you in the fucking head."

Rosie recoils as if slapped. He's never sworn in front of her. Chuy lives mainly in the past, fascinated by the towering sports figures of the old days. Babe Ruth, Jackie Robinson, Hank Aaron—they were heroes before heroes became egomaniacal idiots who performed stupid antics on the internet. The giants of baseball had accomplished feats like smacking balls out of Wrigley Field instead of starring in an online viral clip of getting your balls hit by a yard rake. But this isn't major league sports—this is the World Series of life itself. Life and death. They are at the edge of everything changing.

They already have one out. He stares at Dad standing too close to the edge of the last sinkhole. He can't handle another batter striking out.

Chuy isn't ready to leave his mother behind. He believes she survived the sinkhole. Chuy remembers the lesson on mythology they were studying in literature. Ms. Diaz told them about the Minotaur and the Labyrinth. Mom remains stuck in some ancient catacombs, and Chuy will find a way to get her out.

Before Rosie can recover from his f-bomb enough to scold or threaten to tell Dad, the whole RV shakes like they hit the world's biggest speed bump. They'd parked the RV in a gas station lot. Chuy pitches forward, and Rosie catches him before he bashes his face against the steering wheel.

"Thanks," Chuy mutters.

"I like your mouth better when it's using some manners," she says.

Chuy nods. No more swearing. It made him feel funny, as if he wasn't mature enough to use those words. Like when he'd try on Dad's work boots, which were way too big for him. He didn't want to grow up any faster than he had to. In case Mom…

No. Chuy won't consider that.

He thinks about Davey and Debbie Forderer. They lost their mom to cancer last year. Before, the twins had been as active and adventurous as Chuy, always ready to pretend dragons were circling above or the ghosts of baseball players from the past had come alive for a game. This year, they were solemn and reserved. Life and death slapped the imagination out of them—reality had extinguished all the wonder from their world.

Chuy doesn't want to be like that. He will find his mom because there *is* wonder in this life. Chuy believes in magic.

Dad follows the cop and the others as they walk toward the gas station's front entrance.

"We're not waiting out here while they go for help," Rosie decides for them both. "Come on. We're going in, too. I'm not letting Dad out of my sight."

Chuy lets the unsaid part of her statement go unchallenged—Rosie is saying she isn't going to let another parent disappear and leave her alone to raise Chuy.

They hop down off the bottom rung of the RV ladder as the scary woman in the orange jumpsuit finishes dusting herself off. The outfit is a prison uniform, and she looks like they put her in jail for probably murdering someone. She has tattoos all over half her face and covering one of her handcuffed hands. She glares at Chuy as if sizing him up for sustenance in case she gets hungry and resorts to cannibalism. Or maybe she doesn't need an excuse to chop up little kids…

The grumpy trucker is still shaking from nearly being sucked up by a sinkhole. She came closer to death than most people managed and escaped to tell about it. No one would've risked their lives for her if she got sucked into the tunnels below the desert. She'd have died in the bowels of the Mojave. Not like Mom. They'll rescue Mom when the rescue crews arrive with their earthmovers—a digger, and maybe a drill.

They walk toward the station as a group—eight stranded travelers with no exit out to the main road and no success contacting the outside world. The cop seems to think the guy running the gas station might be able to help. The old man hadn't been much help when the family had stopped earlier to refuel and let Rosie take a crap. Rosie said he was a nasty *caduco*[1]. Neither knew what it meant, only that Dad used it to describe their rude, ancient neighbor.

Chuy doesn't see a helpful digger anywhere in the darkness. Maybe over one of these hills…

The gas station's front door features an old-fashioned sign on a string that says "Closed." The kind you flip around, and it says "Open." Chuy is curious despite the lead anchoring his heart—this setting might be the same thing Babe Ruth would've experienced in his day.

The man who opens the station's front door might be old enough to have seen the Bambino in action. The shotgun cradled in his hands is a few decades newer than when Babe last swung the pine. The words coming out of his mouth aren't the kind of thing the Big Bam would've uttered in his day—

"The first fucking one of you looters who grabs a bag of Cheetos is gonna eat triple ought buckshot."

____

[1] Spanish, senile

5.6 Richter
[Carl]

Carl stares down the unruly bunch of thieving bastards. One's already in a prison jumpsuit and handcuffs. They all look desperate and dangerous. Carl's finger is on the trigger because any one of them might be armed. Somebody even brought their damn kids. What's the world coming to?

"Mister Kennedy," says the black guy in the back like he knows Carl. He steps forward; he's wearing a police officer's uniform. Carl falters and points his gun away from the crowd. He doesn't put it down in case it's a trick, but he isn't going to aim at an officer of the law in case it isn't. "Mister Kennedy, it's me. Officer Hayes."

Carl squints into the darkness. He doesn't recognize Officer Hayes from Deputy Fife.

"I've stopped here for gas on occasion," Hayes reports. "Inyo County Police Department."

The Honanie kid steps up behind Carl. "He's local, Carl. Put the damn gun down. They're not here to steal your Cheetos."

"We need help," the cop says. "Cell service is down. We couldn't get anyone on C.B. radio. I remember some of the older folks on the force talking about your shortwave radio, Carl."

"How do they know about my business?" Carl barks.

Officer Hayes shrugs. He looks nervous. Scared. "They said you had more friends on the other side of the country than here in California."

"I don't have friends, period." Carl examines the assortment of folks before him. Under the canopy over the gas pumps sits an RV—the same RV from earlier. They all appear as scared as he's ever seen anyone. He recognizes the girl who used his bathroom. The mother is missing from the crowd gathered at his door—did she remain in the RV for some reason? Carl figures she'd be front and center, demanding action if trouble had arisen. "What emergency brings all of you to my door at this ungodly hour?"

"We need help," Officer Hayes repeats. "The kids' mother went down a sinkhole."

Carl's heart skips a beat. The mother had been a harridan, but a mama bear protects her cub. Carl didn't hold it against the woman. The daughter hangs her head to conceal her tears. Nice girl. She cleaned up his bathroom perfectly, leaving the chamber the same as she'd found it, less one flush and a few squares of toilet paper. Her mom was the rare person able to stand up to Carl and come out unscathed. Now, the ground swallowed up that woman. Carl doesn't like to think of someone he considered a worthy opponent taken off the board so quickly.

"And my… Uh, my copilot was also victim to a sinkhole," adds a college-age hipster with hair as short as a boy's and smooth Asian features, chest as flat as Officer Hayes's, wearing jeans and a polo shirt—yet Carl gets the sense she's a girl. Maybe. Hard to tell nowadays. And you couldn't ask without getting a sassy retort.

"You," Landry accuses, one dubiously gendered person to another. "You were with that douchebag at Skidoo earlier. You never got out of the vehicle."

"That was me. Now, he's gone."

"My coworker disappeared, too," Landry Honanie says.

"The old man?"

Carl scowls. Old? Bucky was younger than him by a decade. Damn kids are throwing the word "old" around like it doesn't matter. These brats expect Carl to refer to them by their proper ethnicity and chosen pronouns (Hadn't Old Charlie from St. Pete gone on a rant about that very topic last week on the shortwave?), but they could call a man who'd survived war and death and Y2K "old."

"I ain't hosting Thanksgiving dinner. Enough chitchat. What happened out there?" Carl interrupts. "We saw what happened to that big rig."

Carl had seen some shit. The atrocities of war. The horrors of watching Mary succumb to cancer. Life moved on even as Carl had done everything he could to slow it down. But he'd never seen a sinkhole swallow up an eighteen-wheeler. And that was dessert after eating a few people. What is going on?

"I heard some C.B. chatter before mine went silent," the trucker says. Hell, Carl wasn't sure if she was a she, either. "Before the ground sucked up my truck like a Slurpee. There's something funny going on up in Montana, too. Monsters. And Orlando. Some Kraken creature is coming out of the Atlantic."

"Quit that talk now, you hear?" Carl snapped. "You're apt to scare the boy."

"The boy lost his mother," the trucker with an asshole for a mouth says tersely. "He needs to grow up quick."

Carl watches the kid try not to cry. Carl has been avoiding growing up, too, for the last twenty years. He had managed to make each day pass at a glacial pace for two decades. And what did Carl have to show for it? Every goddamn day was the same, so he only managed to make time repeat ad nauseam. That wasn't creating an elongated life but rather simply an unremarkable one.

"Maybe so," Carl mumbles. Maybe there's no other way. "We were trying to raise someone on the shortwave when you came rumbling up."

Carl points to the cop and waves him ahead.

"Let me show him," Carl tells Landry. "Wait outside with the others."

Carl isn't going to let the whole goddamn squadron into his small home. He turns toward his door but pauses. He thinks about the tough mama bear advocating for her daughter's right to poop. Carl pivots around again to look at the family, who now numbers three instead of four. The father appears distraught, and the small boy is too damn young. But the girl who used his bathroom isn't hiding her face anymore. She stares at Carl with a cold gaze. She has the look. Her mama's look. Besides, she's been in his house before.

"And you," Carl says, pointing to the teen.

The shortwave is already on. Carl and Landry barely began the search for someone local who might give them some insight into what's going on or be able to offer some help. Carl knows the folks around Skidoo and the surrounding desert towns who might be able to get some EMS out here. He sits in front of the instruments while Officer Hayes hovers on his left and the girl hangs close to his right.

"Try Sheriff Deekman," Hayes suggests. "He'll send help."

"If the world's as big a mess as you're worried about, the sheriff better not be sitting around on his ass playing with a shortwave radio, officer. A plague of sinkholes and a serious failure in the communication grid at the same time might indicate a coordinated attack by our enemies or some natural phenomenon worse than a little technological hiccup," Carl says. "I know who we need."

Carl scrolls through the dial and gets whistles and a sharp burst of static. "Dorothy? Dot, this is Carl. You there?" Dorothy Krebbs is Sheriff Deekman's mother-in-law. She's always talking about how she lives in the house beside her important son-in-law. Dot will know all the gossip about what's happening in Lone Pine—the closest real town to Skidoo.

Static. Static. Static. Then Carl thinks he hears his name.

"We need help out at Skidoo, Dot," Carl says into the transmitter. "We've got missing people."

"—ple? Try missing a whole fucking town, Carl! This is Armageddon. Lone Pine looks like someone dropped a bomb on the goddamn place! Half the buildings are—" Static drowned out Dot for a moment. "—stay far away from town. Or anywhere. The whole world is go—"

Carl doesn't turn to look at Officer Hayes or the kid. He doesn't want to see the fear in their eyes. There isn't any help out there. Dot's looking for backup, and anyone listening will head to Lone Pine before they trek out to Skidoo. If there's anyone left even to offer help. *The whole world...*

"What is it, Dot?" Carl barks into the handset. "What the hell's going on?"

Silence. Silence. Silence. "—omeone broke the universe." Dot's voice was barely a whisper. "Save yourself. That's what I told Samson Dunphey. I told him to—"

Then the sound cut out. Nothing. Not even a burp of static. Dead air. Carl doesn't want to see the look of the two other people in the room, but what choice does he have? He turns. And it's as bad as he feared. The stunned expression of stark terror reflected on both of their faces.

5.7 Richter

[Landry]

Landry doesn't know how fate had thrust the mantle of second-in-command onto these relatively scrawny shoulders. Whatever skills make for an effective leader have not been honed by the last few years working at a roadside tourist attraction in Skidoo. Customer service doesn't prompt anyone to want to save most of the assholes treading the retail environment. Landry would rather fraternize with the ghosts in town than real people.

The trucker and the convict have gathered near the pumps. The digital readouts glow softly in the night. The tourist who accompanied the douchebag at Skidoo earlier in the day approached and introduced herself as Pi. Now, she's talking to the pastor, who gazes into the desert, perhaps looking for a divine sign. The father and son settled on a bench outside the front door of Carl's convenience store, a sign saying "Closed" hanging in the window.

Landry thinks about Dad. He's in Vegas on a business trip. Does he know what's happening in the Mojave? Is the same thing happening there? Is Dad headed home to find Landry? The phones still show no signal, giving no way to check up on him.

"What're you supposed to be?" asks the man who lost his wife to a sinkhole. He stared for the last few minutes, but Landry assumed it was some empty gaze indicative of a person suffering shock. Instead, it had apparently been a ponderation on Landry's categorization.

"What are any of us supposed to be, Mister...?"

"Hector," he answers with a pinched expression. Maybe being called a mister had reminded him of the existence of a missus.

"I am what I am," Landry answers. "I'm Landry."

"I can't tell if you're—"

"I think there are more important things to worry about right now, Hector," Pi interrupts.

Hector stops, closing his mouth like a good Catholic boy reprimanded by a nun. Landry understands the other "more important" thing Hector needs to worry about is the fate of his wife. She is certainly dead and buried beneath the sand. Hector is probably trying to think about anything *except* something important.

"I like the scarf," Hector's son offers as an olive branch.

Landry can understand the confusion of folks needing to label everything. Especially as the world started turning into something impossible and incomprehensible, Hector wants to put a name to it. Landry wears cowboy boots, a bedazzled vest, a weathered leather cowboy hat, a purple bandana tied around the neck, and tight Wranglers. The belt buckle advertises the ghost town, featuring an old west sheriff mounted on a horse embossed into the big silver buckle—Landry added a unicorn horn onto the horse's head by melting some of the metal with a wood burning torch from Dad's toolshed. The outfit is part costume and part Landry's personality.

Good luck with putting a label on this.

"What's our option if that grumpy bastard can't get anyone to help us?" Pi asks.

Landry hasn't considered a Plan B. What can a bunch of tourists and a couple of locals do about sinking semi-trucks and disappearing coworkers and buried mothers? Not a damn thing. The entire Inyo County PD doesn't have enough workforce to unravel the events of this bizarre night. Landry wants the United States Army to come in and save their asses. What Plan B?

"I never thought about that," Landry admits.

"The roads back the way we came aren't an option. At least, not in an RV and that shitty Nissan over there," Pi says. "I don't suppose the old man has a stable of horses out back?"

"Carl doesn't leave this place. Ever," Landry says. "Besides, why do you think a horse is safer than a vehicle if the ground is swallowing up trucks and people left and right?"

Landry winces, remembering the father and son sitting within earshot.

"Because the only road forward looks like it leads to a whole fuckload of nowhere," Pi snaps. "I want to get out of this goddamn sand trap, not drive right into the mouth of the beast."

The *beast?* What does Pi think is going on here? Earthquakes and sinkholes don't equate to monsters. Was it an expression? Or had these guys seen something before they arrived at Carl's?

The pastor comes closer. "Maybe our fate lies in the hands of God."

"God's left us in this giant box of kitty litter," Pi says. "Fate's a big cat turd, preacher."

"He will provide if we trust in Him."

"I'll take my chances with the cacti, thank you very much," Pi dismisses.

No one seems keen on standing around on the sand and leaving their fate up to divine intervention.

The trucker and the convict come close enough to engage in the conversation. They don't look like the type to let a couple of young people decide the fate of the whole group. Landry considers how hard it was growing up in a place like Inyo County for a kid who dresses and acts so differently from everyone else, but these two women must've endured as much terrible shit in their lives. The story writ across their faces is filled with tragedy to make any YA novel look like a picnic.

"Where does this road go?" asks the woman in the orange jumpsuit and wrists cuffed together by a jangling chain.

"To Skidoo," Landry answers. "A ghost town."

"And then?" asks the other woman, who might've stolen her outfit off a sleeping lumberjack.

"And then nothing. End of the road."

"No backroads? Service roads? Old trails? Anything, kid?" the trucker presses.

"Emigrant Canyon Road forks off into the desert."

"This is already the fucking desert," the convict growls.

"There's more sand," Landry says. "A whole helluva lot more."

The trucker points in the direction of Skidoo. "Is there any way out if we go in that direction?" She seems intent on pressing on rather than waiting for rescue.

Landry isn't sure. There's never been a reason to go farther than Skidoo. Explorers, crazy campers, and adventure seekers have gone out there. Sometimes, someone has to send for gas because they get turned around without realizing Carl offers the only oasis for many miles. An explorer calls out EMS occasionally because they ran into a rattler or got too dehydrated. A couple of years ago, the whole western part of the state was involved in a search for a hiker who'd gotten lost, and they found him dead two days later. There's no town farther than Skidoo, nor any reason to take any fork that ends in only unnavigable desert terrain.

"Maybe some old trails. As old as Skidoo," Landry admits. "But nothing on any G.P.S. Not that the phones are working anyway. And I don't think Carl has a map. He never leaves the station."

"Who else lives out in this godforsaken wasteland?" the convict mumbles.

"God has not forsaken us," the pastor interjects.

"Samson Dunphey," Officer Hayes answers from the entrance to Carl's C-store. The teen girl stands beside him, thin and amorphous, like she's a ghost loosed from Skidoo and haunting their team. "He lives out on Emigrant Canyon Road. Carl raised him on the shortwave. He's willing to give us shelter. If we can get there."

"You don't need to scare the kid," Landry scolds.

"I mean, they didn't build the road up to Samson's for an R.V. or a rundown Nissan," Officer Hayes replies. "It's a rough road. We may have to walk part of the way."

"And why risk it for this Samson guy?" the trucker asks.

"He's a conspiracy nut. He'll have supplies. A bunker." Officer Hayes leaves the rest of the answer unsaid. Samson would have *weapons*. Hayes does have a little compassion not to scare the boy after all.

"Anyone have a better plan?" Pi asks.

Landry gazes desperately around the group. Carl was supposed to be able to call for help and end this harrowing situation. Instead, the terrible events of Landry's present continue. The night might be half over, but the nightmare is far from finished.

5.8 Richter

[Pastor Montgomery]

Monty isn't on board with the plan. The world has begun to suffer the end of times, and he isn't going to wait it out inside some God-forsaken bunker. Monty must get home to Daphne. He wants to find out if Ashley and Cheri are okay. They may need him. Is this craziness really affecting the rest of the world? The others said something is also happening in the north and Florida. Ashley is in Miami. Monty will find a way to reach them.

"I'm not waiting this out," he tells the others. "We won't survive by hiding from adversity in a shelter. God helps those who help them-selves."

"In case you haven't noticed, *mùshī*,[2] God doesn't give a shit about any of us right now," Pi says. "This is the fucking Devil's playground."

The girl's mouth is the Devil's playground. Her tongue is forked, and she says the vilest things. Monty would rather tap into his reservoir of hope. This group has an empty tank. He can't sit around and de-pend on them to escape the desert. He resists their efforts to tempt him with safety and survival. Surviving doesn't matter if his family is

---

[2] Mandarin Chinese, pastor or priest

in danger.

Monty studies the group. Most of them are younger than he—Chuy, Rosario, Landry, Pi, even Brock—all too youthful to risk anything. Suraya and Tasha act like loners who have no one in the world to worry over. Hector is closest to his age, but his reality has been rocked by more than these quakes. He is a widower in mourning. He can't even hold it together enough for his kids. Only the old-timer who runs the gas station is of an age to risk his life for something more important than simple self-preservation.

"What about you, mister?" Monty asks.

The old man stands in the entrance to his store. "I'm not hiding in some bunker," Carl grumbles.

"Then come with me," Monty pleads. "We can get out of here. Get to the nearest town."

"There's a lotta desert between here and anywhere, pastor," Carl says. "And you don't even have a pair of shoes."

Carl lives in the gas station and hasn't bothered to offer Monty a spare pair. The old man's feet are at least two sizes smaller. The only thing worse than crossing the rest of this desert barefoot is cramming them into shoes two sizes too small. He wrapped his feet in dishtowels from the RV and decided they'll work as well as anything.

"God will lead the way," Monty promises.

"I agree with the girl," Carl says. "God has left the building. The monsters are in charge. And I'm too damn old to fight monsters."

"You can't give up, man," Monty says.

"I gave up a long time ago," Carl sighs. "I buried my wife out back, and I wouldn't leave her for the world. I'm staying right here."

Monty looks around at this sorry crew. "Is that it, then? Are you all going to give up? Is this what it comes to? Jesus went up on the cross to die for us, and you're all going to give up on his sacrifice?"

"You believe all that shit, mister?" Pi asks. "All the miracles and wonders and make-believe in your precious book? Angels and devils and all that B.S.? You have such strong faith?"

"Of course," Monty replies. "The word is the truth."

"Well, I went to Sunday school before I woke the hell up," Pi says. "I remember your God flooding the whole world once upon a time. Killed the whole lot. What's to say this bunker isn't the modern version of Noah's ark?"

"God made a promise. He would never destroy the world again," Monty argues. "He made the rainbow as His covenant."

Pi steps forward. He remembers when he first met her and caught her walking on the road. He approached her, and she stepped backward. Now, it's Monty's turn to retreat. The look in her eyes is cold and assured.

"Do you see a motherfucking rainbow, *mùshi?*"

Monty turns away. No one else is coming. No one else has any hope. Carl is ready to give up, and the others think hiding is best. Monty needs to get to civilization. Like the Savior, he needs to make it out of the desert. The Mojave doesn't stretch on forever like the sands of the Sahara. There is an end. Somewhere east, there is an edge.

"Can I take some water?" Monty asks Carl.

Carl nods. He holds open his door and allows Monty inside. The shelves of the C-store are full—sodas and chips and candy row after row. Sin wrapped in colorful little packages. Monty takes a handful of beef jerky and stuffs it into his jacket pocket. He places four large water bottles in a cloth souvenir sack that advertises a ghost town called Skidoo. Monty remembers seeing a billboard showcasing the place while walking along the road with Pi.

Monty heads out of the exit.

"That'll be fifteen bucks, Father," Carl says.

"I'm not a priest," Monty says.

"Neither am I," Carl replies. "Fifteen dollars."

Monty raises an eyebrow inquisitively. "It's the end of the world, and you're going to charge a man of God for sustenance?"

"I'm not one for putting cash in the offering plate, Father," Carl says. "God ain't never done me any favors."

Monty sighs. He's heard that tone of voice before. Carl's wife had passed before her time. Gone too soon. Carl held God responsible for his misery. Monty has lost too many congregants due to grief. Not everyone can find the right path back from the edge of despair. Some souls get lost in the desert and never come out.

Monty could probably exit, and the old man would let him. If the world doesn't end, he has no doubt Carl will report the theft. But Monty isn't going to walk out with his loot. Thou Shalt Not Steal. He fishes out his wallet and puts a ten and a five on the counter. Carl nods. A fair transaction. They're even.

"Last chance, Carl," Monty says. "Have a little faith."

"I already had my last chance," Carl answers, "and I blew it."

Monty exits. The cop pats him on the back. Hector gives him a look as lost as any Monty has ever seen. Pi shakes her head. She thinks he's going to die out there in the desert. Better to die trying than to survive while his family faces danger. He turns his back on the gas station and the bit of humanity too timid to try.

Monty walks away. Soon, the station's lights fade behind him, and then it's just him and the desert. The stars light the world, and everything could be like it was two thousand years ago, when evil tempted Jesus Christ. Maybe Monty would succumb to the temptation to give up.

No. No, Monty's destiny is salvation. His path is of faith. He puts his future in God's hands. The Lord will lead Monty to his rightful destiny. Monty believes he will find his way out of this place. He continues walking.

Through the desert.

To wherever his faith leads.

5.9 Richter

[Pi]

Pi isn't so sure about this. She had hoped for something better than reliance on a nutty survivalist with a desert bunker. The last thing she ever wanted to do was put her life in the hands of a Republican asshole. But no one has offered another option, though, and staying behind with Carl in his gas station sounded awful. The old bastard is biding his time on a house built over fuel tanks—Pi envisions a fireball the size of a mushroom cloud if a sinkhole opens directly under the gas pumps.

Landry pulls the dirty white Nissan into the parking lot and exits the idling vehicle. The rest of the ragtag group loads into the RV. Officer Hayes stands on one side of the RV's back door, ensuring everyone gets safely on board.

"You drive," Landry tells Pi. "I'm going to check on Carl one more time. Make sure he didn't reconsider."

Pi volunteered to accompany Landry in the car and follow the RV in case they needed a second vehicle. She starts heading toward the driver's side while Landry steps toward the station. Carl has turned on the exterior lights under the roof over the gas pumps, making the night more gray than black.

"Grampa didn't sound like he was going to change his mind," Pi says. She really wants to get to that bunker. It sounds a helluva lot better than being out in the open like this.

Pi can still hear Josh screaming. *Don't go.* But she had to. She didn't have another choice. Or rather, the only other option was for them both to die. Pi doesn't *want* to leave another person behind. This time, she has a choice. She can spare a minute or two. Probably. But not a moment longer. She won't die for Carl any more than she was willing to risk her neck for Josh.

"Let me ask him one more time," Landry says. "He's stubborn, but he isn't stupid."

Pi takes measure of the station. It's a lot bigger than a semi-truck. Carl might be safer at home than with the caravan going to some NRA motherfucker's bunker in the remote desert.

Maybe she ought to stay here with Carl. Staying put starts to sound pretty nice. If not for those damn fuel tanks…

A quake shakes Landry enough to cause a stumble. Pi lurches forward, slamming the driver's side door shut and holding on to the roof of the shitty automobile so she doesn't end up on her ass. The RV rocks back and forth on the asphalt parking lot, Officer Hayes getting the door in his face and tripping over his feet. The transformer on the station's electrical pole explodes with sparks raining down. The post topples over and smashes into the metal roof over the pumps, bringing the whole awning down in a ferocious crash.

This is it, Pi thinks. *The tanks are going to blow like a bomb.*

The lights flicker out, and Pi hears the generator out back of the station begin chugging. Red emergency lights come on, painting the whole scene in scarlet. The world looks bathed in blood. Not. Ominous. At. All.

The blackout and the smashed roof on the station aren't the worst of the quake's effects. A sinkhole opens between the station and the pumps, the depression growing in diameter until it reaches the first fuel pumps and the front steps leading to the C-store. Carl is standing inside the front window, interior lights dimmed by the generator. His face is visible in the faint glow, his eyes wide. He's watching the world open before him.

Then Carl disappears back into the station.

The front of the gas station disappears into the sinkhole.

"Get in!" Pi cries.

Officer Hayes is on his feet again but doesn't get into the RV. He slams the back door shut and pounds on the window like he's spurring a horse to get lost. The trucker sits behind the wheel of the RV, and she takes off at the cop's signal. Hayes turns in the direction of the station, running *toward* the building. The guy's insane. That's suicide.

Fuck, I'm stuck.

Pi isn't going down another sinkhole. She gets behind the wheel of the Nissan and screams, "Get in the car, Landry!"

"No," Landry answers, waiting, crouched a dozen feet from the car, watching the world collapse.

"We're going!" Pi demands.

Landry turns to Pi and puts every ounce of fierceness into a stern glare. The red emergency lights catch the steely gaze and turn the expression evil. "You don't touch that goddamn gas pedal until I give permission. We're going to give them a chance."

"There's gonna be two dead or four dead, Landry. Carl made his choice. He's too old to get clear of that station! And Hayes is a damn fool for trying to save his elderly ass."

"Don't call him old," Landry scolds. Pi remembers the leathery bastard's piss and vinegar. He's got as much vigor as any of them. Maybe...

Officer Hayes pauses as an aftershock shakes them again, dancing like her Aunt Zhang at Pi's high school graduation party. Red light paints the cop's black skin, making his face resemble charred embers. Pi thinks about Josh again. The cop wouldn't have left Josh behind. The cop would be dead right now, and no one would be saving Carl. But Pi isn't going to chase toward the station to help Hayes, either. She's only willing to listen to Landry for a while. But soon enough, she'll punch the gas pedal, Landry's demands be damned.

The metal awning that once provided shade for anyone gassing up collapses. The pumps smash like empty soda cans under the debris of the roof. Pi grips the steering wheel and braces for an explosion, but this isn't a movie, and nothing blows up. She saw some blockbuster action flick where The Rock jumped over giant chasms during an earthquake while the ground opened under his feet, but this is real life, not special effects. Even the emergency lights now flicker once and fail. The stars bathe the night in a cool, stark illumination, and Pi can see the hole in the sand growing wider and wider. The entire side of the station nearest Pi and Landry falls in, collapsing like a house of cards.

Officer Hayes regains his balance and moves around the back of the station to where Carl keeps his home. That crazy SOB is willing to risk his life to save someone else. Pi supposes the sense of responsibility comes with the badge, but reciting some oath after graduating from the police academy and actually risking your ass to save someone are two different things.

"Landry, really," Pi shouts from the driver's seat. "We need to leave! Now!"

Landry holds up one finger, a warning against moving the car one inch.

Pi starts counting down from a hundred in her head. If the hole grows any nearer or if she gets to zero before Officer Hayes or Carl reappears, she's going. A chance has an expiration date, and stupidity can spoil the best of intentions pretty damn fast. Pi isn't going to remain idle outside a gas station while death comes for her. She wasn't willing to die in a hole with Josh, and she sure as hell isn't meeting her end in a crappy Nissan.

The countdown gets to fifty, and two more walls of the station fall in, only the backside still standing. The front where she'd stood beside Landry already disappeared into the ground, along with the pumps and the massive flat roof that had shaded the filling area. The pole that held the electrical cables now stands upside-down and straight up inside the hole, like a straw sticking out of a big-ass margarita cup.

Pi gets to ten, and her heart thuds in syncopation with the final countdown, like a spaceship ready to blast off into the sky. She wishes for a rocket right now to take her away from this insanity.

Eight, seven, six...

Pi envisions Hayes running around the corner right as she counts down, dramatically carrying Carl slung over his shoulder as moonlight shines off the last of the sinking station.

Five...

But it's Carl who comes hauling ass around the corner out of the shadows, Hayes on his heels as the caboose. Who is saving whom? For someone of advanced years, Carl moves faster than Pi could sprint. Hayes appears punch-drunk and disoriented, and the only thing giving him forward momentum is Carl's hand clasped around his wrist.

The sinkhole starts widening toward the direction of the car. It starts to collapse right on Hayes's heels. His back foot barely lifts before the ground caves in beneath it. Landry opens the back door facing the escaping men and hops into the passenger seat. Carl ducks and darts into the Nissan's backseat, and Hayes dives in immediately after. Pi punches the gas too hard, and the wheels spin on the sand. Shitty tires have no traction. Pi eases back, then teases the pedal gradually downward, the car steadily accelerating away from the sinkhole.

Pi peers into the rearview mirror to see the last of the station fall into the hole.

Pi points the Nissan toward the RV's taillights and speeds along the barren, bumpy highway.

"That was the biggest sinkhole yet," Pi says.

"They can't get any bigger than that, right?" Landry asks, voice cracking at the edge of panic.

Carl doesn't answer. Hayes doesn't answer. Pi doesn't know. The word "can't" doesn't seem to mean the same thing tonight as it did yesterday.

6.0 Richter

[Bulldog]

Suraya doesn't know if any of the others made it out alive. Maybe only she, Shiv, and the Garcias remained. Were there only five people left alive on the whole planet? Something is coming for all of them. It's only a matter of time.

She stared into the abyss, and the goddamn abyss had stared back.

Suraya saw something in the bottom of the hole. Something that had an *eye*.

Brock explained the general route back at the gas station, and Suraya committed the directions to memory. Getting from here to there is second nature. Suraya shivers as she steers the RV down the highway. She recalls what Holyman said. This is happening everywhere—these events extend beyond the Mojave or even California. Something is stomping around in Montana and Florida. Probably more places than that. The world is being eaten alive.

Something at the bottom of that hole stared up at her.

The eye… She can't stop thinking about the eye.

"Slow down," Shiv says from the passenger seat. Suraya and Shiv make the strangest fucking road trip couple ever to captain an RV together. "The turn's up ahead."

"Yeah."

"You gonna be able to hold your shit together, Bulldog?"

"Don't worry about me."

"I'm worried about your driving skills," Shiv says. "I need you to get me to that bunker in one piece."

"What do you think some concrete shelter is going to do?"

"Same thing it does in a nuclear war or if an asteroid hits the planet. I think it's gonna save my ass."

Suraya opens her mouth, then closes it. She takes the turn according to Carl's directions. She isn't sure she wants to voice what she saw. Suraya has been ignoring it ever since she almost got swallowed. *Swallowed.* It seems impossible. She must have imagined it. But time has passed, and the shock has faded. She still can't unsee the eye.

She must know if Shiv realizes what they're facing. Does Suraya want to lock herself in an underground bunker if there's a monster under the sand?

"Did you see it?" Suraya asks.

"See what?"

"You know what I'm talking about. In the hole."

"It was dark," Shiv grumbles.

"There was plenty of light. And it was *shiny.*"

"Shadows can play tricks on the eye."

Suraya bristles at the comment. "The fucking eye."

"Yeah, I saw it," Shiv confirms quietly, looking over her shoulder so as not to alert the kids in the RV. The convict is tough as nails, yet she has some compassion left. "There's something underground."

"Then why in hell do you want to lock yourself in a bunker closer than ever to that thing?" Suraya hisses. "That's like jumping in a shark cage and cutting loose the tether. It's a matter of time before something hungry comes smashing through the steel bars."

"A bunker like that can withstand a nuclear bomb."

"That thing ate my truck. And it started gobbling an entire gas station. Maybe it can swallow a bunker whole."

"Chance I'll take," Shiv says. "Pretty sure this R.V. is a deathtrap."

Suraya continues driving. The Garcias are quiet in the back, maybe dozing, grief and stress and fear making them inert.

"It was big. The eye," Shiv says.

Suraya doesn't want to discuss it, but Shiv brings it up again anyway—an eye with a pupil the size of the center circle on a basketball court. The shadows might've covered it if the night sky directly above the sinkhole hadn't featured many stars illuminating the scene—a pupil that wasn't the color of a surface but rather the emptiness of an open maw. The pupil acted as a gaping mouth eating up its prey. A red iris with sharp lines in striation away from the nucleus resembled a ring of bloody fangs. The middle was a bottomless hole. Had an eyeball swallowed up the mother of those two kids?

"I don't ever want to see that thing again," Suraya whispers. "If we get swallowed up in a sinkhole, I want you to use that shiv and stab out my eyes."

"Jesus, Bulldog. Get a grip."

"I'm serious. Promise me."

"Usually, someone's got to do something to me to get shanked, lady."

"If that's what it takes, I'll scratch that ugly-ass spiderweb tattoo off your face."

"That'll get you blinded, bitch."

"Then we've got a deal," Suraya says.

The RV's headlights shine along the winding road. Suraya's eyes follow the hard-surfaced route and search for any interruption in the pavement that would indicate a new or previous sinkhole had made their last option of an automotive escape null and void. What are the odds another hole would open on this exact tract of roadway?

"We're being hunted."

The voice from over Suraya's right shoulder almost makes her jump out of her skin. For the last two decades driving a big rig across this country, she hadn't been afraid of the monsters who preyed on women along these American byways. Or the racist assholes who could make her life miserable. But Bulldog has been jumpier than a timid toad since the world swallowed up her truck. Holyman would be calling her Bull*frog*.

The voice had come from one of the Garcias, and the sound had been so hollow and harsh she'd have sworn it was the father. But Suraya peers into the rearview mirror, and the teenage girl stares back. Her eyes are as alien as the gaze Suraya had seen staring up from the pit. That isn't a pleasant comparison. Gooseflesh runs up and down Suraya's arms.

"What're you talking about?"

"Of all the places in the desert, the sinkholes have opened under Mom…under Pi's companion…the prison transport…the gas station…your truck," the girl drones. "The chances of it being a coincidence are impossible."

"That's absurd, kid. It's a kind of seismic event or some shit," Suraya dismisses. She isn't going to tell a teenager about the eye under the sand.

"My name is Rosario, and I'm not a kid. Not anymore," she says. "I heard you talking. You saw something down there."

Suraya doesn't answer. The father and brother have managed to fall asleep—the grief of exhaustion overcoming the guys—but the girl is wide awake. She knows what's what. The teenager stares down the circumstances rather than closing her eyes to them. Bulldog has been tough like that since she was only a pup. Shiv had probably been tough like that when she was only a sharp little stickpin. Rosario. Rose. Doesn't a rose have thorns?

"Alright, Rosario. They call me Bulldog, not Bullshit, so I'll level with you. We saw something underground. Something that shouldn't be there. So, instead of holding hands and crying about it, let's work to-gether and keep ahead because I won't stand my ground if I face that thing again. The ground is the dangerous part. Next time, I'm gonna run.

"Six eyes are better than four. So shut your mouth and open your eyes. You see anything that doesn't belong, that's when you have per-mission to use your mouth. Understand?"

Rosario doesn't make a peep. But she does keep her peepers wide open and alert. Good girl. Bulldog hopes the kid doesn't die. Because if someone as fresh and feisty as Rosario doesn't have the nerve to survive, an old dog doing old tricks is royally screwed.

6.1 Richter

[Brock]

Brock has trained for countless emergencies since becoming a cop—car chases, school shootings, hostage scenarios, terrorist attacks, riots, kidnapping, domestic situations, and underage gunmen. But nothing on underground monsters. His only training on burrowing creatures was when he'd gone out into the desert with his cousin Shad when they were teenagers, and they'd shoot a .22 at the fringe-toed lizards.

A lizard hadn't swallowed Carl's station.

Pi follows the RV down the roadway. Brock barely registers the big motorhome's taillights in the distance. He is in shock—what did he see back there? He ran after Carl without thinking because his job was to save people. Rescue. Protect. Serve. But he'd encountered the unfathomable. What was under the sand?

"You gonna shake it off, Officer Hayes?"

Carl stares at him. He witnessed Brock's breakdown back at the gas station. When Brock came around the back of the building, Carl was braced between the door jamb of his back door with his shotgun against a shoulder, aiming straight down into the growing hole beneath his home. Carl fired the weapon, reloaded, and fired again. Brock skidded to a stop at the sinkhole's edge and peered down at Carl's target. Shadows concealed the object at the bottom of the hole. But Brock knew he wasn't looking at the bottom of a sandy sinkhole.

It wasn't a lizard.

Brock stared down at the impossible.

Then Brock made a fateful, terrible decision. He shined his powerful police flashlight down the pit and immediately regretted it. An eye as big as one of these hot-air balloons they sometimes take over the Mojave peered up from the bottom of the sinkhole. Like someone had buried Godzilla and the kaiju gazed up from its grave. But this thing wasn't dead. As Carl blasted away, the eye shifted. It *looked* at Brock!

Going forth on foot in the darkness makes Brock nearly break down in a panic attack. The vehicles don't afford them any more safety than his own feet—he'd seen the Earth swallow up a semi-truck and gobble a gas station as quickly as it had gulped a full-grown woman. And wouldn't the most logical explanation for the disappearance of his police cruiser and the prison transport bus be that they'd sunk into the ground back before Brock understood what was happening? His partner and a whole load of prisoners inside reinforced police vehicles hadn't been safer than the two people on foot.

They search for a solution at the edge of civilization. Samson Dunphey is a bigger crackpot than Carl Kennedy, and now the refugees depend on him for help. When the world goes nuts, the crazy ones are best apt to assist. When in Wonderland, look to the Mad Hatter for help.

The RV's brake lights paint the route red and stay bright. Then the recreational vehicle is put in Park, and the lights go out. The stars brighten the world enough to see the barren wasteland in every direction. Brock compares the Mojave to the surface of Mars. They might as well be on some alien planet because Earth has become unrecognizable. Fantastical creatures have taken over the world...

Pi puts the Nissan into Park, and all four exit. The prisoner in Brock's care and the burly trucker get out of the cab of the RV as the Garcias exit the back door.

"You made it," the teenage Garcia says to Carl. She sounds relieved.

"I'm a stubborn bastard," Carl says.

Yeah, he is.

Carl looks back the way they came. "I left her there."

"You didn't have a choice," Brock says. All the locals know that Carl's deceased wife, Mary, was buried out back of the gas station. Brock used to think it creepy but lately had found it romantic. "She wouldn't have wanted you to stay and die."

"Right," Carl replies, although he doesn't sound convinced.

The world rumbles again. Brock puts his hand on the roof of the Nissan. Those closest to the RV steady themselves against the vehicle's side. Landry extends both arms like a professional surfer, although no one born and raised in Inyo County has ever done much surfing. Pi and Carl are near enough to use the car as an anchor. The quakes are getting more severe with each occurrence. That is what happens when a goliath moves through the underground sand.

Brock sweeps the area for a sign of a sinkhole. The world quivers, but the ground remains solid. After a few seconds, the shaking subsides.

When the ground settles, Brock assumes the lead. Carl takes point on Brock's right side. Brock can't shake off what he saw in the sinkhole back at the gas station, so he appreciates Carl's unwavering forward momentum.

The night surrounds them on every side—vicious vegetation, venomous creatures, dangerous terrain. There isn't a drop of natural water in any direction for a hundred miles. Sudden drop-offs and loose soil can provide hazards to leave any of them with a broken leg, and there is no rescue in the middle of nowhere. They can't even phone someone to find out what is really going on. This frightened group of people is all alone out here in the desert. They had to rely on each other.

Another aftershock arrives, but Brock doesn't even pause. He doesn't fear a natural phenomenon like an earthquake. There are worse things that exist under his feet than seismic activity.

"Shoot, goddamn it," Carl commanded.

Brock had finally fumbled his sidearm out of his holster. He'd put every bullet in the gun into the thing below the Earth. He could barely hear the gunshots over the sound of destruction as the station ripped apart. The gargantuan eye didn't even blink. Brock froze as the eye ate, sucking huge sections of the station into its hungry gaze. Carl had run out of ammo, and they had run out of time as the station's foundation collapsed. Carl leaped away from the back door, and Brock snapped out of his shock in time enough to grab ahold of Carl's arm so the man didn't fall into the hole. And get eaten by the eye.

"Move, dammit," Carl had demanded, but Brock's legs wouldn't listen. He couldn't budge. The sinkhole started expanding, and Brock couldn't twitch a toe. He had come to rescue Carl, and moments later, his muscles froze as a subterranean kaiju attempted to eat him with its eye. "Now!"

Carl had grabbed him by the wrist and yanked him forward, practically dragging him around the growing sinkhole, sprinting around the station and heading toward Landry's dirty white car. Brock had meant to save Carl's ass, but Carl instead managed to rescue his. Long minutes later, Brock still can't get over what he saw.

Carl is calm and collected, like he'd been nearly swallowed by a gargantuan underground predator before. This whole situation is impossible, but Carl takes it in stride. After one has seen everything under the sun, maybe something so nonsensical starts to make a perverse sort of sense.

"Gimme a minute," Brock says. "I'll get there. I gotta get there."

"What did you see back there?" Landry asks.

"No," Brock warns. "Not yet. Can't talk about it yet."

His mind feels like it's undergoing seismic activity, little cracks appearing in his psyche with every new challenge presented to the refugees. Fissures appear in his sanity, and Brock fears a quake of too large proportions would shatter his foundation and make his mind crumble into pieces. He froze when he had the chance to save Carl; what will happen when the opportunity arises again?

6.2 Richter
[Shiv]

Shiv knew her fair share of violence, but she'd never stabbed an innocent victim in the eye with a sharpened tool. Blinding Bulldog is the last damn thing she wants to do, but she isn't going to let the trucker claw a tattoo off her face, either. And Bulldog is serious. If Shiv doesn't shaft her before they get swallowed by the sand, then Bulldog will die with a flap of Shiv's cheek clutched in her fist.

Bulldog doesn't want to get eaten by an eye.

Shiv doesn't want to get eaten at all.

They're walking the last part of the route to the conspiracy nut's secret bunker. Aren't these kinds of guys usually white supremacists or neo-Nazis? What if this Samson turns away all the brown and black people and only rescues Carl? All this way to save one damn old white man.

The final leg of the road to the bunker is unnavigable by RV or even in Landry's shitty Nissan. They'd need an all-terrain vehicle or a damn good jeep to cross this terrain. Since between the hiking refugees they'd lost more modes of transportation than they currently possessed, no one could produce a spare ATV.

Yesterday morning, Shiv had been loaded onto a prison transport to transfer to a maximum-security federal facility. Shiv had gotten in trouble one time too many, and they were sending her away to meaner masters who could maybe keep her on a leash. Not so many hours ago, she was squatting in the bushes alongside a deserted desert road taking a piss, unaware the whole world had already changed around her.

Beneath her.

The starlight illuminates the path well enough so they can spot a sinkhole in their direct route in plenty of time to avoid falling into a pit. But there's no way to account for a crater opening *beneath* them. She saw the massive eye at the bottom of the hole—she could imagine it went with an enormous nose and a gaping mouth. They could be walking across a gigantic subterranean face, moving steadily toward an underground orifice waiting to swallow them whole. Maybe it's waiting until the pedestrians pass over unseen teeth. Then the buried monster would open wide, and they would all tumble like grains down a funnel.

Carl points a crooked finger ahead. "There."

The remote homestead still has electricity. A single lamppost makes a perfect circle of yellow light on a barren front yard. Shiv can hear the *chugchugchug* of the generator as it keeps up with Samson's use of energy. A soft glow emanates from within a small mobile home, eerily reminiscent of the trailer house back home where Shiv had started down the wrong path in life. The artificial illumination is more comforting than the stark starlight, something that gives Shiv an indication that man can indeed drive back the forces of nature.

Technology can prevail. You hear that, you big damn eye?

Shiv stares at the warm light coming from the cabin like a moth careening heedlessly toward the flame. Maybe this is a trap? Perhaps Samson's nest is an ambush? Is the monster with the eye so clever as to have led them right to slaughter? Is this haven merely bait for some buried gargantuan hunter?

Shiv knows the answer. Because there was something else she saw that Bulldog didn't mention. Shiv stared into the big damn eye with a mouth for a pupil, and she recognized malevolence. Intelligence. *Hunger.*

This Samson S.O.B. better have some reinforced nuclear-bomb

shelter kind of shit.

The nine refugees pause as the world rumbles again. The ground shakes and makes things unsteady. They huddle in the middle of the trail ending at Samson's trailer. They all grab shoulders, hands, or elbows to steady against one another. The pooled light from the lamppost jitters across the ground like a flashlight beam in the grip of someone with palsy. No one falls. No one runs away in fear. No one gets swallowed up by the hardpan leading up to the lonely shelter in the desert.

"Why does that sound like something's hungry?" Landry asks and immediately earns Pi's elbow to the ribs.

"It did sound like a rumbling stomach," Chuy mumbles quietly, moving his scared eyes across the ground.

"Let's quit standing here with our thumbs up our asses and get moving," Carl grumbles.

He crosses the remaining distance to the mobile home. The tin can has seen better days—white paint flecked to show silver beneath, the roof tarred and re-tarred, a door rusted in all four corners, dusty windows muting the warm light within. Carl pounds on the door, and particles drift off the surface. It wouldn't withstand too many more knocks.

"Lights are on, but nobody's home?" Landry asks.

"He's gotta be here," Carl barks. "Nowhere else to go."

"Maybe he went to his bunker?" Officer Hayes suggests.

Carl turns and glares like he's suffering a second grader guessing the capital of New Hampshire. "I radioed him and let him know you were coming. I don't *know* where his bunker is. None of you know where his fucking bunker is. He'd have left a note if he wasn't going to wait for you."

"Maybe he left a note inside," Officer Hayes says.

Carl tries the doorknob, and it turns. Shiv bristles. She's never heard of a conspiracy quack who doesn't fastidiously lock their door—unless it's a trap. Maybe the dude's an NRA nut-job waiting behind the door with a loaded gun to shoot down the first stranger who enters his unlocked door.

Carl glances back over his shoulder. Shiv nods. "Go ahead." Let the white dude go first. Carl enters with Officer Hayes behind him. All the others follow but Shiv and Pi. They sit down on the wooden steps leading into Samson's mobile home.

"I don't know if it's safer inside or outside," Pi says. "This place gives me the creeps."

"Probably doesn't matter either way," Shiv replies.

"You think this is happening anywhere else? The sinkholes…and what's beneath?"

"You ever watch horror movies? Those disaster flicks where a whole town gets attacked by aliens or blobs or some shit?"

Pi shrugs. "Sure. Mostly around Halloween."

"A couple of characters always escape the town at the end, and everything is alright after they leave city limits," Shiv says. "That's some bullshit."

Pi sighs. "Bullshit. Right."

"Don't plan for a happy ending, kid. Expect the worst."

Shiv once had a rosy outlook on life, but someone beat it out of her long ago. She learned that you couldn't leave the horrors behind simply by leaving town.

The world rumbles and gurgles again, and a sinkhole opens not even ten feet from where Shiv's boots rest on the trodden sand. She kicks backward, panicking to get off her ass in time to retreat. Pi has already leaped to her feet and bolted inside. Shiv struggles with the handcuffs to grab the handrail up to the mobile home entrance. She gets a grip and pulls herself upright, staring upward at the roof and avoiding looking back at the hole. She doesn't want to see an eyeball. Not again.

A shadow falls on her, a silhouette created by the stars scattered in the sky blocked behind the biggest goddamn man she'd ever seen. Maybe the effect is because he's up on the roof and framed by the universe—God Himself delivered to save her ass. She recognizes the object in his right hand as he pulls the pin and tosses it in her general direction. Not *at* her. Past her. Behind her.

The grenade hits smack dab in the crater's center, sinking sand absorbing the object even as Shiv backs into the mobile home's doorway. She ought to duck and cover. Shiv should slam the door and make herself as safe as possible. Instead, she gets to her feet and stares at the hole where the grenade had fallen. On the ground, the shadow of the massive man matches with her smaller one cast by the interior lights.

Sand explodes upward in a giant geyser. *POOOOF!*

The sinkhole remains half-formed. The previous pits had refilled after they swallowed whatever was near. After it *ate*. This one merely pauses. It doesn't get any deeper or fill itself back in. The grenade maybe stunned it? Stopped it? *Killed* it?

"Hell yeah," the man on the rooftop yells into the night, a deep baritone sound that rolls like thunder. It isn't Santa Claus up there. It must be Samson Dunphey. The first person in their group to score a point against the leviathan under the sand.

They could fight the creature. Maybe even kill it.

"Hell yeah," Shiv repeated, a dangerous smile curling the corners of her lips.

6.3 Richter

[Carl]

Samson Dunphey tossed a grenade down the gullet of whatever wreaked havoc on the Mojave. Carl hasn't considered much about the cause of the quakes. He tried to ignore what the other refugees had been whispering about in intense tones. The idea that some crazy science fiction component could explain this unusual seismic activity is more than this old man could handle. Carl has made every day since Mary passed as long and tedious as possible. All this wonder and excitement is putting the pedal to the floor in acceleration to an end. Carl isn't ready for the future.

The hulking figure of Samson Dunphey looks down through a hatch on his roof. Carl, Hayes, and the teen girl stand around the base of a stepladder. They hold it steady as the massive man comes down, every step on the ladder creaking in protest. Samson is a mess of hair and muscle and accessories—armed up to his ass against Armageddon.

"What happened out there?" Officer Hayes asks as Samson reaches the floor. "Was that a bomb?"

"You askin' as a cop or a man who wants to live to see tomorrow?" Samson asks.

"I'm not making any arrests tonight," Hayes replies. "I'm only a man."

"Then I'll show you," Samson promises. "First, we come up with a plan. We need to time our trip to the bunker just right. Those things under the sand are hungry."

Carl considers Mary buried behind the gas station. He left her there. He isn't sentimental enough to sacrifice himself to stay with her corpse. Carl doesn't claim to know what's after life, but he doesn't believe the body in the backyard was tethered to Mary. Still, the idea of some underground predator swallowing the remains of his wife... Carl can't dwell on the possibility.

"How far do we need to go to get there?" Landry asks the hulking conspiracy theorist.

"A hundred yards," Samson answers. "The first fifty across pure sand. Then we get to some solid stone. I buried the bunker in bedrock I had blasted out decades ago. Fully stocked with survival supplies. There's also an arsenal for general defense."

"Like more of those grenades you dropped down the sinkhole?" the convict asks eagerly, like a kid wondering about a wrapped present under the tree.

"More," Samson confirms.

"What was—" the trucker asks, then glances at the boy and his sister huddled on either side of their dad. She considers tabling the question, but this isn't the time for pussy-footin' around it. "What were you throwing grenades at, exactly?"

"I don't know *exactly*," Samson admits. "But it ain't no different than if a stranger came bustin' in my front door uninvited—I shoot first and leave the questions to the coroner."

"You didn't invite *us*," the smarty, smart-ass college girl says. *What's her name?* Carl wonders again. *It's a dessert... Cake? Muffin? Pie. Like Key Lime Pie.*

Samson nods at Carl. "He was invited. Him and any of his friends. I told Carl I could keep you all safe. We only need to get to the bunker."

"A hundred yards," Officer Hayes repeats. Quite a feat. Ten people must race across a minefield where the threat can swallow up any one of them from underneath.

"We're going to need bait," Samson says.

Carl glances at Hayes and recognizes a glimmer of suspicion. Same with the convict and the trucker. The young folks are oblivious to the nature of humankind, and the father of those kids clings to the desperate hope he can keep his children safe and still go back and save his wife. The man isn't thinking clearly. The more world-weary group members understand why Samson Dunphey invited *all* of them up to his bunker. Samson expects some of them to serve as a lure—not all are supposed to live through this.

"You want a minnow?" Hayes asks. Samson nods. "And not you, because you can get into the bunker."

"Right," Samson confirms.

Hayes gazes into the night, surveying the landscape. Dawn starts to give a hint in the east of daylight coming soon. The night was long and tiring. Carl feels like he's been awake for days instead of hours. They came a long way, but there were still a hundred yards to the goal. And someone must volunteer to run in the other direction.

"You have a vehicle?" Hayes asks Samson.

"A buggy. Faster than hell."

"Maybe hell's what's coming to get us, sir. Reaching up from the bowels of the Earth."

Samson nods. His mangy beard makes it impossible even to tell he's talking. "Maybe. It's been a long time comin'."

"I can take the buggy. Maybe make like I'm trying to escape," Hayes offers. "Think that will work?"

"Whatever is down there, it's a predator," Samson says. "And it has its prey trapped, backed into a corner. A cat may play with a mouse, but it won't let the varmint escape."

"That's the plan, then," Hayes decides. No one tries to talk him out of it or offers to go in his place. The cop is chivalric to the end. His end.

"Let's get you armed before we send you out," Samson says, flipping open a chest against one wall packed full of weapons—most of which were undoubtedly illegal in California. Carl supposes they didn't offer a permit for grenades, after all. "You deserve a fighting chance,

Officer."

Carl turns toward the assortment of electronics arranged across another whole wall. He marvels over Samson Dunphey's impressive communications array. Samson possesses several different radios utilizing shortwave, broadband, CW, Ham, CB, and digital communications. Satellite receivers. Samson can dial into the whole goddamn communications grid.

"Helluva system," Carl compliments.

"You should check out the moon bounce. I can pick up some wicked E.M.E. reception. Send a message to Germany. You might not believe what you get back."

Samson towers over Carl as he sits down at the radio system. The man certainly lives up to his name—wide as a linebacker, tall as a baseball player, muscles like a weightlifter, and hair as voluminous as a model from a shampoo commercial. Veins of hoary gray run through his dark mane. He appears precisely as Carl pictured the biblical character.

Samson turns to start planning the exodus to the bunker with Officer Hayes. They will have to leave access to the Ham radio behind. Before they go, Carl wants to try the moonbounce. EME is Earth–Moon–Earth communications using the lunar surface as a natural satellite to bounce a signal off and return to Earth. It needs a big antenna, sophisticated equipment, and lots of tuning—Samson has built quite the array. This is an amateur enthusiast's dream. Carl hasn't been so delighted since some moment long before Mary died…

Carl tunes the Ham and manages to catch a signal. The message is indeed in German. Carl doesn't know German beyond *Ich bin ein Berliner* from the famous JFK speech. Yet the words transcend a language difference based on the panicked tone full of fear. Whatever is happening in Europe is connected to what's happening in the California desert, Florida, and Montana. Everywhere. Then silence. Stark. Cold. Fearsome.

"Do you want to know what they said?" Miss Key Lime asks. No one answers. Most people would take it as a "no." Not Pi. She translates after no one replies—"They said, 'It's the hungry mountain. It's eating

Hamburg'."

No answer for several beats of Carl's racing heart. Then the boy, God bless him, asks, "The mountain is eating a Hamburger?"

More silence. Then Miss Key Lime snorts. She's been holding back a laugh. "Sorry."

Landry giggles suddenly, the sound of someone descending into madness. "Sorry, too."

Then the trucker barks out a boisterous laugh. "Hamburger," she guffaws. She's chuckling uncontrollably. Then the convict joins her, the scary face featuring a spiderweb tattoo breaking into a terrifying grin and a dangerous chortle. The mourning family starts laughing. Hayes. Even Samson. All are having a raucous release over the kid's innocent comment. Carl is going off, too, and he can't remember the last time he'd laughed so hard. They are all crying. But the tears aren't of joy or bliss. Like some insane clown coterie, they are all shedding tears of terror.

6.4 Richter

[Brock]

"This decision is stupid as shit, isn't it?" Brock asks Carl.

Brock and Carl stand inside Samson Dunphey's back doorway, staring into the darkness.

"Maybe," Carl answers.

"You're really inspiring confidence, Carl."

"The plan is to run away." Carl frowns. "I've been running away my whole life. Trying to escape from the past. Do you see where I ended up? Right in an unholy mess."

"We aren't getting out of this situation by standing still anymore, Carl. Maybe you've just been running in the wrong direction?"

"Well, the plan is for us each to run in *opposite* directions, Officer. That means one of us will be making a shitty choice." Carl pauses. "Maybe both of us. What if every direction is the wrong one?"

Brock gazes into the abyss beyond the illusion of safety provided by the shelter, searching a barren ground lit by a scattered dapple of starlight, checking for any sign of an attacker.

"When I was a kid, I always thought I'd have all the answers when I was maybe twenty-five," Brock says. "Now I'm twenty-seven and have as many questions as ever. Maybe fifty is the new thirty? Tell me, Old-

Timer, when do you get to the point where it's all less confusing?"

"Not in this lifetime, kid."

Brock nods. That's an answer, at least. Better than a question. The two men turn their backs on the night and step away from the open door.

"I saw the buggy out back," Brock says to Samson, the ATV ten yards out the back door. "I'll head due east. Draw attention."

Samson takes Carl's spot at Brock's side. He hands Brock a set of keys with an NRA keychain. Of course. The man is a giant, dwarfing Brock and blocking him from the rest of the group. Samson features a tangled black beard streaked with white, dark eyes peering from beneath a wily mane and unruly brows.

"You sure about this, Officer Hayes?"

"I'm not going to back out. I know my duty."

Samson nods. He has armed Brock with guns and grenades. At least Brock will have a fighting chance, or he'll be able to end it before he starts getting eaten. Like a hamburger.

Brock returns to the back door. Samson follows and waits in the doorway as Brock exits. Brock pauses on the top step, turning to Samson with a question. The giant man stands there like some wizened figure straight out of the Old Testament. "You know what's out there?"

"I've heard some others on the ham radio tonight," Samson says. "Some say it's the future."

"Tomorrow seems pretty grim."

"Look around, Officer. You think there's any other future for this shithole world than something grim?"

This gloomy bastard might be the last person Brock will ever talk to, and he makes the final words Brock may hear the worst damn pep talk the cop could imagine. If Samson is correct, and it's the future under the sand, then what does it matter? The kids back there don't have a tomorrow to fight to save. Their fate is killer kaiju eating up entire cities.

"I gotta believe there's a chance for something better," Brock says.

"Pollyanna bullshit. Why does tomorrow have to be better?"

"It must be because otherwise I might as well send *your* ass out there. Screw the bunker. If there's no chance, anyways," Brock replies. "The only reason I'm doing this is to save a bunch of innocent people. Why bother if we're all doomed?"

"Right," Samson suddenly agrees in a turnabout. "The future is probably as bright as the sun, Officer. The glass is fucking half full!"

Samson is 100% full of shit, but Brock prefers this send-off to the fatalistic claptrap Samson had initially offered. Before Samson could ruin the high note, Brock launches across the yard and sprints to the spot under a corrugated tin lean-to, where the buggy awaits. He shoves the key into the ignition before the subterranean predator can follow his whereabouts, and Brock cranks the motor to life.

He tromps on the gas, and the buggy launches forward. The all-terrain vehicle is popular along the dunes closer to the edges of the desert, where tourists partake in recreation. This far into the Mojave live only the lonely and the crazy. And a small ghost town to snag a little roadside business from adventurous passersby.

The buggy's headlights illuminate the scant brush and occasional cacti, shadows jumping around like the boogeyman is around every corner. Brock's hands grip the steering wheel tightly, every turn a matter of life and death. He could be speeding headlong into a trap or going too fast to hold the interest of whatever behemoth lurks below. He needs to catch the attention of the thing preying on them.

Brock must act like the bait.

A roll cage protects him overhead, but there's no glass on the whole buggy besides the windshield. Nothing between him and the night air and whatever is beneath the sand. Massive tires with aggressive treads bite into the rock and sand, giving Brock excellent control and impressive speed. He wants to think he has enough horsepower to keep out of the next sand trap that might open—

Right underneath him!

The sinkhole makes the buggy drop suddenly, Brock's stomach smacking into his mouth. When he was younger, he experienced the rides at Disney and became familiar with the first plunge of a fast coaster. Instead of the horizon never moving any closer and dawn seeping into the long night, he faces the cosmos through his windshield. The buggy points nearly straight up. The cascading sand sinks and sinks, and Brock guns the engine, slamming down the gas pedal. The wheels spin a little faster than the world recedes, gaining traction and elevation as the next seconds tick.

The front tires gain purchase on the rocky lip of the sinkhole and grab hold, pulling Brock up and out of the depression and speeding him away from the trap. Back on a flat landscape, Brock accelerates. Another sinkhole opens ahead on his left, and he deftly dodges. Another, and he avoids it again. A wide one forms right in his path, so Brock takes a ninety-degree turn on two oversized tires and speeds parallel to the rift in the desert.

Too many sinkholes open to dodge, so Brock pulls grenades off the belt that Samson had slung over his shoulder like Brock was Chewbacca. Brock expertly tosses a bomb into one hole, another, and another. The ground swallows them up, and shortly after, a muted *pathump* and a mushroom cloud of sand. The desert eats four grenades before the world quits making sinkholes.

Quiet.

The creature doesn't shake the earth. No seismic activity at all. The only disturbance is the rumbling of the buggy under Brock's backside. The grenades had packed enough punch to dissuade the burrowing leviathan—or the thing had found an easier target on foot somewhere behind Brock…

He survived being bait. Brock wasn't sure he would. But here he is, alive and unburied. Now Brock turns the buggy around, back toward Samson's place, at a quick speed and opens the throttle up. He could return in time to join them in the bunker, or maybe the refugees need his help. What's east? Las Vegas? He doesn't have enough fuel to keep riding to the east until he reaches the sun.

It's the hungry mountain. It's eating Hamburg. Something would probably eat Vegas, also. If it hadn't already. But Brock can't save Vegas. He can only maybe help the others.

Brock prays he has given the others enough time.

6.5 Richter

[The Garcias]

The Garcias are among the last in formation as the remaining refugees line up behind Samson to journey from the mobile home to the bunker. Samson warns against all of them going at once like a herd of cattle. He wants to keep some distance between each of them. Instead of all thundering across the expanse together and alerting the… the… Hector couldn't think about the thing under the sand.

"The bunker is a hundred yards due west," Samson says as he steps out. "Bulldog, you follow after I get halfway across. Don't wait so long that you lose sight of me. Keep an eye on me at the edge before the darkness swallows me up."

Samson first. Bulldog second. Shiv third. Pi fourth. Carl fifth. Chuy is next.

"I can't," Chuy says.

"Go, son," Hector says, shoving the boy forward. "No time to waste."

"I can't," Chuy cries, dodging his dad's grip and running toward the back of the trailer.

Rosario stares after Chuy, and Landry watches as Carl nearly disappears into the darkness.

"You go next, Rosario," Hector snaps. He must keep these two safe. Chuy is being Chuy, making everything more complicated than it ought to be. They can't let Carl get too far ahead. "Kid, you keep an eye on her." Landry nods.

Hector doesn't pause to make sure his daughter listens to his command. He races after Chuy into the back of the mobile home. Chuy huddles in the corner of a bedroom, shivering like a dog beaten too many times. How often had Hector been *soooo* frustrated with his son? The boy never followed directions or stuck to the plan. He always follows some tangent about hundred-year-old baseball stats or Satchel Paige trivia. More consumed by history than worrying about the here and now.

That's why Hector thought Chuy might like the ghost town. And the boy did. The tour through the old-fashioned buildings had been a happy moment—a perfect detour. A great memory before Linda got sucked into the ground. Buried alive. Could she *still* be alive? Hector dreads the answer. He can't move forward when he's still hoping against hope. Linda—Hector tamps his grief before it gets them killed.

Chuy huddles beside a bed in a room at the back. Hector squats down on his haunches. "What's the matter, sport?"

Chuy keeps his head down and sniffles into the crook of his arm. "I don't wanna go."

"There's no reason to stay here."

"We need to go back for Mom."

"We will," Hector promises. "But not now."

"I don't wanna leave her and climb into that…" Chuy lifts his head. His eyes are running water and red as chili peppers. "Dad, a bunker is only a nice name for a coffin."

"That bunker offers hope, Chuy. It's a chance for us to make it to tomorrow."

"I'm scared of tomorrow."

"Me, too, son."

"Mom's not going to be there," Chuy whispers. "I don't want a tomorrow where Mom's not there."

Hector deflates. He's supposed to pull his son up and push him forth, telling him he has many reasons to live. But monsters are eating the world, and Hector feels his words would be a blatant lie. If she were here, Linda might have been able to find some inspiration to motivate their son, but Hector is fresh out of optimism. In the language Chuy would understand, it's the bottom of the ninth, and their team is down by six. No runners on base, two outs, and the batter's struck out twice already. What would the Bambino say about this?

Who fucking cares what Babe has to say? He's dead.

Instead of rallying the boy, Hector sits next to Chuy. "Let's stay right here, sport."

Let Rosario face tomorrow. Hector agrees with Chuy. He doesn't want to see what the future brings without Linda.

"What's going on?" croaks the voice of an old man from the bedroom doorway. Carl is standing over the Garcias, and Landry is right beside him.

"Aren't you tired of running, *viejo*[3]?" Hector asks.

"I'm not partial to the alternative," Carl snaps. "Get off your ass and save your son."

"He doesn't want to get rescued," Hector says. "You two go on. We're staying here."

"I sent your daughter on to the bunker, and I came back to help you with the kid in case he gave you trouble," Carl hisses, nodding toward Landry. "We both did. We're risking our necks. So, let's drag him out of here and give him a fighting chance."

"No more fighting," Hector says.

Landry puts a hand on Carl's arm. "Let's go. They're not coming."

Carl advances on Hector and Chuy. "I'm not leaving without the kid."

Hector stands up and blocks the old man's way. "I think Chuy knows what's best for himself. Not you."

"His father is supposed to know what's best, but you're a spineless fool," Carl spits. "I could tell your wife had the balls in the family when I met her at the station. She would've had the gumption to save the boy."

---

[3] Spanish, old man.

"She isn't here," Hector replies darkly, tears rolling down his face. "She couldn't even save herself."

Carl pokes Hector in the chest. "Your job is to be strong and forge on, man!"

"It's useless, *viejo*. You're trying to escape something that's every-where. You can't run away from the world. You heard the reports— they're everywhere. There are giants up north. A sea monster in the Atlantic. There's a mountain eating a city. You can't get away from that," Hector counters. "Tell me, who's the fool?"

"He who gives up without a fight."

"Famous last words," Hector sighs.

"Better than being a pussy."

"We gotta go," Landry cries, tugging at Carl's sleeve.

Another quake. The whole mobile home shudders. Carl and Landry stumble backward out of the bedroom to escape, and Hector plops back down on his backside right beside Chuy, father and son wedged between wall and bed. He puts his arm around Chuy. Maybe this will be quick, and then it'll be over. That's the plan—no more goddamned detours.

Then the mobile home tilts at a severe angle. The roof rips enough so Hector can see the sky. It seems so peaceful out there among the stars. The black has become gray as the morning inches incrementally nearer, putting the terrors of the night behind them. Maybe there *is* a tomorrow. He glimpses it. Right there!

Then the mobile home falls into a sinkhole.

The whole trailer tilts ninety degrees. Hector and Chuy slide toward one bedroom wall. The bed gets to the wall first and flips up, the mat-tress cushioning their fall. A dresser crashes against the wall to their right, and clothes scatter everywhere. The windows in the room shatter, and sand starts leaking in. The house sounds like someone crushing the world's largest tin can.

Maybe giving up wasn't the right decision.

Hector grabs his son's arm and drags him toward the bedroom door. He peers through the doorway, now more like a trapdoor in the floor. Below, Hector sees a living area. Nothing is living. There's sand at the bottom of the trailer, churning like a whirlpool. In the center of the swirling sand is an eye.

An eye is eating up everything that falls near.

Oh, fuck, this was the wrong decision.

Across from the bedroom, wedged against the remaining cabinets in the kitchen, Carl and Landry still survive. The cabinets are attached enough to provide an anchor beside the back door. Hector can see the world behind the two other refugees; that end of the trailer is still above ground level. They can still escape.

But Hector can't jump the expanse between the bedroom door and the kitchen. He can't make it so far. The bedroom wall starts to collapse and could completely give way at any moment. The eye is going to eat him. And Chuy.

No.

Not Chuy.

"I'm going to throw my son across," Hector hollers over the din of the crushing home. "Over to you!"

Carl nods and reaches out a hand. Landry, too.

At least my son will live.

Hector reaches for the boy, but half the wall collapses under their feet. Chuy starts to fall as Hector grabs the edge of the division between the bedroom and living room, hand grasping tangled electrical wires. He snags the back collar of Chuy's shirt as the dresser and bed fall, swallowed by the eye. Hector dangles precariously off the smashed wall with a fistful of Chuy's shirt, saving his son from the thing beneath them. Hector must hold on. He has to save Chuy. The old bastard was right. Then the wire pulls free, and Hector falls. He slings his arm around like Babe Ruth, swinging for the bleachers. He knows it's a good one as he lets go, Chuy flying toward the two catchers.

Gravity is a bitch and inertia even worse, spinning Hector around, so the last thing he sees isn't his son being saved in a last-minute rally to win the game, but rather the hungry eye with an open pupil. Black as death.

6.6 Richter
[Landry]

Landry couldn't look.

Hector gets swallowed by the eye, but that isn't the worst. He tossed his kid at the last moment, and Chuy flew in the wrong direction. The kid smacks into the opposite wall, where Carl and Landry reach out their arms to catch him. For one terrible moment, the kid clutches the curtains of a window as the sand pours through the broken glass, some ten feet below where Carl and Landry have wedged themselves between cabinets near the back door. Then the curtains rip, and Landry turns away.

Carl pushes them through the back door onto a stone ledge, barely resisting the sinkhole's pull. They scramble away and crab-crawl to solid ground before they collapse, huffing and puffing. The old man is banged up and bloodied. Landry wears a long gash from wrist to elbow, dark blood spattering a few drops against the shadowed stone.

Landry looks over a shoulder as the top of the trailer house disappears beneath the lip of the sinkhole. The reverberations through the bedrock shake both Landry and Carl, the regular grinding pattern of someone crunching up jawbreakers between molars. The metal of the mobile home screeches as the eye gobbles it up. Then the raucous noise becomes muffled, and a plume of sand and dust exhales like an earthy belch. The result is a dimpled expanse of sand exhibiting no trace that a home once occupied the space.

Sparks crackle and hum from where electrical lines had once connected to the trailer. Other cables for communication now end abruptly. The lean-to where Samson stored his buggy has become illuminated in the brightening light of pre-dawn. Outside the perimeter of the previous placement of the mobile home, Landry spots footprints from where they'd initially walked up to the mobile home after leaving the vehicles behind. Landry finds Officer Hayes's footprints leading to the buggy's tire tracks. Carl points at the path made by those who'd left for the bunker before Landry and Carl so foolishly went back to rescue Hector and Chuy.

"Get up," Carl says after mere seconds of pause. "Get to the bunker."

The "get up" part goes as planned, but the "get to" is interrupted by the biggest quake yet. Landry falls back down on already bruised knee-caps. Carl hasn't gotten up yet and remains on his hands and knees. The world shakes like it has had enough of being eaten and is preparing to fight back. Or perhaps the damage done by the thing underground is tearing the whole planet asunder?

"How big is this…thing?" Landry asks as the rumbling subsides.

"You saw it?" The old man looks paler than ever.

"It saw us." Landry looks back at where the trailer disappeared under sand and stone.

They follow the path of the footprints, and the trail diverges two directions after they walk only a dozen yards. "The hell?"

Carl points to the trail containing the biggest footprints. "Samson was first. He went that way." He heads in that direction.

Landry's gaze follows the trail leading away from the direction Carl takes. The footprints are two different sets and more petite. Pi and the teenage girl went the other way. The last two refugees who left the mobile home. *Why did they take another path?*

"Carl…" Landry calls out, but Carl doesn't stop.

The day breaks, the light just bright enough to illuminate the surroundings without the impediment of night. The world appears so peaceful. The horizon is a flat line in one direction, the glow of impending dawn marked by a straight line across the faint blue in the distance. To his right, a lone butte interrupts the endless sand, gently sloped sides rising into a brightening sky, two stories up and flat at the top. Landry finds no sign of the others. They were safely tucked inside a bunker already, behind the obstruction of the butte, or…

Landry didn't want to consider the "or."

Landry follows Carl's direction because the silence is worse than any noise. It's the quiet at the edge of cacophony, the beat before all the bass begins. Landry doesn't want to experience all that peacefulness alone because the chaos is coming next.

Landry can differentiate between six different sets of prints going in this direction. The cowboy boot with a pointed toe belongs to Carl. The big feet are Samson's. Two pairs of small feet are Pi's and Rosario's. Those same footprints also point back, opposite the way Landry is going, toward the butte. They'd gone ahead with Samson, Bulldog, and Shiv, then turned around. Rosario and Pi retreated and took the other fork in the trail. Why?

The biggest prints end—Samson's, Shiv's, and Bulldog's. Carl scratches his head, staring at the abrupt end of the trail. In the flat expanse of sand before them, the small prints move in a circular pattern, and Landry can imagine the two girls wandering aimlessly. The bunker is as gone as the trailer house. Or something gobbled up Samson, Bulldog, and Shiv before they arrived, and the secret of the bunker's location died with Samson.

"Shit," Carl mumbles.

"What do we do now?" Landry asks.

"Kid, I don't have the first clue."

Carl has lived a long life. He surely experienced a billion different scenarios over his many decades. How many crazy situations did he survive in all that time? How many close scrapes? How many traumatic experiences? Many. But then, Carl has been hiding in his gas station from his last terrible thing for at least as long as Landry knew him. Carl isn't the guy who survives until the end. He's the guy who hides from adversity.

There's no goddamn place to hide.

Landry grabs the old man's sleeve and tugs. Carl snaps out of his indecisive state and follows as Landry backtracks to the fork in the road. Landry points at the butte. If the girls are alive, they might be hiding behind the bluff. Or on top of it. The old tried-and-true advice from every movie Landry has ever seen comes back—get to higher ground. Pi and Rosario's footprints lead up a steep slope that winds higher and higher. The option seems as good as anything else. Maybe they could see new opportunities if they scope out the area from a bird's eye view.

"What's that?" Carl barks.

Landry was so concentrated on what to do and where to go that the noise hadn't even registered. There's a buzzing sound, low and incessant. It gets louder and louder. There's nowhere to go without knowing what they're running from. Is it the sound the creature below the earth makes before it strikes? A prelude to the next quake? A warning of another sinkhole maybe opening right beneath Landry's feet?

No, it's Officer Hayes, coming in fast from a distance in the dune buggy, tires digging up the sand and kicking up dust. He brakes to a halt right in front of them. The look in Brock's eye suggests he experienced as much scary shit as Landry and Carl.

"Get in!"

Carl hops in the passenger seat, and Landry jumps into the back, a cramped cargo compartment that fits Landry's two skinny legs just fine. Hayes tromps on the gas, and the three locals ride off back the way Hayes came.

"You're the only two who survived?" Hayes asks over the revved engine.

Landry and Carl look at each other. The Gonzales guys are gone. The underground creature ate Samson, Suraya, and the convict. Pi and Rosario may have survived for a while, but how long? Landry leans into the front. "Pi and Rosario might've survived. Tracks lead up the butte."

The trail Hayes follows winds around the slope rising into the sky, now devoid of stars and almost entirely blue. He's putting the bluff between the buggy and the former site of Samson's trailer. Landry doesn't know if Samson based his plan on logic or hope, but having a ton of rock between the survivors and that hungry eye suddenly sounds fine and dandy.

"We'll climb up the far side trail," Officer Hayes promises. "If they're alive, we won't leave them behind."

Hadn't Landry and Carl decided the same things about Hector and Chuy? Hopefully, things will turn out better for the girls.

6.7 Richter

[Pi]

Pi and Rosario sit side by side atop a tall, singular butte. It might not save them if the ground opens and a monster starts eating them from below, but Pi likes to think the massive geological lifeboat affords them at least some time to process what might happen next. Their near future may involve becoming sand monster shit.

"It's beautiful," Rosario says as the sun breaks over the horizon. Maybe she thought she'd never see another sunrise. Her tone suggests she believes this one might be their last.

Pi doesn't usually ponder beauty. She's concerned with puzzles. Logic. Explanation. Reason. None of those words describe the last few hours of her life. But she does agree with Rosario—the sun *is* beautiful. Because there aren't any monsters in the sun.

The stillness is omnipresent, engulfing the entire Earth as if nothing dares make a move. Not even the wind soughs softly. It resembles a framed portrait of a desert hanging on a wall in a hotel, and Pi desperately wishes she had awoken in a numbered room, almost home, and Josh Henry in the next bed over. The scene remains static as Pi and Rosario gaze down from high on the hill in the middle of a seemingly endless expanse of desert.

They can see for miles to the west from up here. In this direction—home, family, rationality. As daylight fully illuminates their desert surroundings, Pi observes the world beginning to exhibit some subtle instances of motion. She catalogs sinkholes appearing here and there along the landscape. Like blurry smudges on a pristine photograph, she spots one appear here, then another, and another. The desert sucks up a tree or a cactus, shifting and sifting sand in pockmarks across the scene.

She'd envisioned a single unspeakable thing preying on them. But there are more. Dozens. Dozens just within the vicinity, close enough for Pi to count.

How many across the entire desert?

Then, a worse thought—maybe it's only one massive monster with multiple eye-mouths. A leviathan with hundreds of ocular orifices, all with gaping pupils to swallow their victims whole. An enormous creature featuring many eyes, like an arachnid, rising from beneath the ground. The monster comes closer to the surface with each quake. Pi shudders.

"Do you hear that?" Rosario asks.

Pi nods.

"What do we do?"

"We stay put," Pi says. "If they're looking for us, they'll assume we headed for high ground."

The sound of a revving engine has risen and faded over the last few minutes. It sounds like the buggy the cop took as a decoy. He must have survived. She doesn't know if the cop decided to haul ass across the desert for solid ground or if the sound of the engine is getting closer. He might be ascending the hill behind them or hauling ass to Vegas. The vast desert landscape plays tricks on her ears.

"You think it's Officer Hayes?" Rosario asks hopefully.

Pi nods again. She isn't going to turn this into a pep rally for a rosy outlook on their future. Pi can't formulate a hypothesis that contains much optimism. She considers getting off her ass and trying to follow the noise, but Pi cannot bring herself to move. Does she want to be rescued? The only safe place in the Mojave might be atop the solid stone butte. *Maybe* safe.

"I didn't want to come on this stupid trip," Rosario says. "We usually spend Christmas with *mi abuela*[4]. She lives in Santa Ana, and we stay over for the whole week. She bakes cookies, and we sing Christmas songs in Spanish, and she hides little treats and presents all over the house for me and Chuy to find. I always feel like a kid again there. Not a care in the world. I feel safe with *mi abuela*. This year would've been a great year to feel safe."

"Yeah," Pi says. What else is she supposed to say? No one else from their group made it. The trailer house disappeared into the earth. This kid lost her whole family. Is Pi supposed to hold Rosario's hand or something? Pi doesn't attempt any gesture.

The open expanse continues to exhibit all sorts of sinkholes. The world disintegrates before their eyes, and staring too long is akin to gazing into the sun. Pi would rather look at Rosario's haunted eyes and bottomless grief because at least that makes sense.

"You ever been in love?" Rosario asks.

The unexpected question takes Pi aback. This girl is dealing with some pretty heavy shit, and everyone processes tragedy in their own way. If Pi somehow manages to survive the desert, her most pressing conundrum is how to tell her sister that a giant underground eyehole ate her boyfriend.

"I'm not really into that scene," Pi says. "Boys and girls don't interest me. I like less-complicated things. Like old relics."

Rosario glances out into the distance, where the hungry eye eats the world. "I don't think the monsters care about relics."

Pi sighs. She doesn't want to face what's out there. She isn't eager to confront today's strife. "Neither do most people."

The sound of the buggy's engine is getting closer. Pi reconsiders getting up and trying to put her eyes on the vehicle to flag down the cop for rescue. Then the earth quakes, and both girls press their hands against the stone under their butts to stay steady. The whole region rumbles, and Pi can see small rocks dancing across the ground. The creatures

---

[4] Spanish, my grandmother

beneath the surface are causing significant seismic stresses. Pi sweeps her gaze across the desert plains to see if any fissures have opened to indicate the whole world might be cracking—like the shell of an egg too abused. But the world remains intact. The random sinkholes here and there still appear like pimples on the face of the Mojave, bubbling and festering for a few moments, taking down a Joshua tree, a scatter of stones, or a copse of cacti before falling still.

"There's a boy back home. He likes me. My friends wanted me to...." Rosario's voice trails off. Pi realizes she's talking about sex. This convo is getting awkward as fuck. Pi isn't here to make a new bestie. She doesn't want to hear about Rosario's love life. "But I wasn't ready."

"Hey, you're a kid. You have—"

What was Pi going to say? Time? A whole future ahead of you? Tomorrow? Nothing Pi considers rings true.

"Yeah," Rosario agrees to the incomplete thought. "You think there's still a home to go back to?"

Pi doesn't answer the question.

The girl confronts the reality of this situation. Her mother disappeared in front of her eyes. Her father and brother are gone. She knows they're all dead. They're not trapped beneath the sand, waiting for rescue. The kid isn't so foolish as to hope for a miracle. God isn't answering any prayers today. One might believe the monsters in the sand indicate Hell opened its gates. Pi isn't a believer in age-old myths— she is an archaeologist. She deals with ancient *facts*.

But Pi's life had turned into some kind of fantasy. Josh had disappeared through a rabbit hole in Whatthefuckland, and now he's late, he's late, for a very important date with Pi's sister. With monsters reported in Montana, Germany, and Florida, maybe some other thing has already taken a bite out of LA. She hasn't thought about her parents or her sister much, because this isn't their story.

All of California is probably under siege, too. Or they're next on the agenda.

On the menu, she thinks darkly.

"There's a chance, right?" Pi says. "We're not giving up."

"We won't," Rosario agrees. "Officer Hayes is coming. The sound is getting closer."

Then they only have to traverse a desert landscape rife with deadly sinkholes.

"You watch those Hollywood post-apocalyptic movies? End-of-the-world shit? Someone always survives."

"Why can't it be us?" Rosario asks.

"Damn right."

Pi falls silent. Movies are a bunch of garbage—prepackaged nonsense where the impossible happens. Someone always avoids certain death. A last-minute miracle comes through in the nick of time. The perfect rescue seems to occur at the most opportune moment. No one even ever stops to pee. Well, this isn't a movie. And Pi really has to pee.

And she isn't getting off this rock.

So, she hangs her ass off the steep edge of the butte and does her business as Rosario gazes out toward the west. Tears roll down the teenager's face as urine rolls down the side of the stony slope. Yeah, this isn't a Hollywood movie. A monster has probably eaten Hollywood. This is real life. And real life always ends in real-life death.

6.8 Richter
[Bulldog]

Blackness envelops Suraya so completely that she wonders if she's dead. It's the absolute black of closed eyes against the darkness—and the things *inside* the darkness. Her eyes are wide open, and she's completely blind. More than merely blind. This is the absence of everything. She exists in an abyss with no end or edge—a world unmoored by logic and reason.

Dead might be better than whatever the hungry eye has in store for Suraya. She made Shiv promise to kill her before the pupil could eat her, so maybe that's what happened. Everything occurred so fast she could hardly piece together recent events. Ten refugees had gathered in Samson's mobile home, but they separated to get safely across the sandy stretch of desert to the bunker. The plan put them in mortal danger in a matter of moments.

The cop was brave and volunteered to be bait. That was supposed to give the other nine time to survive. Samson led the way to his bunker, and Suraya went second. Shiv followed behind her, close enough to stick a knife in her if a sinkhole opened underfoot. But no sinkhole appeared. Samson held open the door to the bunker, waving Suraya inside.

The door was a big metal construct on hinges as massive as Samson's gigantic hands. The hatch reminded her of something on a bank vault or a door to seal off a submarine chamber. The opening was oblong and dark. Suraya sprinted toward the entrance, considering the thought of the eye at the bottom of the hole that had swallowed her semi-truck—how it had wanted to eat her. The doorway was as dark as the pupil in the pit. Was the monster waiting beyond the threshold with an open mouth?

Suraya ran inside. The bunker's interior was more illuminated than it had appeared from outside, running lights exposing the parameters of the chamber. The chamber was about the size of her bedroom. Big enough to hold ten refugees. The walls featured latched cabinets made of more metal. The storage inside was half the overall space. Samson had stocked it well enough to survive for a long time inside these chambers.

Shiv followed her inside. As soon as the woman in the orange jump-suit stepped through the door, the world outside started to quake. Shiv grabbed a handle of one of the storage cabinets as Suraya steadied herself against the metal bunk at the level of her knees. The shaking continued to increase. Samson cursed as he entered the door, pulling it shut behind him and engaging the lock.

The whole bunker moved.

"What's that?" Suraya cried.

"Quake," Samson said through gritted teeth. Then the whole bunker rolled. Suraya banged her head, and then darkness.

Now, still darkness. How long was she unconscious? Long enough. Everything aches. She tastes blood in her mouth but can't spit. She doesn't even know her surroundings. Suraya pictures the belly of a beast, an eye digesting her slowly. Shiv agreed to stab her in the skull if it came to that, but she feels too much pain for this to be death.

"Shiv?" Suraya mumbles.

No answer.

"Samson?"

Silence. Darkness. Nothingness.

She manages to fumble her phone out of her pocket. It hasn't gotten a signal in hours, but she doesn't need it to call for help. There's no one to help them against this. Her screen had cracked in the tumble, but it gives enough light to reveal the bunker still surrounds her. She uses the flashlight, really showing the interior.

Shiv stares at her from across the room.

"Are you alive?" Suraya asks, unsure if maybe the woman died with her eyes open.

Shiv blinks.

Suraya sweeps her light around. She finds Samson on the opposite end of the bunker. On the floor. Or rather, on the ceiling, which is now the floor. Samson doesn't move. His massive form remains still as Suraya stares at him. She crawls closer, a million bumps and bruises protesting the effort. The shell of the bunker is cold, metal. Samson built this thing like a tank, and the creature couldn't breach it.

She shakes Samson. He groans. She examines him with the flashlight and finds a wicked gash across his head. He moves and comes around, hissing like a pissed-off snake. Samson manages to sit up, touching his head. He winces.

"It's deep," Suraya says.

"There's a first aid kit by the door," Samson directs. "Third cabinet on the right…or the left, I suppose, since we're upside down."

Shiv gets the kit and bandages Samson's wound to the best of her abilities. The massive man is hairier than most truckers. What other injuries might be hiding under the mat of hair? That isn't the most important thing right now.

"What happened?" Suraya asks.

"A sinkhole opened right beneath us. We started going down," Samson says. "I jumped in before sand started pouring through the hatch. Slammed the door shut and locked it behind me."

"The others…"

"The cop didn't distract the son of a bitch long enough," Samson complains. "We didn't even have time to get half of us to safety."

"Maybe there's more than one of those things out there," Shiv suggests. None of them have a satisfactory answer to that.

"Where are we now?" Suraya asks.

She might not want the answer. Could they be inside the belly of the beast? Did the eye swallow them and doesn't even know it? Perhaps it would take time to be digested by the creature's innards?

Samson gets to his feet with a mighty groan. He's six-and-a-half feet of muscle and man. Unkempt and unshaven, he's a burly grizzly bear who would've been the beast in most stories—this isn't most stories. Their life is a horror movie. But it isn't a psycho named Jason or Michael or a zombie sniffing for brains. The words of the Germans ring in Suraya's ears— *It's the hungry mountain. It's eating Hamburg.* Now Suraya is in the belly of the beast.

Samson takes a shaky step forward and grabs the large steel wheel that locks a vault door like something that belongs in a submarine. Suraya puts a hand on his large upper arm. He pauses and looks into her eyes.

"What are we going to find out there? Sand? Darkness? Death? Nothing at all?" *The eye?* Suraya thinks.

Samson sighs. "Why are you asking me? I'm just a crazy hermit."

"The whole world is crazy, but that world is on the other side of the door. Maybe we should leave it that way."

"We need to open up and take a look," Samson says. "Sooner than later."

"What do you think is happening?"

"Some of the nuts on the ham radio suggested a rip in spacetime— creatures from the future. Li'l Lulu lives near Area 51. She says the egg-heads were trying to combat global warming in the future and unleashed these unholy creatures to battle climate change. Turns out these things think humanity is the enemy. These are monsters from our tomorrow."

"Time travel?" Suraya says. "Sounds like bullshit."

Samson shrugs. "A giant eyeball doesn't make any fucking sense no matter how you try to explain it."

Suraya could agree with that.

Samson pulls a metal tool out of one of the cubbies upside down along the walls. He swings and strikes the metal door, and the loud clangor makes Suraya and Shiv wince. Samson tilts his head toward the reverberation as it dies off.

"I thought we might be buried alive," Samson says. "Or—" *Swallowed,* Suraya thinks. "But that hollow sound… Nothing is blocking the door. There is air on the other side of the hatch. So, what exactly *is* out there?"

The three refugees locked in the bunker look at each other. No answers are forthcoming.

6.9 Richter

[Shiv]

Samson turns the steel wheel and opens the hatch of the bunker. The world beyond is inky darkness. Shiv is sure the world out there presents a helluva lot more danger than the world inside the bunker. The steel shell should be tough enough to withstand any attack. Attempting to eat the bunker would be akin to a four-year-old trying to crack a walnut between two teeth. Shiv doesn't want to step outside. Samson exits into the pitch.

"What do you see?" Shiv asks.

"Underground caves. No sign of the eye," he answers.

Bulldog pushes past Shiv and leaves the bunker. She aims a flashlight at their surroundings.

"Are there underground caves under the desert?" Shiv asks from inside the bunker.

"Not before," Samson answers.

Shiv steps into the doorway but remains inside the bunker as Bulldog aims her light at the surface of the subterranean caverns. "The walls of the cave look like… glass."

Shiv could stay and close the door—maybe wait out this unexpected Armageddon. Hadn't she prayed to God the previous afternoon on the prison transport bus on her way across the Mojave? She never had faith in divine intervention, but she did believe any place was better than prison, even running off and making a new life in the desert. And wasn't she suddenly stricken with a full bladder? If she could've gotten the drop on Officer Hayes, she'd have broken his neck and run for the hills.

She would already be dead.

Instead, she faces uncertainty in an underground trap.

"What's the plan, Samson?" Shiv asks. "If we get back to the surface, what next? The bunker was supposed to be salvation."

Shiv isn't going to explore the strange glass tunnels if it only means delaying eventual ingestion anyway. She has to know there's a plan to escape—a chance to live.

"Plan B. I've got a map of the trails leading out the eastern part of the desert," Samson says, squinting against the light Bulldog shines on his hoary face, patting his interior chest pocket. "There are old routes from the Gold Rush still winding through the sands. The paths follow ancient riverbeds between the foothills and wide swaths of soft sands."

"You've seen these trails?" Shiv doesn't trust this nut. He believed the government was out to get them—it turns out it's just giant fucking monsters.

Samson nods. "That was always the second part of the plan. Wait out the initial incursion. Whatever it was. Nuclear war. Government takeover. Alien invasion. Then follow the map out. Escape the desert and find a suitable place to regroup."

"You had plans for an alien invasion?" Bulldog quips.

"Seems awfully proactive right about now, doesn't it?" Samson says.

"I was going to say 'paranoid.'"

"A giant eyeball swallowed us up and spat us out."

"I thought it was a giant eyeball from the future," Bulldog drawls. "Now it's a giant eyeball from outer space?"

"We don't know for sure it's from the future. That's one theory," Samson dismisses. "It might be alien. Maybe a demon from hell. It may have come from a Petrie dish in China. Perhaps there is a rift in time after all, and it *did* come from the future. All I know for sure is that it wants to eat us."

"Maybe we should sit it out. Plan A might still work," Shiv says. "There are still plenty of supplies in the bunker. And it withstood the first attack."

"We can't stay here," Samson says. "The creature tore the bunker free from the ventilation system. Three people sucking up air in there would suffocate after a day."

"We leave the door cracked unless the eyeball comes back."

"And if it comes back? What if it returns and waits us out?" Samson challenges. "Then we're trapped inside. Counting the minutes until we run out of oxygen."

"You guys go on," Shiv suggests. "Three people for one day equals one person for three days. Maybe it'll be over in three days."

"You can get out now, or you can stay and live in your fairy tale, Pollyanna," Samson says.

Shiv is damn sure no one has ever accused her of being an optimist.

"C'mon. Let's get outta here, Shiv," Bulldog prods. "Wouldn't you prefer to have a chance to fight for your life rather than die trapped in a fucking tin can?"

"Aw, hell," Shiv finally says, stepping out of the bunker behind Bulldog and Samson. "I've fought my way outta darker holes."

Samson re-enters the bunker and rummages through the storage cabinets. He re-emerges with extra flashlights and tools—a shovel for Bulldog and a pry bar for Shiv. The end is a wedge rather than a sharp point, but Shiv can work with that. Samson carries an electric lantern in one hand and a pistol holstered at his hip. What they need are more of those grenades…

Of course, an explosion would bury them alive.

Better than being *eaten* alive.

"It's like the tunnels made by ants or left behind by worms," Samson marvels, as if fascination could dispel some of the horrors of their circumstances. He starts walking, and the women follow him. The beams of their flashlights mirror off the smooth surface. Blurry reflections move like ghosts along the circular tunnel extending away from the buried bunker. "The sand is fused into a glass shell. Heat? A chemical reaction?"

"Don't start falling in love with the monster, Sam," Shiv warns. The cavern makes her think of catacombs where some cultures used to bury their dead. "It wants to make you into a steaming pile of eye shit."

"It's pure awe," Samson says. "And utter terror."

"That's the same damn thing as love," Shiv mutters.

They follow the tunnels. The world muffles all noise—even the labored breathing of the three humans sounds like cotton is quieting their exhales. Shiv listens intently for the sound of movement. She prepares for any sign of a massive eye burrowing through the sands. Only silence pervades their pathway. For the moment, these three aren't the target of the evil eyeball that had attempted to swallow the bunker. Shiv refuses to imagine what might be distracting it.

If the eye is eating a handful of Garcias or a cop in a buggy or the oddball youths, then that's better than Shiv having to deal with a staring contest with the ocular abomination. She'd been hella ruthless in lockup—she could make newbie convicts shit their shorts by merely giving them a look. Now, Shiv is the one worried about being on the wrong end of some deathly stare-down.

"I didn't think I was ever getting out. I thought I'd live out the rest of my days locked up. Someone else making my choices. My whole life at the whim of someone else," Shiv says as she walks beside Bulldog. She doesn't know why she needs to talk. Maybe the silence is worse than any confession. "Then I was set free. I could go anywhere. Nothing for miles in every direction. No metal bars east, west, anywhere. But now I only wish I was locked up. I don't want to make these damned decisions. Maybe freedom isn't the answer. Being free is only an illusion."

"I don't think the people locked in cages are any safer than we are," Bulldog says.

"Maybe the responsibility of a chance is worse than no chance at all," Shiv says.

Bulldog shines her flashlight on Shiv's handcuffs. "No one chooses to be in chains."

Shiv doesn't have an answer for that.

The world starts to shake. Cracks run up and down the glassy surfaces of the tunnels. Sand sprinkles down from the ceiling like they're standing under a colander sifting granules upon their heads. Samson falls to his knees. Bulldog lands on her ass. Shiv presses her cuffed hands against the surface of one wall to keep steady. The glass beneath her palms cracks and cuts. She flinches back. Shiv bleeds from a dozen little slices as she stumbles around.

She refuses to fall.

Shiv doesn't go down.

She is going to confront the fucking future face-to-face.

Maybe there's an eye coming to eat her. She'll stick a crowbar in it before its first chomp. She's ready to put up a fight.

Then, the tunnels collapse before Shiv can even scream.

7.0 Richter
[Carl]

Carl holds on tightly as Officer Hayes climbs the buggy up the side of the largest hill in the vicinity. The vehicle must take an indirect zig-zag route up the steep, sandy slope of the butte. This back-and-forth path allows them to ascend incrementally and avoid flipping onto their back like an overambitious turtle. Rolling down the incline to the expanse of sand at the base of the hill could be their death. Better slow and steady than too aggressive.

Carl thinks about Mary. Mary had been ardently resistant to innovation. "If it ain't broke, leave it alone," she'd say. New TV? "This one works fine." New radio? "We can make our own music." The latest and greatest SUV? "I'm driving my car until the engine falls out."

One Christmas, Carl bought her an electric can opener. She didn't like it. "My manual one works fine."

"It can save you time," Carl cajoled.

"I've got time enough," Mary said. "What's a few seconds here and there?"

What Carl wouldn't give for a few seconds here and there. It turns out she hadn't had much time left. The woman who had ignored innovation and embraced the more straightforward ways needed all the inventive ways to make life easier at the end. Machines to help her breathe, measure her heartbeat, check her oxygen levels, and monitor her every remaining moment. There hadn't been enough goddamn remaining moments.

What would Mary have thought of this shit? Time-traveling gophers as big as fucking Boeings. Monsters from tomorrow—could that be right? What else might it be? There weren't spaceships hovering in the sky. Perhaps these monsters came from below? Are they ancient subterranean creatures that resurfaced to reclaim Earth? But if there are Kong-sized Yetis in Montana and a marine monster the size of an island off the coast of Florida and mountains eating European cities, they sure as hell hadn't been hiding in the wilds of Canada.

Where else—*when* else but from the future?

Mary wouldn't have taken it well. She disliked the machines blipping and beeping around her as the end drew near. "People shouldn't be poked and prodded as such," she had complained to Carl one afternoon in hospice.

"These machines are keeping you alive," Carl had said.

"What happened to dying a dignified death?"

She couldn't stay with him for as long as he'd wanted her to. At that time, it had already become not a matter of "if" but "when." She could determine somewhat the time left on her clock. She could choose to keep the machines pumping her lungs and heart or go out when it was time for those organs to give out. Mary couldn't abide Carl sitting in a hospital room for weeks, waiting for her body to follow after her mind had gone. She hadn't wanted him to sit bedside as she began to decay slowly. All she had left was the past—the future had wanted nothing to do with Mary Kennedy.

"Get me out of here," she'd told him one early afternoon in April.

Carl took her home. They sat on their front porch watching the birds twitter and the squirrels chase each other up and down their street. Neighbors came by and waved as the day grew long and the sunshine waned. She smiled as the people passed in a steady stream, ostensibly out for a stroll but actually around to say their goodbyes. Carl counted every single one of their neighbors walking by that day. Mary enjoyed a pretty sunset, the deep oranges and reds reflecting augustly upon the previous day rather than offering bright hope for the next one.

She died sometime after dark.

Carl never went back to the house after that night. Not once.

Because the home wasn't his home anymore.

Now, this whole world feels as though it isn't *his* world anymore. Officer Hayes fights gravity, the big wheels of the buggy grabbing the loose soil up the side and slowly climbing the slope. Landry sits behind Carl, hanging on for dear life to Carl's headrest. Carl releases his memories of his dead beloved and focuses on the task at hand. Two girls might be at the top of the hill, scared and needing help.

Officer Hayes starts to lose control of the buggy as they reach the apex of the high hill. Carl might have to offer to take over—he may not have driven a car in twenty years, but whatever Hayes is trying isn't working. But then the vehicle crests the butte and plops down at the summit. Pi and Rosario are waiting, sitting atop the bluff.

Landry stands up in the back. "Need a ride?"

Carl offers the girls a hand. Rosario is taller and gangly, the teen girl folding herself into the buggy. She collapses like a tripod in the backseat next to Landry. If she wonders about her father and brother, she doesn't ask. Rosario tucks her face into her knees and shuts down.

Pi is more clumsy, short, and uncoordinated, eventually climbing over the side and landing in Carl's lap. The buggy is overfull.

"Did you see what happened to Samson and the others?" Officer Hayes asks.

"We got to the bunker, and the footprints just ended," Pi says. "Gone. Like some fancy magic shit in the middle of the Mojave."

"You ever see the bunker before?" Carl asks Landry and Hayes, the two other locals.

Landry says no, but Hayes pauses.

"Once, a while back. We got a call from the A.T.F.[5] about somebody flagged for excessive munitions. It was Samson Dunphey, of

---

[5] A.T.F., Bureau of Alcohol, Tobacco, Firearms and Explosives

course. I had to drive out here and make a visit. I'd taken a land cruiser, so I'd been able to pull up right to Samson's front door. I asked him some questions, and he was an open book. Completely cooperative. He fessed up about how many guns he had and what kind of ammunition he could bring to bear. He even gave me a tour of the compound and let me peek at the bunker. It looked like a Hilton hotel room and a Sherman tank had a baby. The door featured one of those spinning locks you see on a submarine. It seemed like he'd survive with the cockroaches after a third World War."

"Now it's gone," Pi says. "The thing *ate* it."

"The thing probably swallowed it, but I don't think the eye in the sinkhole is strong enough to crack the bunker," Hayes opines. "I bet that shelter could withstand a nuclear blast."

"It took quite some effort to eat the thin metal shell of Samson's trailer," Landry points out.

"The p.s.i. required for breaking open a steel bunker would be a hundred times that," Pi estimates.

Another quake shakes the ground, making the buggy bounce. Carl watches the ripple of the landscape from high on the hill—he can *see* the world quiver. Like goosebumps across tanned flesh, bubbles of displaced sand fester along the landscape. The sand makes a blur of the grainy plains, the granules dancing as far as his eye could see.

"Where was the bunker?" Carl asks Hayes.

"There," the cop points, a spot with nothing but a flat expanse.

Carl stares at the place where the shelter disappeared. If it was as solid and steel as Brock said, Carl agreed that the monster probably couldn't have cracked the container if it tried. But a sinkhole had swallowed up the bunker. Samson, the trucker, and the convict might be buried alive.

"Let's get back to the R.V.," Pi suggests. "If it's still there."

Officer Hayes nods. "That's a good plan. We can regroup there and maybe figure a way out of here."

The stone butte is high enough that they might not get eaten if they stay. Without food or water, they will die soon enough. But dehydration might be better than mastication. Carl sweeps his eyes across the crowd—Hayes, Landry, Pi, and Rosario. No one disagrees. The only guarantee of the future if they stay here is a less painful and more typical death. But they all want a chance to survive.

"We need diesel. There's not enough fuel in the R.V. to get us very far," Landry says. "There's a reserve tank in Skidoo. We can refill up there."

Carl holds up a hand. "There's one other thing. Before we leave, let's check the spot where the bunker disappeared. Just in case anyone survived."

7.1 Richter

[The Garcia]

Rosario is the last living Garcia.

Carl and Landry didn't tell her what happened to her dad and brother, but they're gone. Rosario doesn't know what happened to California, but she knows her *abuela* and all her other cousins and kin are gone. She can *feel* it. Her Aunt Tonya attends the *Universidad Autónoma Metropolitana*, and Rosario believes she's also dead. Mexico City hasn't been the subject of the rumors floating around today, but Rosario feels singular loneliness in her soul. She is the *last* Garcia. The only one left. Her soul contains the legacy of all her ancestors.

Fifteen, and the weight of the whole world rests on her shoulders.

Officer Hayes parks the buggy at the edge of a barren stretch that had recently contained the bunker where they were supposed to be able to wait out this invasion. Conquerors from tomorrow? Or outer space? Both? Aliens from the future? Instead of sanctuary, the monster had gobbled up the bunker in one big gulp. Carl thinks the creature couldn't chew it up, but Rosario believes being swallowed whole inside the belly of a beast might be a worse fate.

Rosario considers Jonah and the whale. Samson isn't Jonah. She remembers Monstro ingesting Pinocchio. Shiv isn't Pinocchio. She once saw a video online of a python swallowing a gator whole, and the snake splits open from its meal while the gator walks away. Bulldog isn't an alligator.

Rosario considers her mother's destiny and how the sand had sucked her down. Buried alive or swallowed whole? The same with her dad and brother. What fate had they suffered? Which was worse? What is Rosario's future?

Rosario has never been like her friends. The other girls back home have always been eager to grow up, act like adults, gain freedom, and experience things beyond their years. They'd always run pell-mell toward tomorrow without appreciating today—boys and parties and smoking and jobs and tattoos and drugs and cars. Rosario never wanted to grow up too fast—she still likes the books the tweens read, playing action figures with Chuy, or watching a Disney Princess cartoon. She hadn't been eager to start working, driving, or worrying about dating.

She had always been comforted by the past. Lately, however, the past had fully ejected her into today, and tomorrow is creeping below her feet, ready to swallow her up like the rest of her family. Rosario can't think about Mom and Dad and her brother without tears overtaking her. She wants to curl up in a ball and close her eyes against the world.

But the thing underground isn't closing its eye. The monster lurks below. And it's still hungry.

Rosario can't end up like the rest of the Garcias. Sharp and focused, she sweeps the ground for the slightest disturbance. Her feet are ready to spring in another direction at the first sign of a sinkhole. She was always the fastest Garcia—faster than Chuy. He always got his feet tangled up and tripped out of the gates. Chuy…

"Oh, God," she whispers, holding her face in her hands so it doesn't break apart.

Landry puts an arm over her shoulders. "Push it back. Save it for later. When we can grieve."

Landry suggests there's little hope for any of their families. If the rest survive long enough to escape the Mojave, they can pick up the pieces afterward. Rosario couldn't think of the past without falling apart, but the future also makes her feel helpless.

Rosario needs to focus on the here and now.

She can't save those they've lost, but she can help rescue Samson. And Bulldog and Shiv. If the bunker was pulled underground but left intact, they could perhaps dig out the entrance and set them free. Or mark the spot for rescue in case they find help later.

Rosario stops short. A few feet in front of her, the sand starts shifting. She's too close to turn and run. Maybe if she stays still, the thing might not sense her. Like a T-Rex, perhaps it only registers motion? Or is she scared stiff, unable to move a muscle even if she wants to?

Landry is still beside her, and neither of them moves. They both stare at the place in the sand where the granules shift and sink. Rosario fears the same fate as her family. She has maybe only outlived them by mere hours. The last living Garcia will simply be the last one to die.

Instead of the sinkhole opening like it had, a fist punches up from underground. The hand opens and flails around, just a limb from the elbow up, waving at the aboveground survivors. Rosario gawks with her mouth agape, blinking dumbly, unable to move. She's watched enough stupid zombie movies with Chuy to imagine an undead Samson or Bulldog rising from the grave.

Officer Hayes races forward and grabs the arm, pulling upward. Landry and Rosario snap out of their state of shock and join the cop left and right, all of them pulling upward like the arm is a boot stuck in the mud. A head and shoulders soon join the arm, then a second arm, and an entire torso. It's Bulldog. They pull her up and out of the ground.

"What the hell?" Carl yelps.

Another arm rises out of the hole in the ground Bulldog had left behind. Officer Hayes, Rosario, and Landry stand at the edge of the sandy orifice that had expelled Bulldog. Rosario notes the sharp shards of glass around the hole Bulldog had come up through. She suffered several minor cuts and scratches coming out of the ground. Like being birthed back into the surface world. Delivered by some monstrous mother.

Rosario shivers.

The aboveground survivors help Samson and then Shiv up through the hole. The three who escaped the underground are covered in dust and look like mummies resurrected after thousands of years instead of being buried only a few minutes. They are a kind of zombie—the three of them ought to be dead.

"The bunker worked," Carl observes.

"The bastard couldn't eat us," Samson confirmed, "but the thing pulled us entirely underground. Buried us."

"It makes tunnels underground," Bulldog says. "Fuses the sand into glass."

"With heat?" Carl stares at the hole with trepidation. None of them want *fire-breathing*, carnivorous, underground eyeballs.

Samson shakes his head. "I don't think so. Maybe chemically?"

"Why?" Landry asks.

"It doesn't matter," Pi dismisses. "We need to get away from here."

"We have a plan," Officer Hayes says. "We retrieve the R.V. Refuel in Skidoo. Escape east through the backroads."

Samson nods. He pats a zip-up pocket on his chest. "I have a map of the old trails. Hardpan riverbeds left behind long ago. Made the map myself. Good, solid ground through the fields of sand. We can follow the route out. If we can avoid the eye."

"There's more than one," Rosario says with a haunted voice. She recalls sitting up high on the butte, watching the numerous sinkholes across the expanse of desert.

"Then let's move our asses," Carl barks.

The eight refugees retreat to the buggy. All eight will not fit in the vehicle, especially with the huge Samson in their group. Bulldog drives, Carl as copilot, Pi and Rosario in the back. Landry, Samson, Shiv, and Officer Hayes walk. The hike back to the RV will take half an hour. Rosario stares at the road before them. A half hour. She's lived several hours longer than any other Garcia, but she must make it through the next half an hour if she hopes to keep their family name alive.

The idea of getting back in the RV hurts her heart. But the idea of being buried with the last remaining memories of Mom and Dad and Chuy aches even more. To keep the past alive, the last Garcia must survive into the future.

7.2 Richter

[Samson]

"Spread out," Samson commands as they start the trek to the RV. It's the best plan to live through this alien incursion, but they must be smart about it. Let's face it, the average IQ of these assholes is in the single digits. The trucker looks like she'd get confused if Samson asked her to add two and two. The convict is mean and cornered, dangerous as a rabid animal. Carl might've been competent when he was younger, but his screws went loose and fell out long ago. The kid named Landry doesn't seem to know whether to sit or stand to pee, let alone find a way out of the desert. Samson isn't sure how a damn one of them made it this far.

The subterranean eyeballs have better senses than the foolish bastards on two legs wandering around the desert like goddamn sheep. Samson notes how ironic it is that these morons who'd been blind to the truth of the world for all these years are now prey to giant, hungry monsters. He's been trying to tell everyone about the world's secrets for as long as he can remember. They only laughed at him. Called him a fool. Now they're all being turned into eyeball shit.

Maybe they're from the future. A lot of the other truthers online certainly seem to think so. Perhaps they're from outer space. Areafifty4ever, who hosts one of Samson's favorite podcasts, swore the invaders were set loose from the secret base out at Roswell, alien captives that had finally broken free. He was dumping his files into Samson's inbox when Areafifty4ever disappeared online. Kicked off or erased? Was Areafifty4ever eliminated or eaten?

The deep state would do everything in its power to keep its secrets. If this were a leak from the government, they would destroy the evidence posthaste. Feed it to a fucking eyeball. Bury it under the ground. Maybe a military lab made these monsters and loosed them upon the world. They'd done it before. Covid. Killer bees. Chemtrails. The 5G network.

Motherfuckers.

Samson is maybe the last line of defense in California against the horrors unleashed by the entrenched autocratic bastards who want to tear down the world. The woke lost their war against the strong, and now they attack like a cornered honey badger. Some accounts pin the blame on climate alarmists who created these buggers in a lab to combat global warming—an accidental effect of trying to save the planet. *Bullshit*, Samson thinks. They want to destroy. Eliminate. Well, Samson isn't going to run scared. He's standing his ground and fighting to survive. He'll outlive this effort just as he had every other ploy. Monsters… Bring it on.

He is armed to the elbows and ready to stand up to the biggest sons of bitches they can throw at him. This is the moment he's been planning for his whole life. He thought maybe Big Pharma would make a play for his mind by disbursing chemicals in the air. Had Pharma gone nuclear, or had they already succeeded, and this was a freaky fucking hallucination? Samson also predicted Big Brother would someday come for his guns. His last stand would've made the O.K. Corral look like a skirmish with peashooters. He prepared for Big Tech using the cellular networks to take over the airwaves and all electronics, enslaving the population by controlling information. He'd had his shortwave radio network set up for the very occasion. The old ways had become essential in communicating the real threat—Big-ass Monsters.

Landry walks in front of Samson about ten yards ahead, and the convict behind Samson an equal distance, the chain on her cuffs jangling quietly. Samson stares at the attire of the person in front of him. Landry wears the same clothes Samson sees desert rats wearing around the Mojave—leather boots handy in case a rattler decides to taste some toes, a weathered cowboy hat with a wide enough brim to keep off the sun. The belt buckle is the size of a slice of bread. That was all well and good for any honky-tonk from Amarillo to East County. But then it went off the rails with a purple handkerchief around the neck, Wranglers two sizes too tight, and a vest covered in sterling gemstones. Jesus H. Christ.

Landry turns and asks, "You sure we're far enough apart?"

Samson shrugs. "No way to be certain since I've never seen this shit before. I know that if a sinkhole opens under your feet, I'm far enough away to run the other way."

Landry glowers at him. Samson isn't here to make friends and hold hands.

"What about the buggy?" Landry says. "Think we're okay by walking at a slower pace? Is the vehicle quiet enough to escape notice?"

"Don't know. That's why I told them we'd go first. Something gets them, then at least we're out front of the sinkhole and not behind it."

"They're bait?" Landry asks, slowing down.

"Keep movin'! You ain't going back to warn 'em," Samson barks. "You keep up the pace in front of me cuz I'll slit your throat and leave you with the cacti if you try to double back past me."

"You're cold, dude."

"Ice cold." Samson doesn't know whether the other person is a cowboy or a cowgirl. The amorphousness bothers him—gender-fluid claptrap. John Wayne never declared his preferred pronouns. The world had made more sense back then. Black and white. Right and wrong. The truth versus liberal hypocrisy. Now everything is blended—families, races, politics, virtue. When Samson was young, they called the muck when everything was mixed up "mud." Nothing special about mud.

It's all been going downhill for decades. Men are all pussies now. The food killed testosterone levels and emasculated virility. Women have the balls now. They run the world. Until they need a man to fix their problems. Until the car won't start or the toilet backs up, or the heavy sofa needs moving. Or they need to live long enough to get out of the desert. Then even a badass like the cuffed convict or the pugnacious trucker deferred to the mountain of man and hair named Samson.

Samson isn't sure which of the various theories he buys. Areafifty-4ever believes it's aliens. Some of his other contacts over the airwaves from the north contend Bigfoot was simply a lot bigger than anyone expected. A flat-earther from Flagler Beach thinks Atlantis released the sea creature threatening the Florida coast. The latest from Germany purports the monster in Hamburg had escaped from a secret NATO genetics laboratory.

Samson only knows his unique talents will keep him alive. The lame liberals have attempted to debunk his theories over the last few decades, but Samson persisted. He refused to be caught unawares by a clandestine Illuminati bent on subjugating the American population. *Hell, no,* Samson thinks. He prepared for aliens, witches, mad scientists, and genetic mutants. He was even ready to survive a zombie apocalypse if the undead came 'round hungry for brains.

Because he has guns.

Samson had fully stocked his stores for an "any of the above" situation.

Then a cold thought strikes him. He prepared for *almost* everything. Future creatures—*check*. Goliath fossils from the past resurrected to wreak havoc—*check*. Mutant animals made in a Silicon Valley think tank—*check*. Alien invaders intent on global domination—*check*. All of those things attacking at once?

No.

He prepared for any of the above, but Samson isn't ready for *all* of the above.

7.3 Richter
[Brock]

Brock Hayes is on foot and thinks about the creature underneath the ground with every step. He sweeps his eyes across the land with each footfall, following the training he'd learned at the police academy, alert for the slightest hint of danger. The instructional exercises would feature a reenactment of an apartment building where there'd been reports of violence, a school scenario with an active shooter, or a crowded arena with a bomb threat. Brock examines his route for the first sign of a sinkhole.

Brock suffers a flutter in his stomach every time he takes a stride. His midsection is aching as they cross the distance back to the RV. He blames damn Pascal Reyes. Brock was only eight when Pascal snuck his parents' DVD of *Jaws* into his bedroom at a sleepover. After that, the image of a predator swimming below him popped into Brock's mind every time he swam in a pool or lake. Even as an adult, the idea of the shark coming to attack from below flickers briefly in any water more than waist-deep.

Now, Brock has the exact image repeat. A predator rises from below on a perpendicular intersection from the horizontal plane. Only it isn't a great white coming for him. It's a great big eye with a hungry aperture—a mouth that can swallow someone whole. Did it have teeth within the darkness? Had it chomped the transport bus and the patrol car with Deputy Donnie Davis? Did it chew up the rest of the Garcias?

Brock doesn't want to get chewed.

Smith walks ten yards in front of him. Her hands remain cuffed, the keys swallowed into the desert along with Deputy Davis. The chain jangles like bells between her wrists. If he could, he would've set her free. Whatever she did before they met, it doesn't matter anymore. None of it matters. All that counts now is what's ahead.

Brock doesn't look back. He can hear the soft murmur of the buggy's engine keeping pace. Landry leads, keeping the pace slow enough for everyone to keep up. Bulldog drives the vehicle at the same speed as the pedestrians. They all leave ten yards between each other so as to not alert the underground monster. How well did that work before?

Brock has no doubt Bulldog would tromp the buggy's gas pedal at the first sign of monsters. Speed like hell to the RV. She would choose saving four asses instead of all eight ending up dead. Brocks believes she would leave those on foot to die.

Samson might survive. He probably has a couple more grenades on him. He isn't sharing.

The ground could open beneath Brock at any given moment. The difference between life and death could be his next step. Or the next. Or the next. Mrs. Garcia didn't know her end was coming. Deputy Donnie Davis never knew when he'd taken his last breath. Hector and Chuy sure didn't think they'd never see Rosario again when she walked off toward the bunker. Every step. Every moment.

"I'd set you free if I could," Brock says to the woman walking ten yards ahead.

"These chains don't determine whether or not I'm free," Smith answers.

"Still, if I could…"

"You don't even know what I done."

"Does it matter anymore?" Brock asks.

"It matters."

"Not to anyone here," Brock says. He looks across the desert to the horizon. "And there might not be anyone else."

"I ain't ready to die yet."

"Neither am I," Brock says as they keep walking.

The rock formations along the route are beautiful reds and oranges and tans. The sand features mica flecks that twinkle in the sunlight. The world is so beautiful. Brock can't imagine it all comes down to monsters hunting humankind in the end. Does the future feature creatures destroying every corner of creation? Storms in the north and east, across the seas, and here, earthquakes make the ground split and swallow.

How can they fight against such overwhelming odds?

Brock can only think of one answer.

He might not be ready to die but sees no other tomorrow waiting for him.

"Fuck," Bulldog hollers behind him. The riders are ten yards behind Brock when the buggy swerves severely to the left. The vehicle doesn't move fast enough, and suddenly the headlights point at a precarious angle. A sinkhole has opened, sucking on the back end. Brock barely sees Bulldog and Carl peeking over the plunging dashboard.

Bulldog tromps the gas, the front wheels spinning and kicking up sand. The tires whine as they try to get a grip. The smell of rubber on sand and dusty air makes Brock choke. Still, he runs toward the buggy instead of away. Smith approaches as well, moving nearer more slowly. Cautiously. Landry sprints toward the vehicle. Only Samson hangs back.

The riders haven't fallen into the sinkhole yet despite the mighty efforts of gravity. The buggy tries to keep up as the sinkhole grows larger. Rosario and Pi jump out and scramble up the side of the sinkhole, clawing at the churning ground. Brock and Landry grab them and pull them out.

Bulldog and Carl are still in the front seats. The buggy will fall into the hole if Bulldog lets up on the gas. They all know what's at the bottom. Carl is too old to clamber up the side of the sinkhole. Brock and Landry each grab a headlamp and try to pull, but the sand and grit choke them out, and they stumble away. Bulldog still has the throttle open, friction and torque against the forces of gravity.

Then the hood tilts back even more, the buggy at more than a forty-five-degree slant. Brock moves along the edge of the growing sinkhole, dancing away as the edge grows larger and larger. He glimpses inside the pit, and sure as hell, the large eye gazes back from the bottom. Like the Earth itself is staring him down. It wants to eat the buggy and anyone inside. Brock tears his eyes away from the ocular abyss and meets Bulldog's gaze. Bulldog has the intense expression of someone with a dangerous plan.

Brock watches as Bulldog yanks the wheel hard to the left. The buggy turns sharply, the passenger right wheel popping out of the hole, and the vehicle swings counterclockwise. Suddenly, Brock faces Carl as the buggy skirts the upper lip of the bowl shape, like a race car going around a steeply inclined track. Carl extends his arm, and Brock grabs it as they pass. He clasps the old man's elbow as Carl holds Brock's biceps. Brock pitches forward, saved from being eye-food only by Landry grabbing the back of his belt. Inmate Smith and Rosario both lend a hand. They all throw themselves backward like a fisherman reeling in a massive marlin. Brock goes over rearward, pulling Carl out. But Carl was the minnow and Bulldog the big fish. The trucker is wrapped tightly around Carl's waist, legs hanging over the lip of the pit.

The empty buggy, without anyone to hold the steering wheel, instantly spins out and slides down the incline. The eye at the bottom swallows it, the sound of mangling mechanics issuing from the massive dark pupil. All metal, no meat.

"Move, move, move," Brock hollers, pulling Carl back along the sand, his hand under one of the old man's armpits while Smith has the other. Landry gets Bulldog to her feet, and they all stumble away from the sinkhole's edge. The ground stops sliding out from underneath them as they retreat far enough away from the depression. Finally, they pause to let Carl get his feet under him.

"Saved our asses," Bulldog says.

"Think I pulled half the muscles in my arm, but worth every goddamn ache," Carl adds. "Thanks."

"No time to pat each other on the back," Pi snaps from the sidelines. She was no help at all after she escaped the buggy. "It's eating up accessories. The truck. The trailer. The bunker. The gas station. We might be a nice snack, but it really wants the raw materials."

"For what?" Landry asks.

"It's building something," Samson says ominously.

"What would a *monster* be building?" Carl barks, irritated.

"Nothing good," Brock answers.

He stares at the spot where the ground swallowed up the buggy. Samson is right. It's taking things like vehicles and buildings. But Brock doesn't think it's digesting the parts. The creature breaks the pieces apart—so it can put them back together? But into what? Why?

During December, the desert isn't as hot as in the summer, but the ambient temperature is still warm enough. Yet Brock shivers. He's cold.

7.4 Richter
[Pi]

Pi doesn't like the situation. She's watched a hundred disaster movies, and there's always some muscular oaf around to save the day. Samson is as big as a goddamn Sasquatch, but he's not saving anything but his own ass. The cop looks a little like a young Jaden Smith, but he's as clueless as a detective in a comedy movie. This situation isn't some progressive tale where Pi saves the day—she hasn't ever been able to rescue anyone from anything. Just ask Josh Henry.

The threat is unquantifiable. Not a natural disaster like a tsunami to survive or a cosmic crash of some asteroid, supervillains, serial killers, or nightmare clowns. People want a specific enemy with ulterior motives so they can root for the hero. There isn't a hero out here at the edge of nothingness, and the villain is a mindless beast from the future—no tales of a brave knight to pass the time.

They enter the final leg of their hike to the RV. Pi waits with every footstep for the world to turn unsteady and a sinkhole to try and swallow her. They came to Samson for shelter, and the haven turned out less safe than moving on. Now they depend on Samson to get them out of here—Pi feels like a freakin' Jew following a random idiot out of Egypt while Moses went the other way. But the RV is still there, and no additional sinkholes appear.

"Everyone, get in," Brock tells them, opening the back door to the RV. "Let's haul ass into Skidoo. We refuel and then head east."

Bulldog climbs behind the wheel of the RV. She's best apt to handle the big vehicle if there needs to be quick maneuvering. She managed to get the four passengers out of the buggy alive—with a valuable assist from Brock, Landry, and Shiv. Landry points toward Skidoo, and Bulldog drives at the fastest possible speed where they can brake if a sudden sinkhole appears in their path. Creeping along slowly in stealth mode didn't help—the buggy still got swallowed.

"Your plan sucks ass," Carl grumbles from his spot at the table right off the kitchenette.

"It's the only way out," Pi says. She takes the measure of the group of refugees. She's the smartest one. Samson maybe had a strategy to stand his ground and fight, but the crazy hermit believed hiding and waiting out Armageddon would work. That had almost gotten them all killed. Samson had prepared for insurrection or Commie infiltration or zombie hordes, not a giant damn monster burrowing beneath the desert. None of his right-wing conspiracy theories had involved fucking kaiju. There wasn't any fighting against these things. The ants didn't take up arms against the humans. They could only run.

"There's a whole town in Skidoo," Brock says. "We can maybe make a stand there."

"We can't stay in the desert," Pi says. "We need to escape."

"There are a lot of miles of Mojave to the east," Landry warns. "The monsters will try to swallow us before we get out of the sand."

"We can make it easy by staying in one place, or we can keep moving the target," Pi says. "We're going to be hunted either way. But it's easier to shoot a fawn if it's standing there like a goddamn deer in the headlights."

No one disagrees. No one has a better plan. The refugees ride in silence. Another quake causes Bulldog to brake, the shaking making the survivors inside the RV hold on to something to keep from toppling to the floor. The RV dances like it's bouncing over speed bumps. Then the tremors subside, and they keep on toward Skidoo. They would re-fuel and make a frantic exodus out of the desert.

Pi calculates their odds. The creatures below the sand have been primarily targeting materials. They gobbled buildings and vehicles, every bit of manufactured property they came across—a semi-truck, the gas station, Samson's trailer and the outbuildings, the bunker, the buggy. The RV was surely a delectable morsel. They only swallowed up Mrs. Garcia alone. Maybe she was a snack they slurped like a little kid finding a raisin stuck on their sleeve. But for the moment, the creatures seem focused elsewhere.

Then Pi sees where else…

Skidoo contained about twenty buildings when she visited yesterday. Pi didn't leave the vehicle, but she observed from the passenger seat. Now, about a fourth of the structures are gone. The latest is being sucked under the sand as they cross the ridge overlooking the ghost town. The replica post office disappears beneath the sands as they approach Skidoo. The monsters are busy with their main course.

That's why they've made it this far with minimal obstacles.

What do they want with the buildings and vehicles?

Pi notes the large water tower in the town center, the tallest structure in the desert. The monsters haven't gotten thirsty yet. Pi wonders what she could see from up there. She doesn't like heights. She can't get up that high. But she needs *someone* to go up there and be her eyes. Pi wants to know what these things are doing…

"I need someone to climb the water tower," Pi announces as the RV reaches the edge of town.

"Climb it yourself, kid," Samson grunts.

"I'm acrophobic," Pi says.

"Well, I have a phobia about getting eaten by big-ass worms, but I don't have a goddamn choice but to walk around on the ground," Samson barks. "Get over it."

"You don't get over it. It's an irrational fear, not a logical one. I can override my rational aversion to being swallowed by a sinkhole. I can't do anything about my fear of heights."

"You have an idea?" Rosario asks. She ought to be a puddle of tears right now. Somehow, she manages to keep her eyes dry.

"I want to understand," Pi says.

"Understand the monsters? They're crazed creatures out to eat everything. Probably made in a lab in China, like everything else. We kill 'em, that's it," Samson argues. "We fight, or we die."

"They're not crazed, though. There's a method to their movements and actions. These creatures are probably more predictable than humans. I want to find the pattern. Maybe we can develop a code so we may predict…"

"They're predators, and we're in their environment," Samson argues. "Can you outsmart the shark in the sea? Can you outthink a lion on the savannah?"

"This is *our* world, not theirs."

"A lot of my sources were sure these things came from the future," Samson says. "If they're right, that means these things are *inevitable*."

"I'm not going to fight them. I want to avoid them. I need more data," Pi grumbles. "What did you see underground?" Pi sweeps her eyes over Bulldog, Samson, and Shiv.

"Tunnels," Bulldog said simply. "Fused into glass."

"Like ants?"

"I don't know. Do I look like I had an ant farm?" Bulldog growled. "These things are bigger than ants."

"Larger tunnels are more susceptible to forces of gravity and physics. Perhaps they need raw materials to reinforce the tunnels? Maybe they're recycling everything they take from us. The gas station, the vehicles, the trailer house, with a boulder here and a Joshua tree there."

"What do you think they're building?" Brock asks.

Pi stares at him. She can think of a dozen horrible answers. She says nothing instead.

"I'll do it," Rosario states, breaking the silence. "I'll climb up."

The RV parks in front of the water tower, and the refugees exit the vehicle. Pi about runs right into the back of Brock Hayes. The cop has stopped dead. Pi worries about a sinkhole as she tracks the object of the cop's gaze. It isn't a sinkhole. It's a person—standing in the middle of the street of the abandoned ghost town.

Pastor Montgomery made it to Skidoo.

7.5 Richter

[Pastor Montgomery]

Monty stares at the group that arrives in Skidoo. When he'd set out on his own from Carl's gas station, he wasn't sure he'd ever see anyone again.

Monty had faith God would protect him from being eaten if monsters were hunting beneath the barren sands between here and there. Like Jesus walking on water, he didn't fear becoming submerged in a sinkhole and disappearing beneath the surface. Monty took direction by divine instinct, trusting God to lead him on a righteous path.

While wandering the desert, Monty felt a strange sense of disembodiment—like his spirit had left him. The sand and the landscape disoriented him, and he felt separated from all earthly things. Monty became a wayward soul alone in reality, rising above the terrestrial crust until he was floating in orbit, observing the whole world being ripped asunder by leviathans from unknown places.

He became terrified for his family. He felt fear, the likes of which he'd never known. His heart shattered at the thought of his daughter. Was Ashley facing the terrifying scourge from Hell off the eastern coast? He couldn't handle the worry for his loved ones. The thought of losing any, or all? He wouldn't survive even as long as Carl had after his wife died. Monty would give up instantly. He wasn't strong enough to endure without them.

"Please, God, give me a sign," Monty pleaded in the desert, dropping to his knees as dawn neared. The sky above was still dark, the scatter of stars like a twinkling peek into heaven itself. What beauty. What perfection. The stars are the map of the past, all fixed into points and laid into a perfect pattern. The lights from those points had started toward Earth a million years ago. A billion. Everlasting light breathed out into the cosmos. Beauty unending. Timeless.

The past isn't something that ought to hold him back. His wife is a strong, independent woman who can care for herself. She would tend to their flock, consoling their congregation in his absence. His daughters are grown women. Cheri would be helping the scared and hurt in Chicago. Ashley would find a way to soothe any creature, heathen, hellacious, or heavenly. His beloved family walks with the Lord, and the Lord *will* protect them.

Amen.

Then a feeling of peace came over Monty. Maybe his place in this story isn't saving his family. Jesus had already saved them, and thus, they could take care of themselves. Monty's purpose is something else. Maybe he is destined to tend to another flock—one more wayward than the competent Childes family. He closed his eyes out there in the wilderness and prayed for direction. Hours ago, before dawn, he started walking confidently on a specific path through the unvarying desert.

He received divine inspiration.

Monty arrived in Skidoo in time for the RV to roll up Main Street.

"You're not dead, *mùshī*," Pi says as she exits the RV. "Congratulations."

"You didn't have faith I'd survive, Miss Lee?"

"You said you were going off to save your family, and yet you ended up in the same place we did," Pi points out. "So much for faith."

Monty smiles and nods. He takes stock of the survivors. The massive man with a hoary beard must be Samson. The rightwing conspiracist. He gives Monty a nod of solidarity. The kooks are usually all about

God and country. Some are racist, too, but Samson seems more likely to be prejudiced against liberals than other ethnicities.

One added, but two gone. Monty notes the missing members. Hector and Chuy Garcia aren't among those who exit the RV, and there are no signs of anyone left inside. One look into Rosario Garcia's eyes tells the terrible tale. She is the sole surviving member of her family.

Pi takes Rosario away before the two missing members of the group weigh too heavily on her. Monty limps over to where Brock and Landry survey Main Street. Still barefoot with only cloth wrapped carefully around his abused feet, he sits on a boulder at the base of the fake water tower. After many hours alone, he feels reunited with a group of long-lost friends. Their time together was brief, yet Monty feels a kinship with these people. As if they are knights on a holy crusade against an evil enemy.

"You see any of those creatures out there, Pastor?" Landry asks.

Monty shakes his head. His night and this day thus far have passed without incident. An occasional tremor but no sinkholes. The worst of his adventure has been the deterioration of his feet. He can barely walk anymore.

Carl had returned to the RV and gone inside. Now, he reappears, walking toward Monty, Brock, and Landry. He carries a pair of fresh dishtowels he procured from inside the Garcias' cupboards. Carl holds the towels out to Monty.

"Here, you need to change those," Carl says. He nods back the way Monty came out of the desert. A trail of bloody footprints leads to the place where Monty had sat on the boulder. Monty didn't even realize how much he was bleeding. The rags around his feet are red.

"Thanks," Monty says. Then he adds with a snarky grin, "What do I owe you?"

Carl charged Monty for the snacks he had procured at the gas station. The food and water provided him sustenance to survive through the night.

"On the house, Father," Carl says, giving Monty a wry wink.

"I told you I'm not Catholic," Monty replies with a smile.

"And I told you, neither am I," Carl answers. The old man nods toward one leg of the fake water tower. Weathered and worn rawhide ropes wind around a post and lend authenticity to the replica. "Landry, go ahead and fetch a length of that rope."

Landry detangles a bit of the rope and brings it over. "Sit tight," Landry says.

Brock and Landry carefully unwrap Monty's ruined feet. Monty hisses as they peel away the sopping rags, and the desert air hits the weeping wounds. Carl retrieves a first aid kit and squeezes some antibiotic ointment over each foot. It takes everything for Monty not to curse. He grabs Carl by the shoulder, and the old man remains steady under Monty's pained grip.

Then Landry and Brock tenderly rewrap his feet in fresh linens, using the rawhide rope to secure the towels. Better than barefoot on his ravaged soles. He feels like Jesus having his feet washed by sinners. But these others aren't any more sinful than Monty, his congregants, or anyone else on this planet. They are all in this together—to survive. To overcome the evil plaguing Earth.

"What do you think, Father?" Carl asks as Landry and Brock finish him up. "You still think God's gonna save our asses from these demons?"

"Of course," Monty answers without a doubt. He is surer than ever. His original intention when he went off alone through the desert was to save his family. But they don't need him. The Lord will watch over them. These refugees are the ones who need his watchful eye. These guys need his prayers. He's right where he needs to be.

"We're going to make it out of the desert," Monty says. "I have faith."

7.6 Richter
[The Garcia]

Rosario Garcia is at the top of the world. A memory tries to barge in as her vision sweeps the landscape. The memory contains some triggers—belted into a seat, screaming people on either side, the slow climb of the train up a steep slope, the anticipation of speed and turns, Chuy right beside her as the cars reach the apex. Almost now. It will careen into the forefront of her thoughts at any moment.

Not yet. Rosario can't think about her brother or her family. Not now.

She's high on the water tower. The view is breathtaking. She can see for miles. Desert stretches in every direction as far as she can see. They are very far from any haven. The landscape looks the same all around her. *Almost* the same. Rosario spies *something* in the distance.

She uses the binoculars Samson had given to her before she climbed up the ladder affixed to the water tower. It isn't an operational structure or even an authentic decommissioned tower, but rather a replica like everything else in this town. Landry's father had built this facade in honor of the past. Nothing here is any older than Rosario's *abuelo*. Still, it provides a fifty-foot perch in the sky where Rosario could see miles across the desert.

Rosario watches the RV move to the fuel tanks behind the mercantile, where the sign on the window advertises souvenirs. Bulldog parks the large vehicle near the pumps. Samson exits the back door and starts to fill the tank.

Between Rosario and the edges of what she could see, she could count multiple pockets of sand moving in at least a dozen sinkholes. Something different occurs in the distance. The high sun glints off something metal, but the reflection shimmers. It changes by the second, like someone is twisting a prism in the daylight.

The reflective surface is shifting, moving, changing.

The monsters are making something.

"What do you see?"

Pi's voice comes up through the still day, floating to Rosario on high. She sees the whole world from up here, and it looks barren. Lonely. Broken. Dying. Things changed so much in the last day. She feels like she woke up and realized the rest of her life was but a dream. She'd been sleeping all along. The dream is past. Gone. The future is a nightmare.

"Something's happening at the edge of what I can see," Rosario says. "Activity. Something sparkling in the daylight."

"To the east?" Pi shouts back.

Rosario follows the line of the horizon from left to right. She sees things glittering here and there, like diamonds scattered in a jagged line, catching sunlight before being absorbed. The marks of activity where things are moving at the edge of her vision suggest intent. None of the construction is close enough so Rosario can see what they are building. The bustling work is closer to the farthest edge of her ability to see.

"It's all over the place," Rosario shouts back.

She takes pictures with her phone. Cell service remains nonexistent, but she can shoot photos and take them down to show Pi. Maybe Pi can discern what's happening better than Rosario. The only thing she ever knew about creepy crawly creatures was what Chuy told her.

Chuy…

Grief catches her by surprise, and Rosario grows dizzy and weak. She wobbles, grabbing hold of a handle before she pitches over the wooden rail around the planks making up the walkway around the fake water tower. She places a palm against the surface of the empty water tank painted with the words, "Welcome to Skidoo." Her brown skin against the white paint. If she pitches over the side and breaks her neck by falling off a fake water tower in a ghost town tourist attraction, she would still have the fourth strangest death of the Garcia family on this trip.

She can't die. She's the last Garcia. She's the one to keep their memory alive.

Rosario descends the ladder and stops before she places her foot on the ground. The monsters are under there. She's lost her whole family to the beasts. Maybe it has a taste for Garcias? She plops her soles to the ground—what does she have to be afraid of? The unknown beneath her feet isn't any worse than the unknown of what happens tomorrow.

She's faced death—she's died three times this trip already. Her heart is buried thrice under the devilish sands.

She hands Pi the phone. "I took as many pictures as I could."

Pi sweeps a finger across the images, pinching and peering closely. Rosario doesn't know what picture she's searching for or what she thinks she'll find, but the teenager does understand what Pi's looking for… Hope. Pi needs to find a way out of this situation. They all do. There's no staying put—it's onward or nowhere.

"What do you see?" Rosario asks.

Pi squints at the screen. Swipes left. Enhances the image. Swipes right. Bites her lip. Exhales loudly. Swipes again. Then she flips her dark eyes up and matches Rosario's stare. They pause like that for a long while.

"They're building something."

Rosario equated these beasts to lions or sharks, but maybe they are more intelligent. Like some predatory alien with extraterrestrial intelligence. Could they be outthinking the humans? Perhaps they aren't only big, fierce, and stealthy—they are also cunning. What if the monsters are *hunting* Rosario and the others?

She doesn't want to know. Instead, she'll let it be. Walk away. Ignorance is bliss. But she can't leave it alone…

"What?" Rosario finally asks. "What are they building?"

"My first thought was that it's a trap, but we're already trapped. The creatures could swallow us up from underneath at any moment."

Rosario glares at Pi. She isn't helping Rosario avoid mindless panic.

"Then I wondered if they were building a base. Maybe somewhere to shelter against the enemy. But who's put up a fight so far, am I right?"

"Right," Rosario agrees. She scans the skies—no fighter jets. No missiles flying. No sign of resistance at all.

"Then it occurred to me. I've studied the past my whole life because I believe that yesterday can give us clues about today. What happened before can explain what's happening now. The progression of evolution is linear. The line from then to now is a straight one. So, the line leading to tomorrow will connect to what we know today. To what we learned from yesterday."

"You think you can get the answers from the dinosaurs?"

"I think I can guess what these things are doing out there based on how biological entities have always acted before," Pi says. Rosario stares at her, desperate for an answer. This situation is beyond comprehension. She needs some steady grip to keep from floating away on nonsense. But the answers might be more terrifying than the unknown. Rosario's *abuela* always said, "Ignorance is bliss," as she tuned out the news or ignored the local gossip. Maybe the old woman was right. Sometimes knowing is worse than wondering.

"Well?" Rosario prods. "What's your theory?"

"I think they're building a nest," Pi says.

7.7 Richter
[Landry]

Landry Honanie surveys Skidoo and takes inventory of the structures remaining. Besides the schoolhouse that had disappeared before Landry had left and the post office, which had been sinking as they approached, the buildings featuring the dentist's office, the blacksmith shop, and the livery stables were gone. One-fourth of the town is missing. The ghost town had become even ghostier.

Landry considers Dad's safety. He'd taken a business trip to Vegas to secure a loan to keep Skidoo from going bankrupt. If only Dad knew the whole town was going under whether he got the cash or not. Maybe the insurance covers abominations or Armageddon or alien attacks.

Landry pulls out the cell phone that hasn't worked since this whole thing started. Still no signal. No one was getting any cell reception. Only short-wave communication had brought news of what was happening outside the Mojave. Nothing about Vegas. Landry didn't know if Dad was safe or scared or if he was trying to get back to Skidoo to rescue his only child.

But Landry isn't a kid anymore. There comes a time in anyone's life when their parents can't save their kids from everything. Landry has relied on Dad for a job, security, and general existence for far too long. Tomorrow had seemed an amorphous entity without definition or urgency for as long as Landry can remember. Now, the future is slapping Landry around like the winds accosting a tumbleweed.

Bulldog finishes refueling the RV. Samson stands guard like the three-headed beast at the entrance to Hades. He trusts no one to take the RV without him, fearing they would leave him behind. Brock and Carl wander around the vehicle performing the last inspection. Shiv stews at the edge of the group as her eyes repeatedly dart toward the edges of Skidoo.

"What do you think?" Landry asks Pi as she returns with Rosario from their reconnaissance mission from the top of the water tower.

"I think they're building a nest," Pi tells the group. "There's activity a few miles away to the east. I think the beasts are constructing some underground hive, like ants."

Landry nods. The theory makes sense. The monsters are dismantling the town. As they approached Skidoo, the post office sank faster than an elephant in quicksand. The creatures had taken Carl's gas station, Samson's trailer, multiple vehicles, and dismantled buildings here in Skidoo. There must be a purpose to it. Pi's theory makes as much sense as anything Landry could guess.

"That's the direction we need to take," Samson says, pointing east, the same direction Pi was talking about. "If we turn around and head west, we backtrack through the same goddamn section of the desert we crossed already. We were waiting to get swallowed by a sinkhole the whole time. What are the chances of getting lucky a second time?"

"We ain't going back. California isn't an option," Shiv says. "There's more desert to the west than to the east. We need to get off the sand."

Pi turns white. Rosario's mouth, already sad, turns grim. *California isn't an option.* Shiv is stabbing holes in the prospects of the two hoping to get home.

"We can't go back," Pi agrees. Logic trumps hope. "The only reason we got this far is because the creatures are distracted by building instead of focused on eating."

"What did you see out there?" Samson demands.

"Think of a bird getting ready to lay her eggs," Pi says. "The buildings, vehicles, and even the trees are the sticks and straws that make up the structure. And we're the motherfucking worms."

"They won't let us go," Rosario adds in a hollow voice.

"Maybe not." Pi gazes eastward toward where she believes the monsters are working on a nest. "We can't go around. The sinkholes will swallow us up. Same if we try to go west. But if they're reinforcing underground, it might make for a stable passageway. I think if we want to escape, the only way we can survive is to go through."

"Driving *over* the monsters' underground nest?" Samson challenges. "Like trying to cross a field filled with landmines?"

"More like swimming across a strait filled with hungry sharks."

Landry stares at Pi. She suggests they run pell-mell into the mouth of the mayhem. She believes their only way out is forward. Landry considers the other vehicles and the other buildings and the disappearing structures around Skidoo. If the monsters want to eat them, there isn't anything going to stop the hungry bastards.

"We're left with just hoping things turn out okay?" Carl asks. "Roll the dice? Pray to whatever God we believe in?"

"God will provide, Carl," Monty says. "He kept me safe in the desert."

"Tell that to Rosario's family," Carl grumbles. "I don't want to forfeit our fates to chance or divine providence. I think we have a little more choice in how today turns out."

"Think whatever you like, sir," Pi retorts. "I don't think we're going to convince the monsters with pleas of mercy."

Landry ponders. Pi is a fatalist. Does she believe whether they live or die is out of their hands? Landry can't subscribe to such a theory where none of them affect what tomorrow might bring. Their choices today must be able to turn the course of tomorrow. Landry's attention focuses on one building after another down Main Street Skidoo.

"Maybe we don't avoid these things or even face them head-on," Landry suggests. "Can we distract them?"

"If your outfit hasn't already done the trick, then I don't know what will," Pi says. "Or do you have a buttload of fireworks in your pocket?"

There's nothing in Landry's pocket but a worthless cell phone and a tube of lip balm.

"What does the bird do if the squirrels start to take away the sticks?" Landry asks.

"Attack the squirrels," Pi answers. "Protect the sticks."

"Because no sticks, no nest."

Pi nods. Carl understands and agrees. Samson grunts an approval.

"How?" Carl asks.

"We use fuel from the tanks. Someone stays behind," Landry suggests. "A volunteer burns down Skidoo one building at a time. While the monsters are distracted, protecting the most plentiful resource for whatever they're building, the rest of us run for it. Will they protect the remnants of Skidoo and let some small worms escape? Or will they come for us and sacrifice the town?"

"These creatures are efficient and calculating," Pi assesses. "I think they'll try to save Skidoo. Nest first, food later. I think we'd stand a chance."

"A chance is all we can hope for," Officer Hayes says.

The refugees gaze around, each looking at the other. Slowly, every one of them starts to nod. They are all in agreement.

The only question is, who will stay behind to torch Skidoo?

7.8 Richter
[Carl]

Carl helps as much as anyone. He might be seventy, but he won't let a tiny sprite of a girl like Pi or a skinny person like Landry contribute more to the effort than he does. They work diligently to fill any portable containers they can find to draw fuel from the large tank out back of the mercantile and distribute it to the remaining buildings around Skidoo.

Carl pours the last batch over his assigned structure. He found an old five-gallon bucket with a rusted lid, filled it with diesel, and carried it to the church. He's already spread one batch across the wooden planked floor, and now he distributes a second. The fuel covers the whole surface evenly. He leaves the bucket by the entrance. No one's ever going to need it again.

Carl surveys the room. Wooden pews line the small interior, ten in all. Nice craftsmanship. Landry said Mr. Honanie recycled many of the props in this place from other ghost towns around Southern California. The pews appear authentic. Fine oak. A shame to burn. But the past is done, anyway. No one is going to visit Skidoo ever again.

The crucifix over the altar catches Carl's eye. He hasn't been in a church in twenty years. The last time was for a funeral—Mary's funeral.

His wife had been a devout Christian up to the moment of her death. She'd prayed to Jesus every day as she succumbed to cancer. Carl had listened one night outside her door as she whispered fervently. It hadn't been a plea for a miracle or a bargain for some miraculous cure. She'd asked Jesus to help Carl through the rest of his life so he wouldn't be alone.

But Carl hasn't lived at all since she died. He hunkered down in that gas station and avoided interaction with anyone. Carl stayed stuck in the past. Now, it's twenty years later, and he has nothing to show for it. Jesus didn't help him with anything. What was that poem Mary had held so fondly? The footprints in the sand where Jesus carried a weary soul during those times they thought they were walking alone. Carl turns back and looks at the impressions coming to and from the fake Skidoo church. All kinds of prints. Ain't none are Jesus's.

Right?

Father Montgomery carries a bucket across the dirt road, limping in pain on ruined feet yet doing his part like anyone else. Despite her devastating loss, Rosario manages to lug two jugs filled with fuel toward one of the buildings. Bulldog and Brock are each heading back to the mercantile empty-handed. They've finished their missions.

Carl falls in step and rejoins the group. He's part of this band of survivors. The first bit of society he's been part of in a long time. A congregation of sorts. Maybe it took twenty years, but Carl isn't alone anymore. Mary's prayer had come true after all.

He counts the different marks of many different shoes. Footprints in the sand. What was the other thing Mary had been so fond of saying? The Lord works in mysterious ways.

"The kindling is ready," Samson announces in his gravelly, deep voice as the refugees finish their errands and congregate around the RV. "Diesel doesn't burn like gas. You can't just flick a match. It'll take sustained heat to ignite the fuel."

"Sounds like you're not volunteering," Carl mumbles.

"I'm a survivor, not a martyr, old man," Samson says. "I'll contribute some munitions. There's a handful of grenades that'll light up a building or two to get the attention of these sons of bitches."

"Insulting sons and their mothers all at once," Landry says with an eye roll. "Class act, sir."

"Can't spell class without 'ass,' kid. I didn't spend my life preparing for the end of times to lay down and die for a bunch of strangers," Samson snaps. "If you don't appreciate that I came prepared, I can manage the rest of the way alone."

"You're not taking the R.V.," Landry says. "You can march off on foot if you don't want to be a part of the team."

"This isn't a team where everyone pitches in. This is a military operation where you follow my orders, and maybe you make it through the battlefield," Samson argues. "Someone's got to lead. I don't see anyone else stepping up."

"So, we're supposed to let you pick who stays behind?" Landry challenges. "You choose who dies?"

"I don't see anyone offering on their own," Samson says.

Samson's right. Carl examines the group, and there isn't one of them who seems eager to die for everyone else. In the movies, a noble character volunteers to give up their future so others may survive. Landry, Pi, and Brock are all so young. The Garcia girl is barely more than a baby. Samson is a survivalist. The preacher isn't going to undertake a suicide mission. Bulldog is too mean to give up without some bite. Shiv is a fierce survivor, not a sacrificial lamb.

"I'll do it," Officer Hayes offers. "Protect and serve."

"Protect and suicide is more like it," Bulldog grumbles.

The preacher shuffles from one rag-wrapped foot to the other. He doesn't volunteer. Carl wonders if it is because suicide is a cardinal sin or because he can't bear the thought of dying before he sees his family again. Either way, the decision is selfish, and Carl doesn't hold the choice against the man. Self-sacrifice is a tough choice.

Officer Hayes sweeps his eyes over the young people. Brock isn't much older than they are, but he has a badge. Rosario, Pi, Landry. Does Brock's gaze change as he settles his eyes on Landry? Amid all this chaos and violence, is there a spark of something hopeful? Carl remembers when he had first seen Mary. She was a nurse, and he'd been bringing in an injured coworker to the ER. During an extreme emergency, something had kindled between Carl and Mary—a love that lasted twenty-five years. Their love was born from tragedy. Hope in a hopeless situation.

"No," Carl decides.

He is old and near his end, even if he has been able to live out his days pumping gas, but he is content with his memories. He'd lived the last twenty years with Mary on his mind, as if he'd kept her alive all this extra time through constant remembrance. But he recalls her prayer. For him not to be alone. Now, he's a part of something.

"Carl…" Brock begins to argue.

"I'll do it," Carl interrupts.

Sometimes prayers don't work out.

"He's as old as dirt anyway." Samson isn't all that much younger than Carl. "Makes sense."

"We measure a man by his longevity?" Landry challenges. "Maybe we should pick by who has an empty moral tank, asshole."

Carl puts his hand on Landry's shoulder. He hadn't paid either Officer Hayes or Landry much attention all this time, but apparently, the spunky Landry had been paying heed to Carl. Landry defends Carl fiercely against the shallow, self-centered Samson. The sentiment touches Carl deeply.

"I've borrowed enough time, kid," Carl says. "I've got bills, and they've come due. Time to pay."

"Time to pay," Shiv says. She steps forward. "I've got more to atone for than all you put together. This is my part to play in this."

Carl looks into her eyes. He sees the truth more profound than any certainty he's felt over his fate. Carl feels selfish and shallow as he feels himself nodding, giving the responsibility to someone else. Carl has maybe ten good years left—if the monsters don't eat the world long before then—but Shiv could have another fifty.

But Carl doesn't argue. He steps aside.

"It's settled then," Pi announces.

Samson may have declared himself the commander, but the troops aren't falling in line. Maybe when the fighting starts, they'll follow. But now, Samson's declaration as an essential soldier only indicates his arrogance. Samson thinks he's the center of the universe. But Samson is no better than Carl—and a lot less dignified than a convict with sin weighing on her soul.

"I'll cause a distraction while the rest of you get the hell out of the desert," Shiv says.

"I'll distribute the grenades, and then we'll haul ass for solid land," Samson declares.

Carl heads toward the RV with Bulldog on his left and Pi on his right. Samson sorts through his munitions. Officer Hayes and Landry wait back with Shiv.

Rosario approaches Carl and grabs his hand. "That was very brave to volunteer to stay behind."

"Brave?" Carl questions. He thinks of staying behind, alone, solitary. He'd been doing that for far too long. For Shiv, her sacrifice is her atonement. It would have been more of the same for Carl—embracing the past instead of facing today. "You think staying behind to die is brave? For some, maybe. For me, that would be the easy way out. You can't lose anyone when you're all by yourself. *This* is hard. Surrounded by others who you've come to care for when you know you can lose them at any time."

Rosario holds his gaze as they approach the RV. She still grasps his hand. The girl is more than fifty years his junior, yet she knows as much as he about the subject. At least as much. She nods and squeezes his hand.

Sometimes, it's harder to survive than to stay behind.

7.9 Richter
[Shiv]

The cop and his skinny local companion stay back to keep Shiv company. Shiv doesn't need a pep talk in advance of her impending doom. She's survived her whole life depending on herself and defending herself, always ruthless and unrepentant. Her actions had consequences that gotta come due at some point. She always thought that meant getting stabbed in the back in the shower or poisoned in the prison cafeteria. She never worried too much about an unexpected death because her fate would never be sunshine, daffodils, and unicorns.

Maybe unicorns. Those were horses with a shaft sticking right out of their forehead. Badass.

"What's your real name?" Landry asks.

"Shiv's as good as any name."

"That isn't what your mamma named you," Hayes says.

"It's Tasha," she answers.

"You don't have to sacrifice yourself because of some noble idea of penance, Tasha," the cop says. "We could do this fairly. Draw straws or something."

"We all have things we need to answer for," Landry adds. "You aren't any more guilty than any of us."

"You ever killed anyone?" Shiv asks Landry.

"Samson probably has," Landry suggests. "Maybe Carl. He probably served in a war or something. The others? Who ever knows the secret life of strangers?"

"'Probably.' 'Maybe.' How about *definitely*? Want me to share the details of some of the ones I killed with these two hands?" She offers forth her handcuffed wrists, palms up, jangling.

"We're neither your judge nor your jury, Tasha," Landry says. They're both using her name instead of what everyone's called her for years. It reminds her that she's more than a weapon. There's more to Shiv's story than the sharpest point of her tale.

"I'm not going to vote for your execution."

"This ain't a goddamn democracy," Shiv says. "You don't get a vote."

"This isn't a good answer."

"Sometimes there are only bad choices."

The head shakes side to side on the willowy stalk of the neck that connects Landry's skull and torso. Shiv had seen shits in the community commode in prison that weighed more than the person standing before her.

"I've done some nasty things in my life," Shiv admits. "A noble death is more'n I maybe deserve."

"It isn't up to us what you do or don't deserve, Tasha," the cop says. "We should decide who stays behind more fairly."

"None of this is fair. The system isn't fair." The cop nods like he thinks Shiv is talking about the penal system, but she isn't. Maybe he takes it as a racial thing, but it's a *life* thing. "The story never ends like it's supposed to unless it's only a chapter in some asshole's book of fiction. I don't want to be some fucking martyr or a redeemed hero. I only wanna be free. I don't care if I'm written off as a hero or villain, so long as the story ends."

The cop steps forward. "I found these in the shed by the fuel tanks when I was looking for gas cans." He has a tool in his hand that he was carrying in his utility belt like some blue-suited Batman. "Tasha, I can take care of the chains."

"These chains aren't what makes me free or not," Shiv replies.

The cop meets her eyes. He nods. He puts the bolt cutter back in his utility belt. Most cops she ever met would make a cheesy speech about how nice it was to get to know a convict or how the two of them aren't so different after all, or how he wishes they could've gotten to know each other under different circumstances, or some such bullshit, but Brock Hayes merely turns and walks away without another word.

Landry stays behind another minute. Landry's dark hair is messy and sticking out in erratic angles. The shirt and vest are formless, and Landry's hips are as straight and square as Shiv's sister, Agnes. Or her brother, Ramesh. Shiv decides it doesn't matter whether Landry is a young man or a young woman. They're all just people at the edge of their end. This is the edge of Shiv's end. The pointy tip of her demise. She always knew she'd die at the mercy of a spike. And life is as sharp as any shiv.

Life'll getcha dead.

Samson approaches, and Landry extends a hand. Shiv shakes it. Not worthy of a hug. The moment isn't emotional or some final good-bye. Shiv's grandma had hugged her close before they took her away after the judge sentenced her to prison. Her sister shed tears—even Agnes didn't want to lose her sister. Ramesh had cried, too. But no one in Shiv's life had shown her respect without fear. Until now. Landry turns and heads to the RV.

Samson hands her a rucksack with a half dozen grenades. "This is what I can spare."

"That'll work, I suppose."

"It'd better," Samson says as he turns and walks to the RV.

What an asshole.

But Samson has left her with more munitions than she had guessed he'd be willing to give her. Samson is all about saving his own ass. Shiv can sympathize with that. And Shiv's success will contribute to Samson's survival. He's calculating how much firepower is necessary to sustain a proper distraction while he makes a mad dash for freedom.

Freedom isn't about getting out of this desert and away from the eye. It isn't the thing Samson's chasing. It isn't about sprinting toward tomorrow with her back to yesterday but taking a minute to pause and reflect. To embrace responsibility. The past has always been a ball and chain on her every choice—even this one. But for too long she's held on so tightly to the past and made every wrong decision because of it. Like she was following some fucked-up script. She told Landry and the cop she wanted the story to end. She isn't going to rewrite her whole life's biography with a few nice words in the final chapter. All the terrible things leading up to today have foreshadowed this conclusion. She is right where she was always ever going to be—killed.

The rest board the RV, and the vehicle starts to leave town. It pauses once, brake lights winking as it points east. She can see Brock in the side window, his black hands pressed against the glass and his white eyes wide with worry. Landry stands beside him, a look of admiration making Shiv sure she made the right decision. Rosario watches out the back window. Maybe the young girl could survive for at least a little longer.

The RV gets going. Shiv turns. The chains on her wrists rattle together as she tosses the rucksack's straps over one shoulder. She starts her task. The nearest structure is the old-time printing shop. The smell of diesel is strong as she stands in the doorway and uses the acetylene torch in her hand to ignite the fuel. Diesel is tough to start but burns hotter than gasoline. These old wood structures would go up in flames quickly.

Shiv starts the little colonial homestead in one corner of Skidoo on fire, as well as the drug store. Then the fireworks must begin. She needs to get the attention of these motherfuckers before the RV gets close enough to be ensnared in their trap or swallowed to add to the nest or whatever the hell's happening out there in the sand. Shiv crosses Main Street and stands in the open doorway of the jailhouse. She pulls a pin and tosses a grenade between the bars of one of the cells. The effort feels cathartic. The building explodes behind her as she strolls down Main. That ought to get their attention.

A sinkhole appears in the middle of Main. Shiv isn't ready for one to appear so fast. An eye had to have been waiting under the sand. *Aw, hell.* She dances around the edge to avoid getting swallowed, jumping onto the wooden front walkway in front of the tax office. She rolls another grenade through the door and runs toward the next structure as the building behind her blows up.

She checks over her shoulder as she stands inside the saloon. The sand swallows up the remains of the tax office. The jailhouse is already gone. A sinkhole sucks up the telegraph office and the colonial homestead. Shiv is causing too much havoc for the monster beneath Skidoo. It needed reinforcements if these bastards hoped to save their precious building materials.

The plan is working. Shiv causes more destruction than the underground kaiju can afford to sacrifice. Protecting natural resources must undoubtedly be more pressing than a small band of morsels racing across the desert.

"Come and get it, fuckers."

Shiv starts the saloon on fire. She watched the flames spread across the whole place. This is the largest structure. Pi and Bulldog rigged the site with a rope saturated in kerosene so the fire would trail from here to the other buildings. Like firecrackers with their fuses wrapped together. The mercantile, the veterinary clinic, and the water tower. Shiv wants to ensure these beasts don't know which way to turn.

The burning floor suddenly opens right in the middle of the saloon. A monster created a sinkhole directly below the structure. Shiv turns toward the exit, but the surface already tilts precipitously. She grabs for the threshold, and her stubby fingernails rip away as she holds a slivery slat board. The fire nips at her toes as she dangles on the sinking floor. The eye is in the middle, swallowing the saloon from the center. The pupil opens wide, eating up boards and props and broken bits of building, even the parts on fire. The image of the flames shines in the ominous white of the beast's eye, and Shiv sees her reflection on the reflective surface.

She doesn't want to be eaten by that thing.

But the fire doesn't quite reach her feet. She can't fall farther without sliding down into the beast's maw. She loses her grip, and terror takes over. She's going to get chewed up and made into monster shit. Hell, she wouldn't have volunteered if this was supposed to be her fucking fate.

Then the chain linking her handcuffs catches on a broken bit of board sticking up from the slatted floor. The fire wicks off the end of the board she's caught on, like she's dangling from a birthday candle. The floor beneath and around her is raging flame. Hotter than hell itself. It catches on her cuffs, and enough fuel has spilled on herself that her whole body catches flame instantly. Then she's burning. Melting. Hot to the core. The pain is incomprehensible, but she'd burn any day if it meant that the monster gets to taste only the ash and char left behind.

Shiv dies, and her smile turns molten and runs down her skull.

8.0 Richter
[Bulldog]

The next earthquake would be strong enough to raze a city if it had occurred in Vegas or Phoenix instead of a remote part of the Mojave.

Suraya struggles to keep from losing control of the RV and tipping the goddamn thing before they even take the chance Shiv gave them by sacrificing herself. The tires dance on the shaking ground, the big box on wheels tottering left and right with the rhythm of the rolling earth. Like driving a big rig in a windstorm, Suraya corrects her steering to counteract the quake. She's one mistake away from the whole RV ending up on its side.

The shaking subsides again, and Suraya hopes they're out of the desert before the next tremor. She doesn't think they'd survive another rumble. The quakes have evolved into the kind of events she's only seen in movies.

Suraya checks the side-view mirrors. The town of Skidoo is nearly gone. Shiv had succeeded in lighting up the ghost town, flames dancing like logs burning in a fireplace. When Suraya glanced a moment ago, a half dozen buildings were aflame. Now, only two structures remain—the water tower burning like a massive torch and the church engulfed with the spire acting as a flickering wick. The last quake caused one section of the church's walls to fall outward, and the tower collapses as Suraya stares into the mirror. Then the church starts being swallowed as the other buildings had been, the fire rolling up in great molten balls until only smoke marks where the church had been. A gray cloud acting as a grave marker slowly dissipates into the desert air.

The only evidence a town—phony or historical—ever existed is the fiery remains of the fake water tower. The plan has worked so far. Shiv had provided enough distraction to allow them to get across the open field where Rosario spied the edge of unusual activity. Where Pi deduced a nest exists. They travel along the only hardpan alternate route out of Skidoo besides the highway. They need to get past the nesting area. Are the creatures going to defend it, or are they adequately distracted? The RV is nearly at the point of escape.

Suraya sees the edges of the area Pi designated as an escape route. The landscape is as barren as the rest of this desert country, but like a game of "what doesn't belong," she picks out oddities that one wouldn't expect in a remote section of the Mojave. It looks like quicksand swallowed a town, or these are the remnants of an old, excavated settlement. A yellow road sign shows a corner above the sandy surface, and a scattered smattering of asphalt chunks make a dotted line. Suraya recognizes one of the pumps from Carl's gas station, half-buried in a dune. A weathered portion of wood siding like a gravestone protruding from the sand features flaking paint that reads "cksmith." Were these pieces ferried through underground tunnels to the edge of the monster's territory? Like a bird making a nest—only this bird is from Hell and buried its nest under the desert.

They approach the edge of the sandy territory. Maybe escape *is* possible.

"We're going to make it," Landry says from the passenger seat.

They follow a faint trail Samson has marked on a hand-drawn map. These were old routes the gold prospectors had used when they came west and constructed the original towns in the Mojave. Over ancient riverbeds or a hardpan where the sand never recollected, the paths are still passable, even on four wheels. Barely. Suraya drives carefully to keep the tires from being bogged down in drifts of sand, stuck as surely as if in a snowbank. There had been a real Skidoo back when someone last traveled these trails, something more authentic than the one swallowed behind them. Wagons, horses, and men traveling back and forth over decades had packed down these routes. Now, the RV handled the solid foundation of the path admirably. So long as Suraya stays on the trail.

Samson looms between the front seats with a massive hand on each headrest. "There's a fork ahead. Stay left."

They've nearly arrived at the line Rosario indicated from her observation atop the water tower, and Samson subsequently marked on the map.

"Hang on," Suraya shouts.

Suraya slams on the brakes and comes to a complete stop. On their left is a bowl in the sand ten feet deep, where a monster abandoned a sinkhole and left a small empty crater. On the right, an uneven incline makes climbing a steep hill impossible. Soft sands prevent any possibility of circumnavigation.

Suraya points out the wide windshield. "That's the only route on your map?"

"The hole wasn't there when I surveyed this spot before," Samson defends.

The route between the slope and the divot is a narrow pass, barely wide enough to accommodate the RV. The quakes had shaken loose debris that rolled down the incline and peppered the trail with obstacles. Some stones are too big for the motorhome to roll over. No way to avoid them. Suraya puts the RV into Park and turns off the motor. She gets up and gathers the survivors at the back door.

"We need to clear the road," Suraya says. "Move it quick. Shiv bought us a tight window to get outta here."

"The rest of you move the rocks," Samson orders. "I'll stay with the R.V."

"You get your ass out there with the rest of us so we can clear a path and keep moving," Suraya demands, getting up in the bigger man's bearded face.

"I got the maps. I got the guns. I got the skills," Samson says. "The captain stays with the ship."

"You're not the goddamn captain," Suraya snaps. She gives the keys to Rosario and opens the door for the girl to exit. "And I don't trust you with the ship. This is her R.V. The keys stay with the girl. You can sit on your ass in the driver's seat, but you ain't goin' nowhere."

Samson crosses his burly arms and glares as the rest of the crew hastily exits and starts moving the stones. Dozens of objects big enough to majorly mess with the RV clutter the route. The largest rocks are rolled out of the way and shoved down into the dormant divot by Officer Hayes and Suraya working together. The others clear the smaller rocks as quickly as they can. They all cast suspicious glances into the sandy depression next to the route, waiting for an eye to appear.

Suraya watches the RV in case Samson tries something funny. Can the asshole hot-wire an RV? Is there a spare key behind the sun visor? If he manages to start the RV and begins to escape, she's close enough to get to the back door before he can accelerate away. Where would he go, anyway? Backtracking is sure death, so he must wait for them to move the rocks if he wants to go forward. Samson might have weapons, but Suraya could hold her own. Shiv had passed her a knife before she volunteered to stay behind.

"Where did you get that?" Suraya asked the prisoner.

"It's my lucky shiv," she said. "Now it's yours. Watch out for that big mothafucka."

Shiv was right. Samson *is* a fucker.

One big stone left. Bigger than Suraya and the cop could get by themselves.

"Get back in," she says to Rosario and Carl.

Suraya grabs Carl and pulls him close as he passes, slipping Shiv's sharpened makeshift knife into his hand, "Keep an eye on Samson for a minute."

As the oldest and youngest rejoin the laziest, Suraya, Officer Hayes, Pi, Pastor Montgomery, and Landry shove and roll the largest stone until it reaches the edge of the pockmark in the desert. They push it over the edge, and it rolls down the slope. As the five turn to make their way back to the RV, the ground shakes, and the sand beneath their feet disappears. They all slide down the slope after the rolling boulder toward the center of the sinkhole, like Batman in an hourglass trap. They claw at the amorphous surface as the granules sift down and down and down. There is no averting inertia. The desert wants them.

Suraya reaches the bottom, and then she's swallowed by the sand.

8.1 Richter
[The Garcia]

They disappeared—five of the eight remaining survivors gone in one big gulp.

Rosario stands outside the open back door of the RV, near enough to the edge of the sloped sinkhole to see down. She glances back at her remaining companions to check if she isn't hallucinating. Carl is already inside the vehicle but stands near a side window with an unobstructed view into the pit. Samson presses his hairy face against the glass, staring into the hole. They all saw the same thing.

Gone.

Rosario turns back toward the sinkhole. Pi. Landry. Officer Hayes. Pastor Montgomery. Bulldog. They all slipped down the slope and into the pit. The RV had been two dozen feet away from the lip of the sinkhole, but the depression widened so that the edge of the hole is now only about six feet away from the rear wheel. If Bulldog hadn't dismissed Rosario and Carl when she had, they would have disappeared into the sand with the others.

With Mom and Dad.

With Chuy.

She closes her eyes tightly before the tears erupt. Not now. She can't deal with it at the moment.

"Get in here," Samson roars from within. "We gotta get away from that sinkhole."

Samson appears half out of his mind. She wonders why he hadn't started the engine already and left her behind while she was standing in paralytic shock. Then she remembers—she has the key.

Rosario runs to the door and up the metal step, boosting herself into the RV. She'd complained about leaving home and spending the holidays in this tin can only a few days ago. Now, it feels like home— her only home. This would always be where she experienced her last memories with Chuy and her parents. Maybe she ought to be pissed that the RV expedition led to this end, but she cherishes the space instead. She has become fiercely protective of the vehicle.

Now, Samson takes up half the width of the recreational vehicle. He looms as an invasive presence she doesn't want in her home. Rosario has always been the passive Garcia—none of Dad's rancor, Mom's stubbornness, or Chuy's persistence. She'd been a peacemaker.

She isn't feeling very peaceful anymore.

"Give me the keys," Samson barks. "We're getting outta here."

Rosario stops beside Carl right inside the back door. She glances over her shoulder. The sinkhole is now still again, with no more structural dissolution. But that could change at any moment. They need to put some distance between the RV and the sinkhole.

"I can drive," she says. She's fifteen, and the extent of her driving experience has been using her permit around the slow neighborhood side streets in Mom's old Toyota. *Could* she drive this thing?

"You're a kid," Samson sneers. "Gimme the goddamn keys so we can leave before it's too late."

"We're not leaving," Rosario states steadfastly. "We have to give them a chance."

"A chance for what, kid? To dig themselves out of their graves?" Samson rumbles, taking a step toward her. "Last thing we need right now is a horde of zombies to join up with the underground monsters."

"Back off, Samson," Carl warns in his curmudgeonly voice. "This is the girl's vehicle. She decides."

"This tin can is our only means of escape, old timer. And it will be utilized by whoever has the firepower to enforce possession. This girl doesn't have shit. I have all the things that go bang."

Samson pulls out a gun. Points it at Rosario. Is this how it ends? Is this the way things go for the Garcia family? Shot in the head defending this box on wheels?

Maybe. Maybe, if that's what it takes.

"We're not leaving without the others," Rosario says. "Pi said this is a nest. They could've fallen into one of those underground tunnels like your shelter ended up. You made it out. It could happen again!"

Samson flips off the safety on his pistol. "I can't wait for them to find an exit. We're leaving *now*."

Carl puts his hand over Rosario's, where she clasps the keys. "Let me drive. I'll roll away slowly. You watch out the back, and if you see anyone, give a holler. I'll stop."

She meets Carl's eyes, and he's trying to tell her something more than he's saying out loud. *Trust me.* Does she? She certainly couldn't trust Samson. The alternative is undoubtedly a bullet and losing the keys anyway. Is this empty home worth getting killed? Should she risk her life for a bunch of strangers?

She lets Carl take the keys. He walks past Samson and settles into the driver's seat. Samson keeps a close eye on Rosario as if he doesn't trust she might not attack if he turns his back on her. Carl turns on the motor. The diesel coughs and roars to life. Samson still stares at Rosario when Carl stands up and silently sneaks behind him. The old man pokes a sharp shiv against Samson's back.

"I've served in war, you mean bastard. I know where to stick this knife so you'll have no chance of surviving long enough to leave this desert," Carl warns. "Put the safety on the gun and drop it."

Samson hesitates. Rosario watches Carl jerk his hand forward, poking the big man a bit. Samson cries out and flicks the safety on his pistol.

"Drop it," Carl demands.

"Drop dead," Samson growls. Carl jabs with the shiv again, but

Samson remains steady and grits his teeth this time. He holsters the pistol on his hip. "The only way I give up this gun is if you pry it from my cold, dead hand. You stab me, and I'll shoot the girl before I bleed out. That I promise you."

"Then get out of the R.V.," Carl demands instead. "We'll give the others a few minutes. To see if they survived. You know Rosario ain't leaving without them or me. If no one shows in a bit, then I'll concede. We'll go."

"I'm not getting out of this—"

"I'm going to start moving this blade forward as soon as I finish talking. You can stay ahead of it, or I'll run you right through. I don't trust you as far as I can spit, and since you won't give up the pistol, I need to get you out of range of the girl."

"We're supposed to be trying to survive," Samson hisses, unhinged but taking a step forward as Carl starts moving the sharp weapon. "Not fighting each other."

"Seems not all the monsters are underground," Carl says.

Samson gets to the doorway, the pointed blade still within millimeters of his back as Carl keeps pace. He shoots a glare back at Rosario. "You'll get us all killed, you little bitch." Then Carl herds him outside, and the men are far enough away that Samson can't get a bead on her to blow her head off.

What a jerk!

Rosario runs up to the driver's seat and climbs behind the wheel. She must be sure she's ready when the others find their way out of the sinkhole. And she can watch Carl and Samson in the rearview mirror. Rosario is now responsible for all their lives since it was her idea to wait for survivors.

8.2 Richter
[Pi]

The underground nest resembles some kind of hive.

When the survivors slipped through the sandy sphincter of the sink-hole, they were shat out the underside. Pi couldn't see anything, but the sensation was the same as when she'd slipped and slid down the piles of sand at El Segundo Dunes near LAX when she was younger. She turned on her belly and drove her arms into the sand as deeply as possible to make an anchor. At the same time, she kicked out the toes of her shoes. She slid a little farther, twisting one ankle painfully. She almost cried out and would've gotten a mouthful of sand for the effort. Waves of granules swept over her from above, but at least she arrested her descent.

Moments later, the cascade of sand finally stops. A foot of sand covers Pi, and her resurrection might've looked like a zombie rising from a grave dug beachside had there been any light to see. Instead, she sputters and breathes heavily until she recovers from being passed through the desert's asshole.

The sibilance of shushing sand had accompanied her descent, and she'd heard someone scream as they passed through the darkness. Now there is absolute silence. She pats her pocket to see if she lost her phone in the experience, but it remains where she tucked it. The light illuminates a chamber no more extensive than the average Starbucks. She's three-quarters of the way down the pile of sand. The perimeter of the cata-comb chamber features exits spaced equally where the sand has escaped, like drains around a butcher's floor for excess blood.

She's alone, or anyone may be buried alive beneath this pile. Pi listens and searches for any movement. Nothing. A hungry eye wasn't waiting for them this time. The quake opened a sinkhole into the underground catacombs created by the eating eyeballs. The beasts are still distracted by Shiv's shitshow in Skidoo. No monsters, and no people, either. The cas-cade of sand acted like a swirl of toilet water and flushed everyone else out of the anteroom.

The walls of the cave are glassy, smooth, and reflective. Something has chemically fused the sand into a translucent barrier. The subterranean structure is reinforced with pieces of buildings, trees, vehicles, billboards, road signs, hunks of asphalt, and repurposed girding for steel towers. Pi was right about this being a nest. Did every exit lead to some horrific egg that would hatch another demonic eyeball? Or a pupa stage even worse than the devilish orbs?

"Landry? Officer Hayes?" Pi calls out cautiously. "Pastor Mont-gomery? Bulldog?"

No answer.

She shines the light on the ceiling. Debris clogged the butthole for now, but she can't bet her life on perpetual constipation. No way to go back the way she's entered. Once the eyeballs rescue their precious nest materials from being razed by Shiv, the dreadful fucking things will be back. Pi better move her ass. She slides down the rest of the slope on her backside, wincing as her injured ankle aches. She balances on her good foot, pondering which exit to take, but positive that inaction would only get her killed.

Pi shines her lights along the walls as she limps around, amazed. The orifices all lead to individual underground tunnels. Like the inside of a beehive, the structure is geometrical and organized to maximize space while minimizing support material. Fascinating.

No time for study. Lingering too long will only get Pi dead.

"Bulldog!" she hollers. "Montgomery! Landry! Hayes!"

There's a chance a monster will hear her and swallow her up. There's a chance no one will hear her, and she's lost underground forever. But life's full of opportunities, and Pi isn't the kind who stands by and lets things happen. She needs to *make* something happen.

Pi fishes inside her pocket and finds her roll of lip balm. She shines her light around until she finds an unobstructed section of hard pan. She bends her knees and squats. After experimenting with placing the tube this way and that until it starts to roll, Pi turns in the direction sloping upward and takes the tunnel. Toward the surface.

She winds her way through labyrinthine corridors for a few long minutes, terrified she may find herself face-to-face with a beast. Her ankle is awful, so she tries to put minimum weight on it, steadying herself against the stone walls. Despite her heart racing and nerves on fire, she still calls out the names of her fellow underground explorers. Her voice echoes out and back. The only answer is her own voice.

Until— "Pi?"

Pi's ears are very attuned to how voices echo off stone due to her experience in excavation over the last few years. She volunteers her summers on archeological digs in stone quarries in the Middle East. Pi follows the sound of her name and finds Bulldog struggling blindly down a dark tunnel without any sort of light.

"So dark," Bulldog yammers. She looks scared to death. "I wondered if maybe I was dead."

"We might be if we don't find a way out of this," Pi says. "Have you heard anything from the others?"

Bulldog says no. Pi nods. The two continue Pi's former trajectory. Bulldog notes Pi's struggle.

"Twisted my ankle," Pi says.

Bulldog nods. She doesn't offer to help. Like a lame horse, Bulldog will leave Pi behind if it means saving herself. Conversely, she slows her pace so as not to overextend Pi's tolerance for her injury.

Like a river's source, one must find the surface by consistently moving upward. Pi leads, and Bulldog follows closely. Pi occasionally pauses to repeat her trick with the tube of lip balm. They both know Bulldog would oversee defense if they encountered anything dangerous, but Pi is the navigator and otherwise in charge of their direction.

They call out names again and again—"Landry! Pastor! Hayes!"

"Do you think they're still alive?" Bulldog asks.

"Doesn't matter what I think," Pi dismisses. "We either find them along our way out, or they'll be left behind. These tunnels are a maze. They could be anywhere in a hundred different directions."

Pi stops and turns out her light. The darkness is not absolute— she sees a faint light ahead. She's found the way out. Logic wins the day once again. These monsters follow the same rules of physics as the rest of the world.

Maybe she can outthink these creatures.

"That's it. The exit," Pi says, flicking the light on again and moving forward.

"We're really leaving without them?"

"Wandering around these catacombs searching for them is a suicide mission," Pi says. "Let's hope they answer before we—"

"Bulldog."

The sound issues faintly from down one winding tunnel.

"I heard Landry's voice."

Pi nods. Shit. So much for a fast escape. "I can't tell where the sound came from."

"Landry?" Bulldog shouts back. "Follow the sound of my voice!"

Pi shakes her head. It doesn't work that way. Going deeper, the branches of the tunnels carry their voices in a hundred different directions. Landry could follow echoes instead of the original sound.

"Samson isn't going to wait for us," Pi says. "We have to keep going."

"We've got to try and find them," Bulldog says.

"If we both go, we might never get out of here. Besides, I'm limping worse and worse," Pi says. "Take the phone and mark the way so you can find your way back."

"It's a chance," Bulldog mumbles.

"It's a chance," Pi agrees.

Bulldog wastes not another moment and plunges down the tunnel like a hound with a scent. Pi watches the light from her phone diminish as Bulldog wanders deeper and deeper into the catacombs. Alone again, the silence is as ominous as any sound. In the darkness, Pi can't tell if an eye the size of a satellite dish is staring at her, waiting for her to step forward so the pupil can swallow her.

Not complete darkness. The light remains steady at the end of the tunnel. Escape. No eye blocks her in that direction. She can see the glow promising sun and air and possible survival. How long would the eyes be distracted by Shiv's antics in Skidoo? The monsters would return before much longer.

Pi determined these creatures are building a nest. She has some insight into the way these things *think*. Bulldog doesn't know. Pastor Montgomery, Landry, and Officer Hayes don't know. Doesn't that make Pi valuable to the survival of the group? To the success of the entire human race? Maybe her insight is the key to the whole future.

Only Pi can save the day.

How selfish to sit in the dark. For the slim chance Bulldog returns with Landry and Hayes.

Pi chooses to get out. Just as she decided to leave Josh Henry. Pi knows she's important to the world. She isn't sure about anyone else in their group. Samson might think the same thing about himself, but the man is an egotistical asshole. Pi is trying to think of everyone else. The few survivors in the Mojave and the rest of the world are trying to persist. She could be some modern-day savior.

Pi turns her back on the others and heads toward the light at the end of the tunnel.

8.3 Richter
[Pastor Montgomery]

Monty appreciates solitude. He meditates regularly, finding the little whisper of God in his soul. The soft voice quiets the clamor of the world. Strife characterizes many of his interactions, so those few minutes every day center his spirit and can steel his resolve. He can feel the Holy Spirit in the stillness of those moments.

Now, the world is tranquil and entirely dark. Monty had fallen through the sinkhole, and a rushing river of sand swept him down a tributary of tunnels like a pest down the drain. Only sand made up the stream rather than dirty water. He'd been lucky to keep from being buried alive. The expansive tunnels beneath the sands are vast enough to disperse the grains, leaving him gasping on a stony floor. Monty didn't move for long minutes, waiting for any survivors to turn on a light on their phones. Everyone has a phone nowadays.

Even Monty.

However, he'd lost his phone at the beginning of this escapade, sucked up by the sand. Luckily, Samson had offered him a choice of grenades, guns, and knives. Monty had declined all weapons, choosing a cache of emergency glowsticks instead. He'd been lost in the desert once before on this adventure, and it might be wise to have something in case he ended up alone again. Monty didn't want to repeat his experience of stumbling over the desert scrub in the dark, especially with the sad state of his feet. He also selected MRE packets for nourishment.

Now, Monty finds himself entombed. Underground. Dark as the very depths of Hell. Surely as lost as any wrong turn in the desert.

Monty cracks a glowstick, activating the chemicals within. A sickly green light paints the inside of a small cave. Behind him, the rush of sand drained through the opening, the slope filling the whole accessway up to the ceiling. Monty holds the stick out and moves it in a circle. There are no other exits. The only way in and out is the way he had arrived.

Monty places the glowstick on the floor at his feet. He puts his hands together with his fingers laced up. How many times has Monty made such an effort? How often has he pleaded for divine intervention? Never for himself. Not once for personal gain. He has been blessed his whole life without tragedy enough to request any special treatment from God. But today, he endeavors for one personal favor. His heart is satisfied about the safety of his wife and daughters, but he isn't so sure about the prospects of reuniting with his family. Monty worries he's not long for this mortal plane. But he desperately wants to see them again.

"Please, Lord," he whispers. "Show me the way. Deliver me from this tomb."

Wasn't Jesus freed from the grave? Hadn't an angel come and rolled the stone away? Aren't there miracles in the world, even in the face of such abhorrent evil and unimaginable horror? Maybe God's favor is more apt to shine in the face of demons walking the earth—something heavenly to balance the hellacious invaders.

"Amen," Monty says. And as if his words were lightning, thunder shakes his world. A tremor almost knocks Monty off his feet. He reaches out and braces himself against the cave wall as the quake rumbles for long seconds. The cave could collapse and bury him under tons of rubble. One large stone dislodging overhead would squash Monty like a grape. The eye could come and sallow him whole without any warning.

Monty hears the shush of sand—it reminds him of the sound of Cheri making her favorite dish when she was a teen. Rice with salsa mixed in. She called it Spanish rice, and it was far from anything Hispanic. Yet Cheri always sang a Latina pop song as she put together ingredients and shook the box of rice for musical effect.

Shifting sand. An underground attacker could create it. Perhaps one of the evil eyes is opening its pupil to swallow him whole. Or maybe the sound of sifting sand had been one of the other survivors digging him out? He picks up the glowstick and points it around. The shadows dance in the sickly green light.

Neither. The quake shifted the sand, causing a cascade that opened a gap between the pile and the top of the cave's entrance—enough for even the rounded midsection of Montgomery Childes to squeeze through.

Monty climbs, squeezes through the tight space, and escapes the cave.

Not as dramatic as the resurrection of Christ, the sand had only trapped Monty for a few minutes rather than a few days. Still, he feels reborn as he follows the light of his glowstick across a sizeable central atrium with a monstrous pile of sand—this is where Monty had arrived from the surface. He spies footprints in the shallow carpet of sand around the base of the massive dune.

"Pi! Landry," Monty calls. "Officer Hayes! Suraya!"

No answer. Monty follows the footprints until they dissipate on the stone surface, and the trail goes cold. The tunnels branch off here and there. Monty stands in the large main cave and peers into one tunnel after another, any of them no more likely to be a means of escape than the other. How did anyone choose which way to go?

There had been only one set of footprints in the sand. Monty thought about the famous poem and how it suggested Jesus carries one when they are in need. Perhaps someone was led out by the grace of the Lord?

Monty closes his eyes and stills his thoughts. He thinks about the quietness in the chaos. The lull in an autumn wind. The calm between waves crashing on the shore. The peaceful moment between two breakers. Monty puts his hand out before him to feel for a wall and steps forward with his eyes still closed. Again. Again.

He walks blindly through a tunnel, taking a turn. Another turn. Another. He doesn't open his eyes. Monty is navigating on faith, taking small steps forward. Perhaps instinct could lead him better than his eyes. Or maybe God guides him through the cave, the Lord acting as a light at the end of the tunnel.

"Pi! Officer Hayes! Suraya! Landry!"

The names echo along the stone tunnels until the syllables come back to his ears, rearranged and crying out random nonsense.

"Sir! Ayandry! Hay Pi! Offaya! Erla!"

He follows the glassy walls, feeling his way carefully along the cracked and sharp-edged surface. He puts his safety in God's hands—he gives over all his trust to the Lord. He has lived his life in service to his faith. Monty has tried to be a good man. He believes wholeheartedly that it can't end like this. God will see him through. Jesus will save him from the depths of this desert hell.

Monty opens his eyes. He tucks his glowstick under an armpit, snuffing the light. He can see something through the darkness. A glimmer. A beacon. Something to propel him forward. He moves toward the object with a heart full of hope and a spirit sure of deliverance. Monty doesn't expect damnation around the very next corner.

Monty is faithful. Optimistic. Stalwart.

He can't imagine an end where he meets his Maker in the bowels of the Mojave, eaten by an unnatural eyeball.

Surely not such an end as that…

8.4 Richter

[Landry]

Landry has only ever been so scared once before.

Ten years ago. Swimming at the community pool with Dad on one unbearably scorching summer day. Hot in the Mojave is as wicked as anywhere on Earth. When the temperatures reached degrees where even tourists didn't come out to Skidoo, Dad sometimes closed the attraction, and they went elsewhere to cool down.

The community pool was a place of both love and detestation for Landry Honanie. The site acted simultaneously as an oasis and a purgatory. The water was a place of respite, and Landry loved to swim beneath the water for long, languid moments. Dad marveled how someone born and raised in the dunes could swim like a fish. The pool of calm, clear water was a magical sanctuary among the drought of the endless sands.

But a public swimming arena also accentuated everything that made Landry Honanie different from everyone else in town. Age twelve was probably the worst age to draw attention to anyone in a bathing suit, and Landry felt no more confident than any other preteen. Less so. Perhaps more than any other venue, the attire at a swimming pool was specific to gender. There isn't a unisex bathing suit.

Landry always felt impossibly exposed at the pool. But whenever Dad suggested the destination, the answer was never no. Underwater, the world didn't follow the same set of rules. There was an alien feel beneath the surface, where everyone could exist outside their normal skin.

The scary day ten years ago started the same as always. Stares. Whispers. If Dad noticed, he never said. He walked beside Landry and commented on the serene blue waters, the delicate splash of the pool, and the chlorine smell. Dad settled into his chair and opened a book, as always. Landry ignored the attention brought by the strange swim attire that included a rash-guard featuring the logo for Skidoo—a cute ghost floating over a silhouette of the town, trademarked water tower front and center with Skidoo written across the tank just like in real life— and a baggy pair of bottoms.

Landry climbed into the refreshing pool. It was heaven against the hellacious heat of high summer. When some of Landry's classmates walked in a few minutes later, panic took over. The event always involved stares, whispers, and sometimes outright ridicule if Dad wasn't within earshot. Landry dunked beneath the surface, propelling downward until bare feet met the pool's bottom. Eight feet of water filled the space between the bottom and the surface. With lungs like a whale, Landry could stay underwater for long periods. How long before the gang of classmates cleared out? Longer than anyone's lung capacity.

Landry's chest started to burn. Time to resurface. But Landry couldn't swim up. Without realizing it, one big toe had gotten wedged in the drain at the bottom of the pool. Fighting panic, it seemed a change in angle would help. No. Maybe a harder tug. Nope. Then fear took over, making the world turn black. Landry kicked, flailed, anything to escape.

No way to scream. No way to send up a flare. Drowning in eight feet of water. Dad was mere feet away, reading. Dad wouldn't even know Landry was dying. Dying. Dying.

Dad.

Dad was underwater, working at Landry's feet. He didn't bother with an attempt to free the toe. Dad yanked the whole grate out of the floor. Later, Landry would stare at the stripped screws and wonder how.

It didn't matter how. All that mattered was Dad pushing Landry up into the air.

This is like that day ten years ago. Landry had stayed so still for long minutes, trying not to breathe, letting the darkness swallow the surroundings completely, like the pool waters, terrified to surface for fear of what awaited above. Maybe it's safer down here in the alien world where no one belongs. But people can't survive where they don't belong for very long.

Dad isn't coming to save Landry this time. It didn't do anyone good to think about the fate of their loved ones, so Landry put what might've happened to Dad out of mind. Thoughts for another time. A person must first live long enough to see tomorrow before considering anything besides the present.

The kaiju nest is Landry's new pool. The darkness is the water. The ravenous eye is the pair of classmates making Landry's life hell. At least Greg Harlson and Chaz Lopez wouldn't ever swallow someone whole. Greg and Chaz are probably both dead. Landry doesn't want to end up dead.

After falling through the sandy sphincter, Landry slid through some subterranean flume until the incline leveled enough to stop. After staying submerged in the dark for too long, Landry uses the feeble cellphone light to measure the cavern's interior—a cave reinforced with recycled road signs and reused sections reconstituted from Skidoo. The sandy walls between salvaged materials are smooth and glassy, melted around the buried building materials repurposed to the edge of the Mojave. The chamber's size is no larger than the Honanie family living room.

"Hayes?" Landry calls out.

Only an echo answers. Landry must move forward. The hungry eyes would be back anytime now. Shiv's distraction of destruction could only last for so long. Time to head back to the light and try to escape.

"Pastor Montgomery!"

Bulldog, Shiv, and Samson found their way out of one of these subterranean catacombs after an eye had tried to swallow Samson's fallout shelter. There must be a way out.

"Pi! Bulldog!"

Landry worries about shouting, but the enemy is more eye than ear. Being lost underground without ever finding escape and eventually dying alone is more troubling.

Turn. Turn. Turn. Turn. The tunnels lead from chamber to chamber. Pi called it a nest. It looks like she was right. Landry recalls being even younger than the swimming pool incident and spending the afternoon at Greg Harlson's house when they were maybe eight. That was before Greg turned into a bully. Greg had an ant farm, and the tunnels and chambers against the plexiglass case were like these routes through the subterranean Mojave. However, the creatures crawling through this sand are big and bad enough to eat everything.

"Hayes!"

Quiet. Quiet. Then…

"Landry!"

The response is so quiet, and Landry almost believes for a moment that the faint noise is a figment of hopeful imagination. But then the sound soughs again through the tunnels, and Landry is sure it's a little louder. They call out to each other, and the replies sound louder and louder as Landry follows the voice. Determining direction proves more challenging as the tunnels bounce sound waves this way and that. But noise becomes light as Landry sees a glow in the distance.

Hayes and Bulldog.

Bulldog claps Landry on the shoulder, and Officer Hayes surprises Landry with a hug. Does strife have a way of making acquaintances feel more familiar, maybe? Hayes has patrolled Skidoo for the past few years, so perhaps he feels like Landry is one of the last connections to a world that still made sense.

The world had never really made all that much sense.

"What about Pi?" Landry asks. "And Pastor Montgomery?"

"Pi is okay," Bulldog reports. "She's keeping her eye on the exit. She'll try to guide us when she sees the light. I came back when I heard voices."

"Bulldog found me wandering in the dark," Hayes says.

"And the pastor?"

Hayes and Bulldog look at each other. Neither has an answer. The pastor might be dead. They can't waste time looking for a dead man.

"Which way to get out of here?" Landry asks.

Bulldog examines her options—left, right, ahead, and back. Every direction looks about the same. "I got turned around looking for you guys. I…"

"Uh," Landry interrupts, shoving them both to the right. "Not that way."

The light from Landry's phone had caught the faint glint of something down the tunnel directly in front of them. An eye. Staring right at them.

8.5 Richter
[Brock]

Brock Hayes has been stupid for so long.

He still remembers the first time he ever saw Landry Honanie. The first week on patrol. His partner had been a seasoned officer. Sergeant Lewis. Sarge was showing him the route around Inyo County. Sarge retired last year to Florida. Brock wonders if the old fart ran into whatever monster they were talking about on the radio. If so, Brock hopes Sergeant Lewis put a few slugs into the beast.

Skidoo was part of the countywide beat of the ICP patrols, but the place was remote, so Sarge scheduled it as the last section of Inyo County to visit. They pulled into town on a quiet Thursday afternoon. The ghost town was a ghost town. The police cruiser was the only vehicle in the parking lot.

"The Honanies run the place. They're good people. Nice place to grab a coffee and chat up Doug Honanie. "

Sarge bought them both coffees at the little mercantile, where Doug Honanie sold souvenirs. Doug and Sarge argued about the Giants versus the Padres, but Brock didn't care about baseball. He was preoccupied with watching the most curious person he'd ever seen. Landry strolled down the Old West street in a shirt that wasn't pink or orange but something between the two colors. Amorphous jeans complemented the top. A flop of hair black as tar and entirely unkempt peeked out from a weathered leather cowboy hat. The vest might've been stolen from an old John Wayne movie but for the hem bordered in blue rhinestones. The belt buckle matched the size of Brock's fist.

What was Brock looking at?

He hadn't known then, but the person had made him smile.

He doesn't know now, and Landry still makes him smile.

Landry grabs his hand, pulling Brock along the tunnel pell-mell, the only light a bouncing glow from Bulldog's otherwise useless phone as she leads the way. They are running for their lives, but is it strange that the galloping beat of his heart isn't only from terror and adrenaline? Brock has imagined holding Landry's hand for as long as he can remember, and now they are *touching*. The sparks travel along his fingers, up his arm, and explode like lightning in his heart, confirming everything he always wondered was true.

He loves Landry Honanie.

It's why his relationship with Jessie never worked. He wasn't invested in a future with Jessie after the first time he'd first rolled into Skidoo. Landry is a wonderful and enigmatic creature who'd always seemed magical, a fairytale related to bedtime stories rather than real life. Landry has a unicorn belt buckle, for chrissakes. How much more mythical can any person be? Yet their hands are clasped here and now, and Brock feels something firm and solid.

His feelings aren't just once upon a time. They're forever and ever kinds of emotions.

True love at the end of the world. Why had he waited so damn long?

They come to a dead end. The asinine names people come up with for things. *Dead end?*

"Fuck," Bulldog curses, sweeping the light around the glassy chamber and toward the ceiling. Then, reluctantly, back the way they'd come. The eye is coming.

It fills the whole rounded tunnel leading to this cavern without an exit. It's a trap. No way out. The eye comes forward, the orb some-how moving along the underground corridor even as the pupil stays fixated on its three prey. The iris around the black center is ochre, a fiery hue that is both beautiful and terrifying. Brock has never considered what's *behind* the eye. Is it an orb at the end of a stalk? Is there an amoeba-like form behind the eye? All they've seen is the eye itself, but what about the body? How does the rest of the monster look? Does he want to know?

Bulldog keeps the light trained on the ocular nightmare. The pupil had seemed depthless and empty before, but now, closer, Brock sees it isn't vacant. There are objects inside the darkness. Something within the eye. *Teeth.* The teeth are the color of the iris, with dozens, hundreds, innumerable fangs, all sharp as knives ringing the circle like spikes arranged around the inside of a wheel.

Brock draws his gun as the eye enters the chamber, the orb stopping as it bulges from the tunnel, turning in the doorway opening like rock makes a socket. He aims and holds his finger on the trigger. Will bullets make it flinch or simply piss it off? Will his valiant last stand instead limit his final moments with Landry?

"I love you, Landry Honanie."

Landry stares at the eye with all color drained from every inch of exposed flesh but turns at Brock's shocking confession. Brock had let go of Landry's hand to remove the pistol. He wishes he could retake it. He wants to die holding on to Landry in those last precious seconds. But like Sarge surely shooting up whatever big bastard beast is eating up Florida, Brock couldn't let Landry get chomped up without at least trying to save the day.

"That's beautiful, Hayes," Bulldog mumbles, voice cracking with fear and maybe something else. She hands her phone off to Landry. "Promise me you two'll name a kid after me."

"Kid?" Landry stutters.

"Or a pet," Bulldog suggests, pulling a hand from her trucker's vest. She holds one of the grenades Samson had passed out. "Whatever you're into."

"I like fish," Landry says.

"Bulldog is a good name for a fish," Brock says.

Landry smiles. Of course, it is. Bulldog gives them a nod, sets her face to the familiar grimace, and pulls the pin. The trucker starts running toward the carnivorous orb. The pupil constricts, suspicious, but it can't refuse a free meal. Bulldog wouldn't have to kamikaze the staring contest if the pupil had opened so she could throw the grenade, but the eye won't dilate for anything but a meal. Bulldog reaches the opening and leaps forward, the pupil yawning wide. She disappears into the opening filled with ferocious teeth. The peeper pauses to eat. Brock hears a horrifying scream and the sound of meat in a grinder, then the count in his head hits *zero*. Brock has enough time to throw himself in front of Landry as the muffled explosion behind him blasts his back with sand, pieces of flesh, and sharp projectiles.

Then silence.

Darkness.

Nothing.

"Brock." Landry's voice calls him from the abyss, pulling him up from somewhere deep, cold, and far away. "Brock!"

Back. Brock's eyes flutter open. His back. He feels blood running down his back. But nothing feels critical. He's able to get to his feet. He feels a little dizzy, but he's able to move forward. His police vest had protected him from the worst of the exploding eyeball.

"The blast blew a hole into an adjacent tunnel," Landry says, pointing to the light.

The phone's illumination is barely strong enough to cut through the dusty air. Brock and Landry are coughing hard as they avoid stepping into the mess of monster mixed with the woman who'd saved them. They need to move their asses before another eyeball arrives. They don't have any more grenades.

"Pi!" Landry shouts. "Pastor!"

No answer. Brock and Landry forge ahead. There's no other option than to try. Brock may have made a fool of himself when he blurted out his feelings, but there's no retracting them now. Landry knows how he feels. But Brock still has no idea what Landry thinks about him.

"What you said back there," Landry says while helping Brock along. He can walk, but the pain in his back causes him to stagger. "What did you mean by that?"

"It wasn't a riddle, Landry. It's something I've been feeling for a long time. Too scared to say before, I suppose. Terrified of what it might mean."

"You're not scared anymore?" Landry asks.

"I found out there are plenty scarier things in the world than how I feel about you."

"Right."

Brock pauses, catching his breath. "What do you think?"

Landry shrugs from beneath his arm and takes his hand. Their eyes meet in the dim light of the underground passageway, and Brock realizes the glint in Landry's eye isn't from the phone's light. The phone's screen has gone dead. It's a glow at the end of the tunnel—the exit.

"I say we head for the light and see what happens," Landry says with a stunning smile.

8.6 Richter
[Carl]

Carl faces Samson. He keeps the shiv trained on the big bastard. If the mountain of a man so much as twitches, Carl thinks he's still fast enough to cross the distance between them and shaft the motherfucker before he can draw the gun from his holster. Of course, Carl isn't as young as he once was, and he might not be fast enough even to take one step before Samson puts a hole between his eyes.

"We've waited long enough, Carl," Samson grumbles in his deep baritone voice. "Time to go."

Carl glances at the RV. Samson might not be right quite yet, but he's *almost* right. The monsters will be back soon. They can't wait around forever for the others to resurface. The rest of the refugees are probably all dead already. But Rosario won't forgive him if he gives up before the five lost members have a chance to—

"Let's get out of here," comes a deadpan voice behind him.

Pi limps toward them. The young woman wears dust from head to toe. She looks like she's survived a battlefield. She shuffles toward them, not asking why Carl and Samson are standing outside the RV, staring each other down like two cowboys at high noon in an Old West movie. If she notes any bit of tension between the men, it doesn't give her pause. Her face registers only pain. She stops and leans on Carl. He keeps the shiv handy in case Samson tries something.

"I can't walk anymore," she says, agony tinging her voice. A sheen of sweat covers her face.

"The others?" he asks.

"No one else is going to make it," Pi says.

Carl thinks she's saying more than the words convey. The look in Pi's eye is off. Not unlike the glower coming from Samson. They'll both leave everyone behind to get out of here. Neither gives a shit about anyone else.

Pi waves at Rosario, who is parked down the road. The teenager stands outside the driver's open door, watching the scene. She is fifty yards down the trail, moved safely enough away that she could get in the RV and escape if Samson tries anything funny. Carl watches as Rosario gets in the vehicle, and the reverse lights come on. She slowly starts backing toward them.

"You waited," Pi says.

"Not all of us wanted to," Carl accuses.

Pi stares at Samson. Something passes between the two. Carl doesn't like the vibe. Maybe Pi is more an enemy than an ally. She's leaning on Carl, but she stands with Samson.

"Now we're done waiting," Pi declares.

Carl observes Rosario's progress. She's coming up on them slowly. Will she give up on Landry and the others as readily as Pi and Samson?

"Depends on what the girl thinks," Carl says. "It's her R.V."

"We're done waiting," Pi repeats firmly.

Samson nods in agreement. There's some language of self-preservation and selfishness passing between Pi and Samson. Nonverbal coordination.

"Goddamn," Carl swears.

Pi leans harder on him, and her effort makes Carl too slow. Samson has his gun out and points at Carl before Carl can even attempt to close the distance between them. Samson is back in charge. Carl glances at the RV, but either Rosario can't see the scene between Carl and Samson, or she's resigned to this fate. The reverse lights stay bright, and the brake lights remain dim.

"I told you, old man," Samson gloats. "Human beings want to survive. We don't keep living by hanging around for the weakest ones to catch up. It's the endurance of the fittest."

Pi is still a heavy anchor on Carl. She isn't helping Rosario or Carl or the missing members. She wants to leave as much as Samson. Ten feet separate Carl from Samson, the distance far too great to cross without getting a bullet for his troubles. Samson is in control, and Carl doesn't have any more tricks up his slee—

Another quake. The three of them dance as the ground moves under their feet. Carl fears more stones rolling down and knocking the RV off the path, but the largest rolling rocks have already been exhausted. They must only worry about further erosion of the other side, where the sinkhole drops precipitously. It had already claimed a majority of them. Now, the ground wears away behind Samson. He staggers forward as Carl and Pi shuffle backward.

The shaking subsides, and the ground quits falling away. The bass of moving rocks and earth reverberates through the air. Samson aims the gun at Carl again as things become steady. But the rumbling sound doesn't stop. Too late, Samson notices the RV hasn't slowed at all. It had sped up. Pi flings herself backward, pulling Carl with her, and out of the way.

It's too late for Samson to move an inch.

Bam!

The back of the RV plows into Samson and sends him flying over the sinkhole's edge. Rosario slams the brakes just as the back tires reach the border. Carl helps Pi to her good foot, and she hops along to the back door of the RV. They get inside and close the door behind them. Locked.

Pi saved him. In the end, she isn't a monster. Maybe out to save her own ass, but she'll help if it doesn't mean *risking* her ass.

"The others?" Rosario asks.

"I think it's too late, child," Carl concedes.

"It's time to go, Rosario," Pi adds.

Rosario looks from Carl to Pi. She nods sadly. "We'll go."

She puts the RV into drive. Pi plops down behind the table in the living area. Carl makes his way to the passenger seat as Rosario slowly navigates the narrower route between the butte and the sinkhole. She looks so small in the driver's seat. Tears track down her face—she's lost so much. Carl wishes there had been more of them who'd survived this evacua—

Blam!

A bullet hole appears in the windshield between Carl and Rosario's heads, spiderwebbing the whole sheet of glass on the passenger side half of the windshield. They both look over their shoulders to see a maniacal Samson staring at them with crazy eyes. He's hanging from the ladder that goes up the back of the RV with his gun pointing right at them. The first shot exploded the back window and then shattered half the windshield. His arm extends inside the motorhome, aiming directly at Rosario.

"Stop the fucking R.V.," he hollers.

Rosario stomps on the brakes hard, and Samson almost tumbles into the RV, his big arm tangled in the ladder anchoring him outside. Losing balance, he uses his gun hand to steady himself against the open window frame. Then Rosario hits the gas and accelerates. He falls backward but still has his other arm clamped on the ladder. The teenager buys them mere moments. If Samson wants them dead…

Carl leaps out of the seat and charges. His body is between Samson and any line of sight of the girl driving the RV. Pi ducks behind the kitchenette bench. Carl runs toward the back, but the thirty-foot vehicle may as well have been the length of a football field. He is never going to beat a bullet. He only wants to give the kid a chance—but Carl doesn't know what kind of a chance. The future may look bleak, but these young people deserve something besides what Samson is serving.

Carl has lived too long in the past. Time to run ahead. Into whatever tomorrow has in store. His future looks to be short, but short is better than nothing. He passed too many years in banality. Boredom.

Blah. His life since Mary died has been more like death. Now, at least, he's living. Running. Fighting.

For a few precious seconds, he's shining like the sun.

Then Carl hears the sound of the bullet and the echo of his whole future.

8.7 Richter
[The Garcia]

Rosario pulls to the side. Puts the RV in Park. This wasn't exactly how she expected things would end when she demanded they stay and wait for survivors. But things often don't turn out as you think. Some divine ranking of good and evil doesn't determine who lives or dies. No one can label those who come out on the other side as heroes or villains. These are all merely people. Good and bad. Some alive. Some dead.

Rosario exits the RV and runs over to the trio of refugees they'd written off as dead. Landry, Brock, and the pastor had all emerged as Samson was climbing through the shattered back window of the RV. Now Brock stoops to check on the lifeless body, and Pastor Montgomery stands nearby the officer while giving a prayer for the dead. Rosario falls into Landry's open arms. They stand there for a long while in an embrace, her face buried in a sympathetic shoulder. This long, terrible ordeal seems no closer to being over now than it had this morning, but at least she hadn't lost Officer Hayes, Landry, or Pastor Montgomery.

"I thought you were gone," Rosario sniffs. She stands back and wipes her eyes with the back of her hand. She better rein in the emotion or devastation will wash over her and sweep her away.

"So did we," Landry says. "Bulldog saved Brock and me."

"Bulldog…" Rosario says.

Landry looks down. "She died saving us."

Rosario sheds silent tears. Just when she thinks the well has run dry, she cries again, stinging her raw eyes.

Officer Hayes glances up from where he's crouched beside the corpse. "She's a hero."

"And the Lord led me from the darkness," Pastor Montgomery said solemnly. "Back to the light. I ran into Officer Hayes and Landry near the exit. We emerged from the underground tunnels just in time to see…." The reverend nods down at the dead body.

Samson's corpse.

"What happened up here?" Hayes asks.

"He tried to get us to go without you. I said no," Rosario says. "Carl kept him leashed for a while, but he went rabid. He tried to shoot me. That's when you…you saved me. Like Bulldog saved you."

"Payin' it forward," Hayes says. He holsters his gun again, short one bullet.

"The sumbitch would still be alive if he'd treated us like human beings," Landry says.

"He was worried we'd stand around pissing and moaning when we ought to be hauling ass for solid ground," Pi says. She limps from the RV and glares at Rosario, Landry, Hayes, and Pastor Montgomery. Impatience is writ across her face. "Now we're sitting targets. Let's go!"

Hayes favors her with a scowl. "Where are we going, Pi? There's more desert ahead, and I don't know my way from here to there. Samson did, but he was impatient. Now he's dead. We need to take his map of trails, or we're gonna get the R.V. stuck in a dune before we get a hundred yards."

Pi drops to her knees and starts sticking her hands in Samson's many pockets, with no qualms about searching through a dead man's clothes. "Then make some fucking haste, Officer. This asshole won't be offended by a postmortem pat down."

Pastor Montgomery scowls at Pi. She doesn't temper her language around the holy man. Pi doesn't care if she offends everyone. Rosario kind of respects her fierce attitude. Officer Hayes helps Pi search through Samson's pockets.

Hayes pulls out the map from one of the endless recesses of Samson's outfit. Pi nods and stands, leading them back to the RV with a pained shuffle. Carl waits onboard, now behind the wheel. Brock killed Samson a split-second before Samson could shoot Carl, saving the brave old man to pilot the RV a little longer. Carl drives it a helluva lot better than Rosario did. As soon as Pi closes the back door, the motorhome moves forward.

Hayes rides shotgun, pointing out the route through the clear half of the windshield on the driver's side. The road is rough sometimes, with ancient trails eroded by the weather and aged by the years. Carl makes good time. Pi, Landry, and Rosario watch through the rear window Samson had broken out, scanning for sinkholes along the span of the sandy surface. The reverend sits quietly with his eyes closed, praying to his God to keep them safe this last leg through the Mojave. After an hour, they start to believe they've escaped the borders of the underground caves.

"What was that, exactly?" Rosario asks Pi.

Pi sighs. "I thought it was a hive made of underground passages. I'd guessed the eyes were making some sort of underground birthing place, but I was wrong. The eyes are more like the mouth of an earthworm, eating sand and secreting it into glass walls. They are shoring up the burrows with building materials. I thought the purpose was as a nest for babies, but that isn't it. The patterns of those tunnels—zigzag shapes, like cracks in an eggshell. The eyes are making the crust of the world right there *pliable*. Weak. So whatever is beneath the scab of rock and sand can break forth."

"Those tunnels crisscross the Mojave for hundreds of square miles," Pastor Montgomery says.

Pi agrees. "Exactly. Whatever is under the shell must be…leviathan."

"Jesus," Rosario whispers.

"How far do we need to go to get away?" Landry asks.

Pi shrugs. "We head east. As far away as—"

"Look!" Landry points out the back window.

Rosario isn't quite sure what she's seeing. It's like the dawn is break-ing in the west, but the rising shape isn't the sun. It isn't bright and doesn't glow. It's a bubble of sand and rock, a bulge that makes the whole hori-zon unsymmetrical. The swell is miles across. The hump rises miles up into the sky. Rosario watched a few minutes of some disaster movie Chuy had been playing once, and this reminds her of the volcano grow-ing and erupting in some planetary cataclysm. It feels like the end of times.

Such destruction isn't without effect. The world starts to rumble, the noise growing until Rosario has to put her hands over her ears. The landscape around them starts to shake, like a scene drawn on some cosmic Etch-a-Sketch, and something is shaking them up. Erased. Time to start over.

The sand around them vibrates off the ground as the Earth quakes. A few feet off the ground in every direction, the world becomes a blur, like a low mist made of sand has descended on this place at the edge of the Mojave. The shaking world makes Carl's task of staying on the road nearly impossible. The RV zigzags from one side of the highway to the other, barely keeping out of the ditches.

Then a shockwave catches up to them, and Rosario barely ducks behind a seatback before a granulated blast slams through the back win-dow, pelting them all like a sandblaster attacking them. On each side of the road, the soundwave sweeps the desert forth. Cracks riddle the dry land to the north and south. Here and there, chasms open wide enough to swallow at least an RV. Fault lines open in long, jagged runs along the landscape under the stress of the thing breaking through Earth's mantle. Carl curses from the driver's seat, the RV almost going over on its side. He barely keeps her upright. Rosario has been on rollercoasters her whole life and has never been on a ride as wild as this.

The sonic boom of destruction subsides, and Rosario peers over the headrest of her seat. The earthen egg dozens of miles behind them has shed its shell and revealed its contents. It's a monster. The creature's curvature rivals the setting sun's size along the horizon. Terrifying appendages cover the massive bulb of the creature's body—hundreds of stalks writhing like snakes stretch out from the domed surface. Like Medusa's head if she was a kaiju. But the ends of the whiplike tendrils don't have the fangs of a snake—the tips feature those familiar hungry eyes. Red irises with striations like teeth. Black pupils that act as the mouths.

The thing is bigger than the highest mountain. Like the moon itself if it was birthed from Mother Earth and launched from its Terran womb out into orbit. But it isn't natural. This thing has erupted from the bowels of hell itself.

"My God," Pastor Montgomery says.

"God damn," Pi swears.

Carl doesn't let off the gas pedal. The RV races away from the thing in the Mojave as fast as it can. The engine sounds like it could blow at any moment. Fear had taken over, and none cautioned Carl to slow down. The event behind them defies all reason, and everyone wants to get as far away from the impossible as fast as possible. Rosario stares as it slowly disappears behind the planetary curvature as they continue eastward. Nightmares of the event might plague her for the rest of her days, but nothing in her imagination will ever equal the reality of the horror she just witnessed. It is beyond understanding. Beyond recollection. She confronted the impossible in person.

Rosario couldn't even cry. She is beyond tears—past all emotional reactions.

They ride in silence for a while. After more hours, the sands of the desert fall behind them, and the world becomes green and vibrant. They head north and east. They drive for days, stopping to talk to other survivors when they see them. The radio works sporadically. Information is terrifying, unbelievable, panicked, and probably outright lies. The people passing stories from person to person seem more reliable.

They saw the real thing.

There are other creatures. The thing in the Atlantic is as big as an island and moves inland with terrifying tentacles. The beasts in the north are gargantuan white monsters as tall as skyscrapers. There is talk of other horrors—something razing New York City, a snakelike kaiju terrorizing Mexico City, creatures resembling horned hawks the size of Boeings owning the skies over Western Europe, and real-life dragons attacking London. Some sounded bogus, but hadn't Rosario seen some strange and impossible things the last few days?

Rosario misses her mom and dad. As they pass a sign welcoming them to Kansas, she wishes Chuy could see this. He had always loved *The Wizard of Oz* so. He'd have gotten a kick out of being here. For a while. He had a fear of tornados. It isn't tornado season, but it wasn't "the Earth cracking open like a giant egg" season either.

"What's next?" Rosario asks as they arrive in a small town called Lawrence. There were people everywhere. It seems many, many others have already started to convene here.

"I have some ideas for fighting these things," Pi says. "I have to find someone in charge."

"You guys go on," Officer Hayes encourages, gazing at Landry with a look in his eye—something familiar to Rosario… Mom and Dad would look at each other like that sometimes. Thankfully, not often. "We'll catch up."

Good for them.

Rosario exits the RV with Carl, Pastor Montgomery, and Pi. They wander through a parking lot containing more cars in one place than Rosario has ever seen. Vehicles clutter a whole field as far as she can see. She notes license plates from Montana and Florida and wonders what horrors those passengers have seen. Maybe they could all compare stories and figure out a way to win. Because people *are* going to win, aren't they? They would figure out a way to beat the monsters. Right?

"You might have a plan, Pi?" Rosario asks. She needs to hear the words. She needs to feel some hope.

"I have an idea," Pi says.

"We have a chance, then? To survive? To beat them? We're going to find a way to make a future, right?"

"Of course," Pi says, although her tone isn't as confident as Samson's when he threatened to kill all the refugees if they stood in his way. And Rosario knows what happened to Samson. "This is our world, Rosario. Not theirs."

"Yeah," she says.

But Rosario isn't so sure. The subterranean eye-worms move through the sand like fish through water. The size of the creature that emerged from under the Mojave bucks conventional physics and defies comprehension. Someone must have designed the monsters in the frozen north for the cold. The sea creature attacking Orlando seems perfectly adapted to the sea. Maybe the world *doesn't* belong to humans anymore.

Maybe the monsters have already won.

The rest of this event is just the monsters licking the rest of the crumbs off their plates.

Epilogue
[Pastor Montgomery]

Monty walks alongside Pi, Carl, and Rosario. The wild ride is over. No one can get a cell signal—communications are out from California to Kansas. The world's technology has been rendered inert by these infernal invaders. Monty wishes he could contact Daphne and the girls, but he isn't desperate for it. He has faith in their safety.

God will watch over them in these dire times. He believes God will protect them from this terrible tribulation unleashed upon the world. Monty has never been the type of pastor who preached fire and brimstone or prepared his congregation for the coming apocalypse—Revelations wasn't his favorite Book of the Bible—but apparently, the end of times doesn't care whether Monty prepared his flock for Armageddon or not. Fantastic and terrible beasts have escaped across the globe.

The others are worse off. Rosario is an orphan. Carl is a lonely widower. Pi has a family in Los Angeles, but she doesn't know if they're okay or not. Brock has friends and loved ones back in the desert who may or may not still be alive. Landry's dad got lost in Las Vegas. They can only be sure that they still have each other.

"There are a lot of people here," Carl observes. "Seems like they've come from all over the country."

"Maybe that's a sign," Rosario suggests. "People are regrouping. Ready to fight."

"Or backed into a fucking corner," Pi notes with characteristic vulgarity. She doesn't respect a reverend's white collar one bit. "Maybe these predators have us right where they want us."

"You think we can maybe find a ham radio in this town?" Monty asks Carl. The aged man knows how to operate such a machine. He had one in his gas station back in California. "I'd like to try to find out about my family."

"Me, too," Pi adds quietly. She's been all vim and vigor, but the mention of family finally dulls her sharp tone.

"Maybe," Carl answers with a nod. "We can spot an antenna. You know the one hooked on the roof back at my gas station?"

Monty nods. He can remember enough to spot the strange metal spire sticking out of someone's roof.

"You all head in each direction," Carl suggests to the crew. "I'll go that way. Meet back here in a half hour."

The four split up. There are people everywhere, and yet the six strangers who survived the Mojave have become like family to one another. They will find each other again and stick together going forward. In addition to Daphne, Ashley, and Cheri, the five other survivors who escaped the California desert are now a part of Monty's circle.

He wanders along a street called Iris Lane and shudders as he remembers the great eye who gulped up the underground of the Mojave. The immense orb ended up being only a small part of a massive monster that was incubating in an egg the size of a small state beneath the desert floor. Now, some gargantuan kaiju the size of an entire county had broken free from beneath the planet's shell. Will such mass tilt the very world off its axis and send Earth catapulting into the sun?

That is up to God Almighty to handle. A bunch of ragtag survivors from the edges of America can't put up a fight against something as big as a city. They will need some significant divine intervention if humans hope to reclaim control of the world.

What better place to put in a good word than a house of worship? Pastor Montgomery Childes stops in front of a Catholic cathedral along Iris Lane. A steady stream of parishioners enters and exits. Even in the face of evil incarnate invading the world, plenty of folks still put their faith in the Lord to see them through.

Monty enters through the narthex and pauses as he spots the familiar cross. It hangs over the altar at the end of the church. The Catholics might have all the bling, art, and fanciness, but they still value the simplest symbols. Monty can appreciate the glitz and glamor of the Vatican, but genuine humility in Christ doesn't come with a price tag.

The priest is an older man with fantastic gray hair and wrinkles for days. He appraises Monty from across the nave, notes the collar, and nods at the fellow pastor in solidarity. Parishioners fill the seats, clog the aisle, line the walls, and sit cross-legged along the front before the altar. Babies are crying, adults are weeping, and the vibe is that of a memorial for some important public figure. In this case, humanity itself is in grave danger.

The world has become an enclave of desperate survivors.

Here and there, believers get up and silently depart as others take their seats. A young man no older than Rosario stands up in the pew next to Monty and looks at the pastor with eyes more haunted than anyone Monty has ever seen. This young man has lost everything. He appears more devastated than even young Rosario. At least Rosario still has Landry and Pi, Carl and Officer Hayes. And, of course, she still has Pastor Montgomery. He walks away in a lifeless shuffle of someone resigned to a doomed fate.

Monty scoots into the pew and takes the seat vacated by the boy. Some of the congregation is singing off-key "All Creatures of Our God and King" and murdering the lyrics. Ashley's favorite hymn. Monty folded his hands and closed his eyes. He pictures his daughter, and she is all right. Monty thinks about Cheri, and she is safe. He imagines Ashley is saving the world.

"You a pastor?" asks the woman on his right.

She's Latina and looks like she's been through hell. They all do.

No one is in this building to thank God for recent riches. The woman appears tired, haggard, and somehow saturated through and through even though she's dry as a bone. She gives Monty the impression of a woman wearing the weariness of a world underwater for forty days and forty nights.

Monty touches his collar. Still there. "Yes," he says. "I am a man of God."

"God's got some serious fucking explaining to do," she snaps. "He needs to get down here and straighten some shit out."

Her language is as foul as Pi's. And she's in a church! Doubly damned.

"He'll deliver us from evil," Monty assures.

His words cause her to touch her belly. She isn't showing, but Monty understands. *Deliver*—the woman is pregnant.

"'Is it not wonderful news to believe that salvation lies outside ourselves?'" comes a voice on the other side of Monty. It's an old woman with white hair. Her lips are edged in bluc, as if hoary frostbite long ago affected her severely and she has never entirely recovered from its effects. She looks like she has been frozen to the bone and cannot shake the chill. Her hands suffer tremors that might be from palsy or fright or eternal frigidness.

"That's a quote from Martin Luther," Monty says.

"Is it?" the old woman answers. "I don't remember where I saw it."

"I hope it's true," the Latina woman says.

"What's your name, dear?" the old woman asks.

"Renata Sánchez," the pregnant lady introduces.

"I'm…" and the words seem to freeze on her tongue.

"Esther, dear," says the no-nonsense black woman beside her. "We should be leaving. The others are waiting."

"Yes," Renata agrees. "I have others, also."

"May I ask," Monty interjects before they leave. "Where have you come from? Before Kansas?"

"Florida," answers Renata. "Where there are monsters in the sea."

"North," replies Esther. "Where there are monsters in the white."

"Right," Monty says. "I think… I think we can maybe learn from each other. Help each other. Find a way to survive."

"I thought you wanted to leave this up to God," Renata dismisses.

"No," Pastor Montgomery Childes states, standing up. "God helps those who help themselves. We can't do it alone. But maybe we can do it together."

The women don't disagree. They all leave together. Monty pauses to dip his fingers as he walks past the holy water font. He isn't Catholic, of course, but he does it without thinking. He peers at the surface of the water before following the women out. Someone has dumped some ice cubes inside, and Monty stares. His fingers cause ripples in tiny seismic circles, moving the water and clinking together the ice. Quakes. Frost. Water. Together.

All together.

A sign? A warning from God?

A wind blows through the front door and Monty shivers.

This isn't over yet.

ABOUT THE AUTHOR

Edward Newton grew up in North Dakota, which inspired book one of the Tempests of Terror series, *Horrorfrost*. He's lived in Florida for the last few years, sparking a sequel, *Horroricane*. He received the Robert L. Fish Memorial Award from the Mystery Writers of America for the Best First Short Story. Edward has published several short stories, a young adult science fiction novel, *The Infinite Minute*, and a fantasy work called *Truth to Light*. Keep up on current works, author news, and bonus short stories at EdwardNewton.blogspot.com.

HORRORFROST
EDWARD NEWTON

def. hoarfrost
hoar·frost
ˈhôrˌfrôst/
noun
a grayish-white crystalline deposit of frozen water vapor formed in
clear still weather on vegetation, fences, etc.

0°

Hoarfrost covers the glass in the small cabin, concealing the world outside. A fire licks the air inside, tasting the cold, snapping and snarling at the precipitous drop in temperature. A storm moves in, wind howling against the walls and whispering through the cracks and crevices of the old place. Snow falls from the sky in big, fat flakes, shushing and scraping against the pinewood logs of the foundation. It was just morning moments ago, but now darkness falls as the thick precipitation blots out the universe beyond.

Roman Carver doesn't even ponder the resort town at the bottom of the mountain slope, let alone the universe beyond it. Twenty years ago, he'd been a successful banker in a big city in the flattest part of Texas. In any given week, he could foreclose on a family home, bankrupt a small business, and deny loan after loan after loan, sending working folks into a financial spiral. He had been connected, corporate, and cold.

Then one day he unplugged. He stood up in the middle of an afternoon in December and walked to his floor-to-ceiling window in the corner office on the top floor of a downtown high-rise. It never snowed in this part of Texas, yet an errant snowflake drifted outside the plate glass, dancing like it did not have a care in the world. Roman had watched as it did some sort of natural ballet in the sky, a frosty kiss that broke a spell he had not even realized he was under.

There'd been a conference call playing on a speakerphone on his desk. His desk had been half the size of the room where he'd spent the past two decades of his life. He'd walked away from the desk, out of the room, and off the conference call without signing off, an urgent "Mister Carver? Mister Carver? Are you there?" following him all the way down the hall to the elevators. He'd owned a million dollar penthouse in the Renaissance district, but Roman did not even bother stopping at home before he left town forever. Six months into a relationship with a stockbroker from Austin, he never even bothered calling to tell her it was over.

Roman Carver had left Texas and came to the mountains of Montana.

He'd built this cabin with his own two hands. A man who had become successful entirely on his own, rising through the ranks to run a multimillion-dollar corporation, he had not asked for help on this new endeavor. Trial and error. His initial supplies had consisted of a flint lighter, some how-to books on survival, a first aid kit, a bowie knife, some tin pots and pans, fishing line and hooks, and a compound bow with complimentary arrows. The first month, he had almost starved. The first winter, he had almost froze. The first spring, he'd gotten so sick he thought he was going to die. That was all twenty years ago.

Roman is still alive.

He sips a mug of hot coffee cupped in calloused hands. Steam issues off the black surface, further obscuring the view out the window. Not that he needs to see snow. This high in the mountains, a storm could easily yield a foot of new powder overnight. Nothing to do but hunker down and wait out the worst. He stares at the fire. There is no electricity in the cabin. No television. No phone. No electronics of any kind. Roman had left it all behind.

A noise outside sounds like a tree giving under a load of snow, the burden beating the ground with a solid thump. The surface of the coffee in his mug ripples like a pond disturbed by a pebble. Roman had not seen a movie in twenty years, but he knew *Jurassic Park*. He is fairly sure he does not have to worry about a t-rex, but the rippled-java effect was certainly not caused by falling snow. Nothing short of an avalanche.

"The hell?" he mumbles, his voice dry and scratchy from irregular use.

Roman has not gone down to the town in the two decades since he arrived from Texas. He did not need supplies. No news. No gossip. He crossed paths with an occasional hiker in the warm months and a skier every once in a while during the winter, but he never stopped for more than a "Howdy-do." When he had come up into the mountains, Bill Clinton had been president, Elway had gotten his Super Bowl ring, and "Mmmbop" had been driving him crazy. He never asked what happened after that.

No one ever comes up here in anything big enough to cause a noise like that. Roman glares at the opaque pane. *What is out there?* He ponders for a while until curiosity finally outweighs the cold.

His coat is bearskin, a grizzly he'd taken ten years ago. Boots are sheepskin. Gloves rabbit. Before he'd left Texas, he'd been a regular contributor to PETA, and now he looked like some creature the organization would seek to protect. Ethical treatment of animals is using every part of the kill, the spirit of the beasts living on by helping Roman survive. He had never had such respect for the creatures of the wild when he'd been using them as a charitable tax deduction.

Maybe it was an animal that made the noise? A moose that bumped into a nearby tree?

Roman opens the front door and a small hill of snow crumbles into the cabin. He pushes through a drift as high as his waist, then pulls the door shut behind him. The wind cuts as sharp as the knife strapped to his waist, ready in case some winter-starved predator dares attack. The white is absolute, the driven snow like a wall that might be solid but for the shifting grains moving before his eyes.

He pushes through the snow. The cabin is in a clearing, and his home disappears behind him after he takes just three steps. He knows these woods like the back of his hand in the dark, but the blowing snow is disorienting. Better off blind than mesmerized, Roman closes his eyes and forges forward. He marks his way by putting a hand on the old tree ten yards from his front door. From there, the denser forest blocks some of the blizzard.

Roman moves in the direction of the sound, forward, forward, until he finds what he is looking for. It is a blue spruce, snapped in two, as big as any other tree in the woods. Boughs heavy with the season's snow must have sounded like an earthquake when it broke. But the weight of the snow could not have made the tree trunk crack in half. Something broke it off. Something big enough to snap it mid-section, some sixty feet up.

"The hell?" Roman says again, the wind whiting out his words.

A gust brings snowy blindness, suddenly obscuring everything. Whatever did this is still out there somewhere, in the white. Did a small plane crash in the woods? There is no other evidence. A meteor? Maybe. Something else? Something else covers a lot of possibilities. Roman has largely ignored the developments of the modern world these last two decades, so maybe they had invented something that could do this kind of damage. After all, man is always inventing new ways to destroy nature.

Another trembling bass, this one thrumming through the soles of Roman's sheepskin boots. Like an explosion deep within the earth, but the sound carries across the winter air, muffled by the thick snow. The origin is back the way he came, from the direction of his cabin.

Roman stares into the white before rushing off. Deliberating. He knows the dangers of this world. He has crossed every type of animal that lives in these mountains over the last two decades, sometimes as predator, sometimes as prey, sometimes as passerby. It feels like something else. There is something else on his mountain. Something new. But he cannot see anything through the snowfall, just a shifting white curtain that conceals everything beyond.

Roman moves back toward his home. He gets to the old tree and stops again, eyes straining against the static of the snowstorm. He cannot pick out a stationary object within all the turgid swirl of the scene. No hint. Nothing he can separate from the constant white noise.

He can't see anything out in the clearing. The blowing snow erases everything. He steps forward, one foot in front of the other. The clearing is about fifty yards in diameter, his cabin at the center. If he loses his way in the disorienting blizzard, he will find more trees. Another step. The snow gathers in drifts now nearly to his shoulders. Forward, forward, forward. Right to his front door.

Or where his front door ought to be.

The walls are all flat, smashed to the ground and nearly covered already by fresh snow. Everything he ever had has been pummeled, flat as the pancakes he made just that morning.

Something squashed the cabin as easily as Roman might flatten a pill bug under his heel.

Whatever it was could be as close as his fingertips, concealed by the white.

And the wind rises, the temperature slips another degree, and Roman Carver shivers.

It has nothing to do with the cold.

-1°

Trevin Mendoza sits on the edge of the bed. Behind him, a tussle of pink hair peeks out from beneath a rumpled bed sheet. The head does not belong to his fiancé. It is someone who had been just a friend before last night. Trevin watches the ice creep up and across the glass of the patio door that leads to the suite's balcony. It is cold outside. It is cold inside.

Maybe he is not ready to be married. That's what Alex had told him last night, before things got out of hand and went too far. Those words had made sense a few hours ago. Glancing back at Alex's pink bangs sticking out from the tangled bedding, they still make sense. His mother had always told him he wasn't the marrying kind. He hates to admit his mother is right about anything, but the evidence still hangs in the air like Alex's musky aftershave.

This is supposed to be a bachelor party weekend. The engaged couple came to Enchanted Point Ski Resort together, with an entourage, ready to celebrate the last days of bachelorhood before tying the knot in Vegas next week. Alex is supposed to be the best man at the ceremony. Yet somehow Alex had ended up in Trevin's bed. And bad things had ensued.

Such deliciously bad things.

Shit.

Trevin stands up, considers pants, then snorts. What goddamn difference did it make now? He walks naked to the icy patio door and peeks out the small corner not yet covered with frost. Outside, snow blankets the small town of Zukunft Falls, Montana. From what Trevin can see of the balcony, the railings look like lumps under a sheet. Like a lover concealed beneath the blanket of sin.

Trevin sighs. The breath turns to condensation on the glass, then freezes, crackled ice radiating out from the edges of the pane toward the center. It looks like broken glass. One more broken thing. He turns away.

Alex is sitting up in bed, watching him.

"You look like someone caught you with your hand in the cookie jar, Trev," Alex says.

"Don't call me that," Trevin says. "Only David calls me that."

"I bet he might call you something else when you tell him about this."

"Who says I am going to tell him?" Trevin challenges. "It would ruin everything."

"The only reason you did this is so you can tell him. You *want* to ruin everything."

Trevin looks away. Modesty has never been part of his personality, but standing here naked in front of Alex, he feels ashamed. Alex is right. He did this so that there could be no turning back. If he simply told David that he did not want to get married, David would try to talk him out of it. David would succeed in talking him out of it. But this?

There is no talking out of this.

"You want me to tell him?" Alex asks.

Trevin glares. Passions can flare between two people, dangerous emotions both dark and bright. So often the extremes occur on opposite sides of night.

"I'll tell him," Trevin says.

"When?"

"Tomorrow," Trevin responds, postponing the inevitable.

One last day together.

Trevin and David have been a couple for more than four years, ever since they'd met online shortly after David moved to L.A. from Nebraska. He'd been an ingenue, and Trevin was a seasoned SoCal social superman. Trevin had introduced David to everything fantastic, and David had showed him what it meant to take a step back and appreciate those fantastic things.

David had told him on their fourth anniversary that he wanted to move forward or he was going to move on. Trevin proposed. And for a while it had been fine. Exciting. A new adventure. But then they'd started planning this trip and reality started to solidify. It got hard to see the future. Then it started to show cracks.

Now, it is in pieces.

"Why wait 'til tomorrow?" Alex presses.

"Tomorrow is as good as today."

"That is the thing about tomorrows, Trev. They never get here."

"Get dressed," Trevin snaps. "Get out."

Last night they couldn't get enough of each other. Now Trevin has had enough. This is the other side of the coin.

Somewhere outside the translucent window, the world gray and gloomy despite the midmorning hour, comes the sound of thunder. Alex, pants up and shirt half-buttoned, turns to the patio door. Trevin, still without a stitch on, approaches the balcony. Another boom. Louder. Closer.

"What was that?" Alex asks.

Trevin steps into a pair of Calvin Klein sweatpants that were crumpled in a corner. He pulls on the white and blue Bogner ski jacket he wore on the slopes yesterday. There are a pair of Hestra mittens that must be Alex's tossed not far from pink bikini briefs that also do not belong to Trevin. He pulls on the mittens. Stepping into his ski boots, he opens the glass door; the quick flick of cold takes his breath. Yesterday had been sunny and perfect; this morning is like nothing a SoCal surfer has ever seen. Trevin likes his water in waves instead of flakes.

The white is absolute. He remembers seeing the white sand of

Coronado Beach for the first time and telling his boyfriend at the time that it must be like walking in snow. Nope. It is nothing like snow. This is endless, oppressive, unstoppable. Trevin feels like he is staring into oblivion, and if he looks into it long enough, he might go blind.

Somewhere in the white, another boom. Trevin cannot be sure with the swirls and eddies of the snow, but he thinks the sound made the flakes *vibrate*.

"That is not thunder," Alex says from right beside him, making Trevin jump. "It sounded like an explosion."

Alex had donned a pair of spare gloves, hat, ski goggles, as well as his own jacket and boots. He looks ready to survive a blizzard. Well, if he wasn't going to leave willingly by the main hotel room door…

"Go check it out," Trevin goads.

Alex gives him a face. "Why don't you go?"

"You're dressed for it," Trevin says. "Goggles and everything. I wouldn't be able to see a thing out there in that blizzard."

They stare out into the suffocating snow. The wind gusts and Trevin cannot see more than two feet in front of him. For one excruciating moment, he imagines David, unseen, in front of him, looking back as Trevin looks out, yet they cannot see each other. Close enough to reach out and touch, yet separated by an insurmountable distance. The space between them is too great to erase.

"Scared?" Trevin taunts.

Another boom.

"Yes," Alex says.

Instead of forward, both men take a step back. Retreat. They close the frosted door and stare at the pane veiled with hoarfrost. Snow had sneaked in while they'd been staring down the storm, tendrils like tentacles winding away from the closed door, quickly melting, fingers of water leaving wet streaks on the gray carpet. Outside, the sounds of more explosions, like someone had declared war on this resort town.

Then the lights go out.

-2°

Rhonda Phelps stares into the mirror. Was that another wrinkle? Another line? Shitshitshit. They popped up lately like weeds in a garden. Every morning. Festering like an infection. Of course, the stress over each one likely caused the next, a snowball rolling down a hill gathering momentum. Her mama, God rest her soul, might hate her for it, but Rhonda plans on going under the knife as soon as she gets back to Rochester.

She had dyed her hair for the occasion, a professional job that she'd driven an hour out of town to get done, far enough away from anyone who might have known her. She has been doing the same thing since the first errant strand of gray arrived some fifteen years ago. She had her regular local hairstylist, and then her secret one, who existed out of town, for coloring, like she was married to one and cheating with the other. All to keep up the illusion. Everything to stave off the realization of time running out.

This trip was a bust. She had been dating Howard online for the last few months. They arranged a face-to-face for a week of skiing in the middle of nowhere, Montana. They'd met for the first time ever in the lobby of the community lodge to kick off the vacation with some drinks and an introductory meeting. Well, Howard's online profile picture was from a good fifty pounds ago. And as he had pointed out before leaving for home five days early, Rhonda's was from a good two decades ago.

She had lied about her age. She has been lying about her age since forty snuck up and stole her future. For a few years, it had been easy to get away with. Perpetually thirty-nine, she looked it until just recently. Something had changed in the last year. Like the borrowed time she had used up on lying these last ten years had all piled on at once, advancing too fast. The woman in the mirror is not thirty-nine. Tomorrow, Rhonda turns fifty.

He had left her the birthday gift he'd brought. It is a gray scarf the color of hoarfrost. She picks it up now and wraps it around her neck. It covers up some of the waddles and wrinkles that seemed to appear overnight. Like her body knows fifty is only a day away.

There is another reverberating bass in the distance, like a drumbeat loud enough to make her bones ache. Thunder? Some local phenomenon? An artificial annoyance?

The old woman in the mirror disappears into darkness as the lights flicker and fail. Like candles blown out on a birthday cake.

Howard had left, but Rhonda had decided to stay. The suite is prepaid through the end of the week, and she was not prepared to go home to New York and face her family and friends about the shitty reality of her romantic vacation. Certainly, Sheila would arrange a night out with the gang for Rhonda's birthday. None of them believed she was still thirty-nine. That had turned from a cute joke to an awkward obliviousness over the last couple of years. No one would be surprised she is turning fifty.

None of them except Rhonda herself.

She had such plans. She had wanted to be married by thirty, two kids by thirty-five, and by now she had expected to be cheering at a high school football game or giving a standing ovation at the state spelling bee. Instead, she looks like a grandmother with no grandchildren to show for it.

The dark is a brief blessing.

Then she feels her way out of the suite. Dim light leaks in from the terrace doors flecked with crystalline frost, a gray ambiance that reminds her of the strands that populate her black hair, more and more and more. Before she had her coif colored for this trip, she'd plucked enough gray weeds to make Barbie's granny a wig.

The light is just bright enough to separate objects from the pathway, barely illuminating the route to the front door of the suite. Rhonda opens the door with the number 438 on the front. In the hall, emergency lights cast everything in a dull red glow. Other occupants stand in doorways and gather in small groups.

"What's going on?" Rhonda asks a woman who looks like she is maybe twenty-five and does not have to lie about her age. Little blonde thing with hair all tussled like she just woke up and still looks as pretty as if she spent hours on her face. The girl obviously exited her suite without putting on a bra, the nip in the air ensuring it is not the only nip noticeable. What is not noticeable is any sag whatsoever.

Little bitch.

"The lights are out," the girl answers, like Rhonda had just asked the stupidest question ever. She does not even look up from the phone she is on, texting away like some stenographer transcribing their conversation. The blonde did not have to ask anyone in the hall what is happening; her phone is the only companion she needs.

Someone ought to slap some sense into the girl, but that someone is not Rhonda. Not today. Instead, she turns away from the nubile youth and walks across the room to a woman who makes Rhonda look young in comparison.

The occupant in the room across from Rhonda's looks like she is in her sixties, a slight, sprightly white woman wringing her hands like she is applying lotions and pissed about it. She is wearing colorful leggings over a fit form and a sweater that looks as trendy as anything the idiot blonde might wear. The older woman at least has the sense to wear undergarments.

Closer now, Rhonda notices the sweater is on backward. Under other circumstances, Rhonda would have honored the sisterhood code and notified the lady—Rhonda is not shy about boogers hanging from noses or a piece of spinach caught in someone's teeth—but there seems to be something more important to discuss than turned-around tops.

"Do you know what's happening?" Rhonda asks.

"No," the woman answers with a worried expression, not wasting words with a stupid reply. "Clarice went down to the lobby. She was concerned after the explosions started. No nonsense, that one. She scooted off before the lights went dark. I hope she isn't stuck in the elevator. With her arthritis, she never takes the stairs. Do you think they have an emergency backup for the elevators?"

"I'm sure they do, ma'am," Rhonda replies. She has no idea.

Someone with a flashlight sweeping the hall left to right starts coming down the corridor. It is a resort employee with a name tag that says "Conner." Conner looks the same age as the blonde still standing braless in the doorway of her suite, the glow of her phone casting shadows across her shirt, highlighting twin nubs that keep getting pointier. Conner gets an eyeful, pausing right between Rhonda and the girl.

"You have some answers for us, Conner?" Rhonda asks.

"Just stay inside your suite, ma'am," he answers without looking at Rhonda, absorbing an eyeful of the blonde's perky bosom.

It's like Rhonda isn't even there. Age has made her invisible. There had been a time when she'd been the one who had caught the boys' attention. Now, she is the incessant buzz in the background.

"Have you seen my friend?" the old woman asks Conner. "Her name is Clarice Otter. She went down to your lobby to find out what this is all about."

"What?" Conner stutters, distracted by delectable tits. Then he finally turns, the task at hand finally resurfacing. He looks at the old woman. "I didn't see anyone on my way up. She might still be in the lobby. She shouldn't be wandering around without a flashlight."

"Why did the lights go out?" Rhonda asks.

Conner looks as clueless as the blonde across the hallway. "For your own safety, please return to your suite until the electricity comes back on." He is reciting the company line, like an automated message repeating on an intercom.

Another explosion sounds outside. Closer. The maid's cart parked under the emergency light two doors down rolls a few inches up the hall from the reverberation, a bottle of cleaner shaking off the edge of the cart. Rhonda grabs the door jamb to steady herself, her other hand cupping the old woman's elbow to make sure the senior citizen does not topple over.

"What the fuck is that?" Conner swears, eschewing company protocol in favor of stark fear.

The blonde looks up from the glowing screen of her phone like she has just witnessed someone murdered right in front of her face. "I lost my signal."

Conner pulls his own electronic device from the pocket of his resort uniform. "Me, too." In the pale light from his screen, he looks like a ghost. "The tower must be down."

"No Wi-Fi, either," the blonde adds.

Another explosion shakes the entire building.

"My last message," Conner whispers, reading, professional mission now entirely abandoned. "It's from my buddy who works out at the lifts, up the mountain. He says there is something in the snow."

Rhonda looks over Conner's shoulder and reads the last text message on his screen from someone called "Doobie," a dubious eyewitness account from someone named after a marijuana cigarette: "cant see it jist shadows theirs somethng trrble in the white."

The bass sounds again, this time shaking Rhonda so hard she stumbles forward, almost knocking into Miss Braless Blondie. *There's something terrible in the white.* For so long, she has dreaded turning fifty. Wished tomorrow would never come. But now, Rhonda Phelps wants nothing more than to see just one more day.

HORRORICANE

EDWARD NEWTON

def. hurricane
hurr·i·cane
ˈhər-ə-kān/
noun
1: a tropical cyclone with winds of 74 miles (119 kilometers) per hour or greater that occurs especially in the western Atlantic, that is usually accompanied by rain, thunder, and lightning, and that sometimes moves into temperate latitudes
2: something resembling a hurricane, especially in its turmoil

0"

[Leo]

Leo's laboratory is a mess. What would his mother say? Surely curse him in Japanese because that's what she's good at. Galileo Enomoto is good at something else. He's *great* at something else. When it comes to science, Leo is a *rockstar*.

The rest? Well, the rest sucks.

"C'mon, Leo," Arianna complains. "It's Friday, for Chrissakes. Let's wrap it up and get out of here."

"Out?" Leo asks, pausing for a moment from looking for the last printout that he put…somewhere. "Like for drinks?"

"Whatever shakes your maracas, dude," Arianna says. Then she catches his meaning. "Oh, you mean, like me and you? Are you shitting me? My boyfriend would kill me if he ever saw me out with another guy. Or you."

She says it like she isn't sure if Leo is a guy or something else. His face turns red and he goes back to looking for the report. "You can go. I'll finish up here."

"We're partners," Arianna sighs like she just told her family she has cancer.

"Yeah, partners." Arianna hadn't contributed more than a full helping of boobs to their work so far. But at the end of the day, Leo has as much chance of experimenting with her physiology as Arianna has in mastering paleotempestological reconstructions. "Go on. Don't worry. I've already got your name on our report."

Arianna leans across the desk where she's been sitting for the last half an hour, scrolling through social media. Her cleavage is on full display today. It looks like her breasts are ready to party for the weekend. She lets him get an eyeful, gives him a knowing grin, and thanks him before she skips out the door.

Leo finds the paleotempestology report tucked between an electronic tablet and his clipboard charts and remembers he was distracted when Arianna dropped her lipstick and bent over to pick it up, her top *allllllll-most* spilling out from the straining black lace bra. Damn gravity never seemed to work quite right when you needed it to. This afternoon, science had let him down.

The entire east side of the UCF laboratory is a window, blinds drawn. Leo checks the weather app on his phone to see what it's like outside instead of walking over and looking for himself. He is trained to trust technology over his own eyes. Bytes and binary don't lie, but visual input may be corrupted by any number of variables.

It isn't supposed to rain until overnight. But the weather in Florida works like a science geek and smooth moves—can't ever quite figure out what's next. Leo certainly doesn't want to get caught in a rainstorm. He's wearing a white polo shirt today because he forgot to do laundry all week, so he couldn't allow himself to get soaked in a downpour; he would look like a sorority girl in a wet t-shirt contest. His man-boobs aren't quite as big as Arianna's tits, but his hairless chest could be mistaken for feminine under the translucent material. His roommates are planning a weekend party that starts tonight, and Leo refuses to walk through a dozen girls showing off his strangely oblong aureoles. People are shits, and Leo doesn't want to give them a reason to throw their shade in his direction.

The app still promises no rain until after midnight. That gives Leo another few hours to crunch research numbers. His semester assignment is a mammoth research project about using the past to predict the future in a paper co-authored by Arianna. (It doesn't matter if her name is on it or not. She wants to be a meteorologist on a local newscast. That means being photogenic rather than scientific.) Meteorology is guessing the future—his mother often teased that astrology is as respectable a science as meteorology. His father sometimes taunted Leo about studying "meteors." "Awfully specific," he would jibe. "Like studying only comets." Once, he spent an entire afternoon joking about the Avon lady being a "cometologist."

As it happens, paleotempestology *is* a rather specific field of study. Leo studies past tropical storm data. He also collects information from the job site following every hurricane. He charts the past to indicate future storm patterns. Field research takes him onto atolls and into marshes, trudging through coastal lakes to gather samples and data from overwash deposits. Leo primarily concentrates on oxygen isotopes as reflected in coral, tree rings, and even in fish bivalves. All this research indicates the frequency of the storms and can be predictive of tomorrow's inclement weather.

Leo likes working in the laboratory more than working in the field—he's more comfortable analyzing data rather than collecting it. The information gathered by himself and others in the program is entered into a database and correlated into a record covering storm events over several millennia. In theory, Leo and the other paleotempestologists ought to be able to come up with a model to someday accurately forecast tropical storms.

They'll be able to predict hurricanes.

Predict the *future*.

Outside, the wind howls like a wolf baying at the moon. The sound seems mournful—as if the state of all things has saddened the world. Why wouldn't it be? The world is a shitty place. Leo sometimes wonders if he took up paleotempestology not to determine *if* the ultimate storm is coming but to predict *when*. Humanity has pushed the planet to the brink of a breakdown. Pollution, overpopulation, global warming, the rape of natural resources. Soon, the world will push back.

Leo isn't trying to save the world or discover some useful warning; instead, he's trying to discern an expiration date so he can determine how much longer before this suffering ends. The world's suffering. And his own.

He thinks about Arianna, somewhere with her boyfriend, laughing and showing off her chest. He thinks about any girl, anywhere, everywhere but right here. There are sixty thousand students at UCF, yet Leo has been lonely ever since he arrived in Orlando. The world is ending, and he's fine with that. Let's get it over with.

"How long you gonna be?" asks a janitor popping his head into the room.

Leo looks away from the charts hanging on the wall. The janitor is way past retirement age, maybe eighty even, old as hell and bent over like a wilted palm tree. The old man squints across the room as if unsure whether Leo is a student or a teacher, male or female, man or mannequin. The janitor seems surprised when Leo answers.

"Not long," Leo says. "I want to get out ahead of the rain."

"Might be too late," the janitor replies. "Gonna start any second now."

Leo rolls his eyes as the janitor turns and trudges away. What does this old man know about the weather? He certainly didn't check the app before commenting on the forecast. Leo had another few hours before the precipitation is due to arrive.

Leo turns back to the data. Vague. Disparate. Incomplete. Indecisive. Like a message written in the sand after the tides have scrubbed at the shore. The data could mean a hundred different things. It suggests the next storm could arrive in a hundred years or a few weeks. The one thing science says for sure is Central Florida isn't going to see a hurricane tonight. Too bad, since Leo would love to see Arianna's night completely ruined by natural disaster.

He checks the instruments along the wall opposite the windows, machines attuned to the world outside these four walls. He notices the needle on the barometer is moving fast enough that he could *clock* it, like it's ticking off time instead of millibars. It's at 31.2 inches and falling. Fast. He has never seen it drop so precipitously. The weather app said he had until after midnight, but as the pressure drops right before Leo's very eyes, he suddenly doubts technology. That makes his stomach instantly queasy. If you can't trust machines, then who can you trust in this world?

The elderly janitor had warned Leo the rain was coming. Maybe something could be said for old-fashioned *observation*.

Leo goes to the window and looks outside. Palm trees blow in the wind. Clouds gather overhead, big gray puffs that blot out all the sky Leo could see. Lightning reaches from one roiling thunderhead to another before the rumble rolls across the sky. There had been no major storms brewing in the Atlantic lately—the hurricane season is over. It *should* be over. But this looks like there's a storm on the horizon. A big one. Leo examines the air pressure again. Already under 29 inches. And still spiraling fast.

.01" (trace)
[Amaris]

Amaris Azmi is seventeen, but she's all ready to set sail solo, say *namaste* to her siblings, and put her parents in her past. They wouldn't understand. They wouldn't let her do what she wanted to do. The only word they know is "University," and Amaris isn't going to freaking college. With a name like hers, she's not destined to get a Bachelor's in mind-numbing Physical Therapy like her mother wants her to. "Amaris Azmi" is going to look *epic* on the top of a blockbuster summer movie poster.

Epic!

"What're we doing here at Disney if you're leaving tonight, Amaris?" Ryan asks.

Ryan fidgets nervously. She's the one who will lie to Mr. and Mrs. Azmi for the next two days. She must cover for Amaris until she's far enough away from Orlando that they won't come after her. She might be almost eighteen, but "almost" isn't the same as being a legal adult. Amaris needs a head start.

"Two reasons, Ry," Amaris says, smiling ear to ear. Her heart is racing, her skin tingling. The excitement makes her pee herself a little. She has never been so eager for anything in her whole life, not any

Christmas, not getting her puppy Mr. Waggles when she was ten, not that amazing night she spent with Scott Masters last October. *Nothing!* "First, my parents track my phone, so I'm gonna answer one last call and let them hear the Disney noises in the background and see my location here and now. Say 'goodnight' and 'I love you' and all that crap. That should cover it for tonight. You take my phone, and you cover me for a couple of days. Phone audio glitches out, so you text them something from me—you make excuses."

"Yeah, I got it," Ryan says, sounding miserable. "But what's the other reason we're here?"

"The Beast," Amaris announces like it's the premiere of her very own blockbuster movie in the near future. "One last time."

It had always been *their* ride. Amaris and Ryan. Since they'd been tall enough to both get on the coaster. It was third grade, and Amaris had finally hit the mark they'd made on her bedroom door jamb. They'd begged their parents to take them to the park, and Amaris's father had accompanied them on the attraction for the first time. It had been thrilling, a feeling that came in second to everything after. Even the night with Scott Masters. They had ridden the Beast a dozen times that day.

So now Amaris and Ryan wait in a line that's long and slow-moving. There's a quartet of boys who pass them regularly in the serpentine queue, the hungry pack eyeing the teen girls with every pass. One wears a black leather jacket despite the balmy December weather, and Amaris wonders if he has a motorcycle and what it would take to make him drive her to California. In the end, she decides that she doesn't want to sleep with him, and he probably wouldn't accept anything less in trade.

"Are we going to make it?" Ryan asks, looking at the gray clouds gathering in the distance, forming a disconcerting cyclonic pattern.

"We have to," Amaris answers. "This is my last wish for Florida. I want to ride the Beast before I go."

"The weather doesn't care whether you get to go on it or not, Am," Ryan says.

But the line moves forward, and no announcement comes that the attraction is suspended as Amaris and Ryan get closer and closer to the

Beast. They know the turns of the queue by heart, and this is the final run-up to the ride. The boys who'd leered from the line get on the Beast, all of them screaming like babies cutting teeth as the coaster starts moving. One more set of riders in front of Amaris, then—

"Due to inclement weather, this ride is shutting down for the safety of our guests," comes the disheartening announcement. A collective groan issues from the crowd, interspersed with a smattering of four-letter words. "Please proceed to the nearest exit."

Sometimes the suspension of rides in Disney lasts for a few minutes, but Amaris knows this weather will shut down the Beast indefinitely. And she needs to get the hell out of Orlando. She and Ryan make their way to the exit as instructed.

The sky is overcast, and Amaris stares up at the thick clouds as a smattering of raindrops falls. One can always count on random rain to ruin any plans in Orlando. She scowls at the sky as if nature gives one crap about her sullenness, then turns to Ryan with a pouty face.

"Looks like I'll have to get a raincheck on our last ride, Ry."

"Once you get to L.A., I don't think you're ever coming back, Am."

"Then you can come to see me in Cali. We have a Disney there, too, y'know."

"I know," Ryan sighs. She stares at Amaris like it's the last time she's ever going to see her friend, and Amaris doesn't even notice in the moment. But she'll look back on this convo soon and she'll wonder if Ryan is still alive. Soon enough, Amaris will understand these next moments will have been their last moments.

The girls take shelter in a souvenir shop selling stuffed versions of every conceivable character, eyes all glaring at Amaris. A poster on the wall advertises the Tomorrowland attraction with the caption, "Where tomorrow is today." The clerk slides a bin containing umbrellas out to the main entrance, indicating they don't believe the precipitation will be a passing shower. Bottles of water fill a refrigerated bin by the door, trapped H_2O taunted by the free-falling raindrops outside. A hole in the ceiling of the shop lets through an anemic *dripdripdrip*.

"I'm going to call Mom," Amaris says. "You ready to back me up?"

"I guess," Ryan agrees unenthusiastically.

"Do your part. I'll do the talking."

"You'll start the lie. But then I have to keep it alive."

Amaris glares at Ryan as the phone rings once. Ryan has already agreed to this arrangement, so it's bullcrap that she's now heaping guilt on Amaris about it. If Ryan hadn't wanted to lie, Amaris had a half dozen other girlfriends who she could've convinced. She doesn't have time to deal with Ryan's waffling.

Amaris hears her mother's voice before she even answers the phone, but it's in her head and from the past, from earlier this year, after Amaris had told her mom she wanted to go to Los Angeles and be an actress. "This is America, Amaris," her mother had said. "They're living in Hollywood, not looking for Bollywood." Her mother had been right about one thing; this is *America.* It isn't the racist place her mother grew up in anymore, especially in California. A dreamer with Indian ancestry has as much chance at making it as any white girl.

Her mother answers after the first second. "Amaris?" Like her caller ID isn't showing Amaris's name and displaying the face from Amaris's third birthday with her face full of strawberry frosting and playing the ringtone that's the theme song from *Tubbytots* even though Amaris hasn't watched it since she was in kindergarten. Yet still, every time, her mother answers like it's a question.

"Hi, Mom," Amaris says, putting as much excitement and happiness into her voice as would be expected when one's at a place like Disney. "It's raining a bit, so I thought I'd call and touch base before we hit the rides again. I don't know if I'll have another chance before you get to bed."

Her mother's a nurse and works at 5:00 a.m., in bed by nine every night.

"Well, text me when you get to Aryanna's house," Mom says. She can't ever call Ryan "Ryan" because her mother is convinced it's a nickname for boys. Her mother is *so* last millennium. Everyone born in the twentieth century is like that. "Rain, you say? Did you bring a slicker?"

A *slicker?* Mom won't even say a swear as mild as "darn," and yet she uses terminology that somehow sounds dirtier than even a snappy "mother-fucker." Who the hell doesn't call it a *raincoat*? Someone born when phones still had cords, Amaris supposes.

"We're in a souvenir shop. We'll stay under shelter until it passes. Can't be much longer," Amaris says.

As soon as the conversation ends, whether rain or shine, Amaris is getting the hell out of Disney. She has five hundred dollars on a pre-paid Visa card, money put on there by her grandmother throughout the last two years' worth of birthdays and holidays. She also has two hundred in cash from working at Molly's Diner and stashing her tips over the last few weeks. Finally, she has some funds in her PayPal account from stuff she had sold to friends the last few days—extra clothes, shoes, make-up, electronics. Things she isn't taking to L.A. And she's never coming back.

After a stilted conversation, Amaris says, "All right, Mom. Gotta go."

"Okay, sweetheart. Be careful. I love you."

"Love you, too, Mom," Amaris mumbles and disconnects. "All right, Ry. Stick around the park for a couple of hours. Here's ten bucks for some snacks. Text her tonight. Cover me for tomorrow with some texts from my phone and maybe call her once and tell her I fell asleep or whatever. Try on Sunday, if you can, but she'll start to get suspicious. It'll fall apart sometime Sunday. But I'll be on the other side of the Mississippi by then."

Ryan looks miserable, but Amaris can't let her off the hook. This is the only option now. "I guess this is goodbye."

Amaris hugs her friend. "Come see me in Cali."

Then she turns to the rain. Sprinkles. Making the world a haze, like the scene before her is a dream that isn't fully realized. An idea that might turn out bright and sunny or could as easily stay gloomy and gray. The structures of Disney look undefined, as if Amaris is watching something as it fades, a painted picture washed away by running water. A curious effect, one that portends an unformed tomorrow. Amaris takes it as a sign.

She steps forward into the rain, and she doesn't look back.

.25"

[Carlos]

Carlos Licha paddles out from the beach off the coast of New Smyrna. The swells are pretty good today—lately, conditions haven't been conducive to catching some serious waves. At sixty-five, there are some days when his body might not agree with his surfin' spirit; such some days aren't today.

He takes a moment out on the water. His suit fits ankle to neck; the cool December water is a nice contrast to the bright sun warming his black attire. He loves the smell of it, the wax on his board mixed with the salt water and the musky scent of sea life, and the sound of the crashing waves on the sandy shore and the slap of water all around him and the whisper of the wind in his ears. If he could live right here off-shore…

But he couldn't. Man wasn't meant to be entirely aquatic. Evolution-arily, Carlos is out of his element. No gills. No fins. No blowhole. The salt water feels fine for a while but would deteriorate his skin after pro-longed exposure. Nothing to drink. Food is elusive without the right adaptations to hunt in the water. Man has been made for land, so why does Carlos feel such affinity to the sea?

Because the ocean is a capricious lover, taunting him with its charms before rejecting him outright. Even the waves push him in, then try to send him back to the beach, expelling him from the watery world where he doesn't belong. This lifelong love affair with the sea has always been a one-way relationship.

Carlos exhales, making a wish to be a fish, but that wish would never be granted. There's no magic in the real world. The days are entirely predictable.

Carlos used to come out here every day. Half his life while living in Florida and the first half back in Puerto Rico. Always the ocean. Carlos and the sea. His older brother, Diego, had been all about work and success and power—Diego had become a multimillionaire by age thirty-five. Carlos and Diego had argued whenever they'd been together about working hard versus living the easy life. Then Diego was diagnosed with terminal cancer, and all the money in the world couldn't save him. He'd bequeathed Carlos a house right on the beach and a monthly stipend enough so that Carlos never had to work again. Diego had left Carlos a short and simple message in his will: "You were right." Carlos had just turned thirty when Diego died.

That was half a lifetime ago. Carlos has never had a real job ever since. He gets up in the morning and surfs or sleeps late and surfs or goes for an evening surf. Carlos has been in the water nearly every day for all these years. Only hurricanes have kept him out for an entire day. He is as much a staple of the beach as the shells along the shore-line or the sight of a cruise ship along the horizon.

But lately, there have been aches and pains, and getting out on the board has sometimes been a trial rather than a blessing. Like hard work rather than living the easy life. Age is catching up to him. He has taken a day or two here and there and skipped surfing. He still swims or walks along the shore, but sometimes he leaves his board behind. The tide of his life is going out.

But not today. Today, he feels good. The waves are nice. He had been up and out early. Now he feels the tug and push of the current, urging him to take the next wave, take the next wave, take the next wave. But he knows which one to take. He knows enough to wait for the right one. He lets one after the other pass. Because there's always a next one. And a next one. Until it's the one he wants to ride.

He times it perfectly without thinking, then he's upright and moving, a man walking on water, defying the natural order, giving the sea one massive middle finger by rising, rising above, and being a master of the moment. The ocean is powerful and mercurial and cares not one whit for Carlos any more than the next partner who dares dance the dance for a while. But in those few seconds, Carlos is in control, and the ocean has met its match.

Then a wave crashes and he's underwater. The moment had been glorious but, as always, short-lived. The ocean never fails to remind Carlos who is a god and who is a mere man.

Mere man.

Carlos treads water offshore, deep enough to stay submerged but near enough to see the people stretched out along the beach. It's December, and the combers are limited to locals out for a walk and penny-pinchers who found an off-season deal on the Internet. He doesn't feel the affinity for his fellow man that he does for the ocean all around him. But the sea doesn't feel the same about him. The waves push him forward, away, like a piece of food stuck in its craw.

Carlos turns to swim back out as a smattering of rain drums his board. There wasn't any precipitation in the forecast today, but then the weather in Florida has always had a mind of its own. He could still surf in a quick shower, but the skies have become more ominous than a momentary passing system. Out east, he sees lightning flash across the sky, cloud to cloud, and cloud to sea. He isn't going to surf in a lightning storm.

The occasional annoying tourist would sometimes ask if he were worried about sharks. "Leave 'em alone, and they'll leave you be." Implied was that the same rules ought to apply to man. But lightning? Lightning will kill you any day of the week.

Carlos feels something in the water. Is it the tingle of a current from a lightning strike far offshore? The ambient static charge of the coming storm? The vibrations of the raindrops across the endless stretch of water? It feels like something else. Like the quiet hunger pangs of the entire ocean.

He looks around. The waves go up and he's in a trough, the world blocked by water. There could be something nearby. Something over the next crest. Or something swimming beneath him right now. That is always the situation out here in the sea. What you can't see. It never bothered Carlos before. He never worries about maybes. But maybe…

There's something else in the water.

He imagines a school of sharks acting irrationally, stirred up by the unnatural electrical storm. Supercharged by the unexpected weather. The waves raise him toward the top of a crest. Higher. Higher. He sees a shark fin nearby. Too close. Then another. Another. A dozen. He has never witnessed a group of predators all concentrated so near the shore at one time. The sharks are acting oddly. Carlos reaches the apex and jumps on his board, catching the wave, letting the sea take him toward shore and away from the frenzy of sharks.

Leave 'em alone and they'll leave you be.

The wave crashes in the shallows, and Carlos is safe from the shark-infested depths. He gazes back as a dozen fingers of lightning shatter the sky. Seconds later, thunder rolls over him in waves of bass. The clouds offshore turn in a meandering rotation. Carlos has seen his share of hurricanes and lived through a handful. He has always stayed, never evacuated. He knows how the storms come and go. They form with plenty of warning, somewhere other than right off the Space Coast of Florida. This spot is *never* where they originate. And he knows damn well that there were no hurricanes out in the Atlantic when he suited up this morning.

So, what is he looking at?

Like the birth of some great new force, he witnesses the contractions of nature. The process of something new being unleashed upon the world. Mother Nature is in labor, and this is what it looks like when she's fully dilated. Something original is straining to come forth, something the whole world isn't prepared for.

Something different.

Something disquieting.
Something wrong.

Press
Presents

In a far corner of space, orbiting a massive black hole, the research ship DARC12 discovers a strange asteroid—one that seems to be alive. After loading the rock on board for study, the ship quickly descends into madness. It begins with voices, whispers filling the shadows and the minds of the crew. A once-sane man declares that their discovery is not just a rock, but a god. Then the killing begins, and a cult rises, swearing allegiance to their newfound deity.

As the murders mount and the dead themselves begin to rise, a small group of survivors clings to the hope that they can somehow escape the hell they've been plunged into. But their problems escalate as they face an army of undead crewmembers, the reanimated corpses of hundreds of failed genetic experiments, the murderous cult, and—worst of all—the rapidly evolving creature in…

CONTAINMENT ROOM 7

Frantic, hungry claws scraping against wood…
The whining of a drill as it grinds through bone…
The ravings of a lunatic amid the honking of gridlocked cars…
Agonized shrieks through the phone line, followed by the rending
of flesh…
The hypnotic, deadly tones of a calliope on a warm summer night…

When the sun goes down and darkness claims the land…
When the silence descends, isolating the lonely, the desperate,
the weak…
These are the

NIGHT SOUNDS

you would hear, should you care to listen.
And just below it, if you strain your ears, you will hear
what the night sounds mask…
The sounds of human suffering,
the music of the night.

NIGHT SOUNDS: From Podcast to Print is a collection of scary, sometimes humorous stories, mostly written for popular fiction podcasts. The book is a throwback to Anderson's earliest fiction influences, what we now call Old Time Radio.

An embittered farmer.
A New York corporate raider.
Two teenage high school girls.
A failed small business owner.

Past and present collide, secrets are revealed.
These disparate people gather at a desolate Kansas farm
for a hellish night not everyone will survive.
Godland is a dark psychological suspense horror thriller.

A Midwestern nightmare.
Farm noir.

Martin "Wags" Wagner, an aging catcher relegated to a minor-league affiliate of the San Francisco Giants, is offered a new assignment— take a promising young pitcher under his wing and show him the ropes. Martin's manager is cagey about the new player, giving only his name, Andrei Dinescu, and his country of origin, Moldova. Despite the mysterious circumstances, Martin accepts the assignment, hoping to earn a return to the big leagues.

After his first bullpen session with the new pitcher, Martin is stunned by Andrei's lack of physical ability and his unfamiliarity with baseball. However, with each passing week, Andrei's strength and skill grow exponentially, and his miraculous leaps in both ability and pitch velocity frighten Martin. His fear is compounded by the organization's obvious attempts to keep Andrei separated from the rest of the team.

When Martin discovers the shocking truth about Andrei Dinescu, he realizes his path back to the big leagues is one stained with horror and blood.